**Pre-publication Reviews**
**For**
**The Last Parade**

<u>Don Charest:</u>
   I loved The Last Parade. The plot and action held my interest from the first page to the last. I must say you owe me one night's sleep because I could hardly put this thing down. It took me only two days to finish it.

<u>Pat Breland Shumock:</u>
   The Last Parade is the fifth book in Shumock's Letter Series. It's evident that he loves research and clearly hits the target in all scenes throughout this book. Full speed ahead drama and suspense as the story unfolds and will not disappoint.
   Guaranteed to keep you engaged with constant surprise. With a well devised plan to take over the U.S. Government, a global pandemic helps set the stage for the highest-ranking officials in our government to execute their plan. Greed, murder, and broken trusts challenge Rage Doyle's experienced team to answer the president's call for help.
   I could not put the book down until I had read to the end!

<u>Elmira Tanner:</u>
   Shumock has developed a series of interesting books.
   *The Last Parade*, his latest, takes the reader down many roads of discovery ultimately ending in our nation's capital.
   All this while the country fights to overcome the effects of Covid 19.
   Characters race to uncover suspected conspiracy at the highest levels of government and our military.
   As with other suspense novels in Shumock's series, the reader wants to keep turning the pages. What happens next…

*The Last Parade* is fiction but is it that far from the possible?


<u>Bobby Carmichael:</u>
Joe Shumock keeps the suspense, mystery, romance, murder, and the intriguing characters alive in his latest book, *The Last Parade*.

Once again, when you start reading, you can't wait to see what the next chapter brings. This plot is filled with international characters and espionage within our government.


<u>Rosie Mistretta:</u>
As in the last book, I get lost in the descriptions of the characters, which I know are necessary. I kept waiting for something to happen at a parade in New Orleans since he used a lot of time there. I was completely shocked at how much research was required to get to the plot. Toward the end, I could not stop reading. My husband left the house for about an hour, and I was still in the same spot reading when he got back. I fixed his dinner and read more. fed my cats and read again.

A really good read. Can't wait for the book to come out.

I mentioned it to one of my Newcomer friends. She has read all the *Letter Series* books and can't wait for the new one.

# Books by Joe Shumock

* * *

## The Letter Series

*A Letter to Die For*

*The Lost Letter*

*Letter from the Dark*

*Sacrifice of the Lambs*

*The Last Parade*

## For Young Audiences

*Briana and the Dog*

## Others

*The Shepherd's Crook*

# The Last Parade

~

*Fifth in The Letter Series*

~

# Joe Shumock

To

The Memory of

Eldon Gene Shumock

My Son and Cindy's Brother.

1973 - 2020

# THE LAST PARADE

# Chapter One

Traffic on St. Charles Avenue was slow, typical for a late Thursday evening in New Orleans. A streetcar was passing; the clickity-clack of its wheels beat out a rough rhythm that settled softly into the misty night. A few solitary passengers, most appearing deep in their own thoughts, were scattered throughout the car. Several were punching at cell phones.

Signs of an earlier thunderstorm were mostly gone now. Scraps of trash driven by the wind darted here and there among the empty parking spaces.

With no current shoppers in the neighborhood convenience store, the clerk walked to the door and looked out. He had heard the gusts as they ripped across the lot.

The cold rain had been pushed by the wind since mid-afternoon. Gusts appeared to be coming from the north, off Lake Pontchartrain. The temperature was in the low forties and falling—cold for New Orleans. After all, this was mid-March. Around the city, spring, with its profusion of azaleas and other blossoms, would arrive in the coming days.

Buds were already giving promises of what was to come.

Peering out the door, the clerk allowed his mind to wander.

*Night after night, aways the same.*

Leading such a mundane life, he had little to look forward to except the occasional streetcar passing in the night. He smiled a sad smile and slowly shook his head.

Streetlights along the avenue cast eerie shadows among the ancient oaks. Spanish moss, damp with rain, hung from branches like regretful tears on the cheeks of a N'awlins lady of the night. He had imagined that on some past stormy evening.

As he turned back inside, the clerk's thoughts drifted to a young Marlon Brando in *A Streetcar Named Desire.* Having watched the movie countless times, the clerk often imagined himself as Stanley Kowalski. Grinning, he doubted if his 5'7" frame and skinny physique would do honor to Brando's tempestuous character.

Willing his attention back to the present, the clerk tugged the neck of his sweater tighter and shook his head, amused at his own imagination. Stepping behind the counter, he casually stacked a carton of cigarettes on the rack. Finished, he turned to scan the parking lot again. His old beat-up VW was the only car there.

As he watched, a young woman rounded the street corner. She appeared determined to hold her hair in place, but it was being tossed all over by the wind. Head down and into the gale, she headed for the store.

He recognized her; she was a sometimes customer though he didn't know her name.

Stopping just outside the door, she hesitated, fighting an uphill battle to slip a mask over her ears while keeping some semblance of order to the hair.

The clerk slipped on his own mask.

As the young woman pushed through the door, the clerk glanced at the clock. Almost 10:30. A rush of cold air accompanied the opened door and triggered an involuntary shiver along his spine.

*If it stays this cool, I'll be wearing a scarf tomorrow night. It should be warmer.* He pulled the heavy sweater even closer around his neck and wished the registerwas not so close to the big glass doors.

Watching the woman, the clerk guessed she lived in the neighborhood at least part of the time. She would come in a couple of times a week, but periodically, to pick up things she'd probably forgotten at the grocery store—milk, bread, eggs. This was her usual time, late evening.

"Whew! That wind," he heard her say as she came through the door. She was still dealing with the hair.

Smiling at her from behind the mask as she passed the counter, he received a pleasant "Hi" and a wave in response. Tonight, her heels clicked as she headed for the cooler.

Standing behind the counter, his eyes were still following her when another blast of the cold hit him. Looking toward the door, he saw a bedraggled individual enter and glance around the store. The clerk's eyes went immediately to the man's hand. The pistol he held appeared large and threatening. Then the clerk took note of the man, his clothes, the long hair, and dirty cap. The hair didn't go with the way the man was dressed. It hung long and was too…nice.

"Open the register," the man said softly, "and then turn toward the wall." He was visually checking out the store while giving the clerk instructions.

When he was hired, the clerk's manager advised him to follow orders but to notice details if anyone came in to rob the store. "Do what they tell you," the boss had said. "A few bucks aren't worth getting killed."

The clerk's thoughts were on the killing part now.

Intending to obey, he opened the drawer and then glanced toward the back of the store. The woman was facing away, almost hidden, obviously unaware of the action at the register. He could tell she was holding a cooler door open with one hand and reaching for eggs with the other.

~~~

When the clerk regained his senses, he was propped upright in the back of an ambulance. He glanced at his watch out of habit. Nearly 11:00 p.m. He would have been off and gone in another ten minutes. His relief person was standing at the edge of the parking lot.

The back of his head hurt. Touching it, he could feel a big knot. There was a sticky substance too when he took his fingers away—blood. He wiped them clean on a pant leg.

"I'll have it bandaged in a minute," the masked female EMT told him. "It's a nasty cut. You're going to need stitches when we get you to the emergency room."
~~~

Outside, he could see several onlookers watching from behind police tape. A half-dozen patrol cars were at angles in the small parking lot and up and down St. Charles Avenue. There were a couple more he could see around the corner on the side street. The clerk wondered why a robbery would require so many cops in the parking lot and in his store.

It didn't take long to figure it out.

From his vantage point, the clerk had a sweeping view inside the store. His eyes were drawn to the coolers. He could see a body there covered by a sheet.

*Who ...?*

The clerk's heart seemed to skip a beat as his thoughts jumped to the man who had come into the store carrying the big pistol. He said to the EMT, "Someone was killed?" thinking an officer might have happened along as the cash register was being emptied.

"Yes," the EMT said, "... a woman." She didn't elaborate, becoming still for a moment, also watching the action inside the store.

As they both stared, the clerk saw something that he hadn't noticed before. There was a foot visible under the edge of the sheet—a woman's foot. She was wearing heels.

His familiar late-night customer often wore heels. She always dressed nice.

The clerk's emotions did a little flip-flop. *It's her.*

He watched as a man wearing a suit and a serious expression walked out of the store. The wind had calmed a bit, and the rain had become a mist again.

Glancing around the area, the man in the suit turned and headed over to the ambulance.

Placing a foot on the step and leaning against the door, he said, "I'm Detective Belou." Then he flashed a badge. Running a hand inside his coat, the detective came out with a small notebook and a pen.

"You were behind the counter when the shooter came in?" It was both a question and a statement. "That's where your relief found you."

The clerk nodded, his face immediately twisting, and his eyes slamming shut for a moment. *Oww... That hurts.*

*The shooter?*

"Just you and the woman in the store at the time?"

"Yes." The clerk spoke up this time. Nodding his head had hurt. Squinching his eyes, he said, "She had just walked in."

"Tell me what happened."

The clerk told what he remembered. He mentioned the guy's hair and his own earlier conclusion. "I think he was wearing a wig."

Belou made a note in his book. The medic attending him had backed away but was listening.

"Did you know the woman?"

The detective had piercing eyes. When he zeroed in on her, the EMT found other chores to keep her busy.

"If it's the same woman, she comes in a couple of times a week. We'd say hello—things like that. I didn't really know her." He thought for a moment before adding, "She must not live here full-time.

Sometimes I don't see her for a while, and then at other times, she's in a couple of times a week."

The detective jotted in his notebook again. Then, "Did you recognize the gunman? Do you recall him coming in before tonight?"

The clerk hesitated, thoughtful, and then shook his head—carefully. "I don't think so," he said. "Weget a lot of regulars, people from the neighborhood. I would have noticed if he'd been in more than a couple of times."

"Anything else you can tell me?" Belou looked at the clerk expectantly. "Anything at all?"

The clerk thought about it. "No, nothing else comes to mind."

"Would you take a look?" the detective asked, motioning toward the store. "Verify it's the same woman. We need to identify her."

"Sure." The clerk glanced at the EMT; she nodded an okay.

He stepped out of the ambulance and followed Belou.

"Are you the queasy type?" the detective asked over his shoulder. "There's a lot of blood."

The clerk shrugged. "I'm okay."

"The jerk shot her twice. Once in the chest and another in the head." Stepping inside the door, the detective was almost talking to himself. "She didn't stand a chance."

The two of them walked back to the covered body. The detective, careful of the broken eggs, squatted and turned back the sheet to expose her face. The material near the back of her head was saturated with blood.

Leaning over, hands on his knees, the clerk looked at her face. He couldn't help seeing the blood pooled on the floor. Then his eyes came back to the face. It was her—his friendly late-evening patron. *What a waste...*

"Is this the woman who came in just before the shooter?" Detective Belou wanted confirmation.

"Yes," the clerk said, almost whispering. "That's her."

Covering the woman's face, the detective stood and said thanks, adding, "You need to get back out to the ambulance and let them take you to the emergency room. They said you'll need stitches."

Glancing again at the covered body, the clerk had a different thought. *I'll miss her coming in. She was nice.*

He walked a couple of steps, then turned and asked, "You haven't identified her?" He'd forgotten what the detective had said, and for some reason he wanted to know.

Belou hesitated, then said, "We haven't. We didn't find a purse." He looked at the clerk. "Was she carrying one?"

The clerk thought back to when she came in, when she'd given him that little wave and said "Hi."

*Could that have been only a half-hour ago?*

He looked back at the sheet-covered body.

"I don't remember if she was carrying a purse." Hesitating then, he said, "I guess she was, though." Remembering previous late evenings, he added, "In fact, I'm sure of it. She always had to dig around for money or a card when she checked out."

The detective listened, then ended the conversation with, "It's missing then, along with her identification."

# Chapter Two

Rage Doyle was stuck in Prague's Václav Havel Airport.

The message said there was a problem with their aircraft requiring a short delay. After an anxious hour, he had given up hope for a short delay and approached a refreshment stand. Glancing at the selection, he chose a pack of crackers to go with his coffee, then reached for an English language newspaper.

*No way I'm going to make the connection for Atlanta.*

With his paper, coffee, and crackers in hand, Rage considered the options. "Doesn't make sense to waste the time," he said softly to himself as he gathered his bags. Rage moved his things into a corner away from the gate. Taking a seat as far from other passengers as possible, he opened the crackers and unfolded the newspaper.

Scanning the headlines, he took a sip of the coffee, savoring it for a moment on his tongue. Just the way he liked it—hot and in his hand.

Nothing in the newspaper tugged at his attention until he started to fold it for the trash. He noticed a small article with a headline that read, "Covid Virus Origins Becoming Clear."

Thinking he'd read and heard enough about covid, Rage touched his chin with a finger and then smiled, realizing that he had gotten so accustomed to wearing his mask that it had become second nature to him.

Glancing at his fellow passengers, Rage breathed a sigh of relief to be headed home. He hopedno one was carrying the virus onto the plane. *Sick or not, I'll be sitting beside some of these people for the next several hours.* Glancing around, he saw that almost everyone was wearing their mask. Rage knew it had become a requirement with the airlines.

When he'd left the Tennessee mountains three weeks earlier, most of the people in his area were wearing face coverings. Without thinking, he touched the extra mask in his coat pocket. Glancing back at the newspaper, he expected he'd see almost everyone in a mask on his return to the U.S.

He'd read enough. Skipping through the remainder of the article, he tossed the newspaper into a nearby trash receptacle. He had other important subjects to consider.

Thinking of the things he wanted to accomplish, Rage unpacked his MacBook Pro and placed it on his knees. Over the last several days, he had been pondering plans for the future. Settled in and as comfortable as he was likely to get, Rage slipped the mask down and took another sip of coffee. Then, staring out across the concourse, he considered the last few weeks.

A year ago, he lost the woman who had been very dear to him. Kateřina Bambenek had waited for him... *and waited*

*The years had passed so quickly.*

Other duties had kept him away. Then it was too late. Kateřina was gone. Only a buried urn with a small headstone marked her passing. He'd said his last goodbyes a year ago at a Prague cemetery.

Even as she'd neared the end, Kateřina had planned a surprise for him. With her attorney's guidance and without telling Rage, Kateřina had him made her sole heir. She had left him a mindboggling amount of cash. And there were other assets.

Her lawyer had told him there was more to come. Many hard assets had not yet been liquidated— the house and its furnishings, her jewelry, the Porsche, and whatever else the old attorney and his young associate might turn up. The last time he met with them, they were still finding possessions. Though Rage hadn't gone to the attorney's office on this visit, he'd had two lengthy phone conversations with the young assistant. There had also been papers to sign, but those had been brought to his hotel.

Rage's main purpose in coming to Prague this time was to visit Kateřina's and her daughter's shared gravesite. Details involving the estate had been unexpected.

Finally, with all business put away, Rage had reached the airport. He was ready to get back to his mountain cabin.

Sitting and waiting for the flight, Rage considered a plan to use his newfound wealth. The original shock had worn off and an idea had taken form. Liquid funds had already been sitting idle too long. The old attorney had called his attention to that several times.

Turning back to the computer, Rage began opening files. One folder contained a list of individuals. Mike Webster was the first name he typed.

Thinking, he turned and picked up the cup, tasted it and made a disapproving face. The coffee was getting cold.

Except for casually listening to announcements, Rage hardly looked up for the next two hours. Deeply engrossed in the work, he was startled when the gate attendant touched his shoulder.

"Mr. Doyle?" The German accent was harsh,and she looked a bit aggravated. "We have finished boarding your flight." Even with her mask on, Rage knew there was no smile, and her words were biting and sharp.

"You will need to get aboard immediately and take your seat. Yah?"

Rage glanced around; he was alone in the seating area.

Quickly gathering his things, Rage realized their routing had probably changed. He asked where they were going.

"To Stuttgart," the attendant said. "You will have a five-hour layover and then fly directly to Atlanta." Motioning toward the walkway to his plane, she said, "Now, please get aboard."

The waiting routine in Germany was much the same as in Prague. Rage found a quiet corner and continued laying out plans on the laptop. He was relieved when the Atlanta flight was called on time. By then he knew what he wanted to accomplish over the next several days.

His new plans required a side trip to Washington, D.C.

~~~

Doyle's flight touched down in Atlanta on Wednesday night at 10:10 p.m. An hour later, he was on a flight to Washington. Upon arrival, three hours of sleep in an airport hotel room had him ready to use most of Thursday to achieve goals he had posted on the computer.

Rage made three early morning calls. Then he waited.

The first returned contact came an hour later. The voice on the other end belonged to Bernard "Bernie" Sladen, Chief of Staff at the National Security Agency. After friendly greetings, a short conversation ensued, and a meeting was arranged. Two other calls followed Sladen's—one from the FBI and another from an individual representing the CIA. Groundwork had been laid for the next couple of days.

~~~

A few minutes before nine that evening, Rage was finishing dinner at Washington's Rooster & Owl restaurant. As he leaned back taking a sip of coffee, a tall, handsome black gentleman passed on his way out of the restaurant. Appearing surprised at the encounter to any who might see them, Bernie Sladen said hello to Rage. No mention was made of their early morning conversation.

Sladen was invited to sit and have coffee. He accepted. The two men spoke casually at first, mostly about the coronavirus.

Rage listened but was anxious to get on to the business at hand. He wanted Sladen to be aware of his new endeavor.

Sladen wanted to move on too and soon asked Rage, "How can I help?"

For the next half hour, Rage, in a soft voice, laid out his plans to Sladen. Finished, he leaned back, waiting for a reaction.

"So, your organization would be available for assignments where we would rather not use our own NSA agents?"

"Yes," Rage agreed. "That's a good summary."

Nodding, Sladen said, "You know there are others doing this."

Rage nodded. "But do they have the CIA experience I bring to the table?"

Sladen smiled. "Let me take your idea back to the office. Can I reach you on the number I used this morning?"

"Yes."

"I'll be in touch. This will probably require another meeting."

The men stood and shook hands, and then Sladen was gone.

During the day on Friday, similar meetings were arranged with Robert E. Cummings, Associate Deputy Director of the FBI and Eldon J. Patterson, Deputy Executive Director at the Central Intelligence

Agency. In face-to-face discussions, the men were each informed that Doyle was speaking with the other agencies. Questions were asked and clarifications made to both contacts.

The end results of all three meetings were verbal agreements that the services would keep Doyle's contact information and reach out to him if his skills were needed.

The CIA even provided a special encrypted phone for communications.

# Chapter Three

Though St. Patrick's Day was only a weekend away, a light blanket of snow covered the Capital on Friday morning. Green reminders of the upcoming holiday were scattered in offices throughout Washington. At his desk in the Russell Senate Office Building, Senator Wayne Washington Rayburt wore a tie trimmed in green. His green covid mask lay on the corner of the desk.

Leaning back, Rayburt considered immediate plans. Two days earlier, a furtive meeting with his top people had been scheduled for the weekend. Then he expected to be back in his office early on Monday. The clandestine operation they were planning was close—only weeks away—and there was much to do, many preparations yet to complete.

The senator's spacious office was luxurious; tasteful antiques accented large and comfortable furniture befitting a United States senator. Mementoes representing Rayburt's five terms in office were displayed about on bookshelves, tables, and his desk. Special photos and paintings decorated the walls. He was only sixty-two years old and a poster image for health and fitness. How he stays so fit with the incredible schedule he keeps had been a topic of light gossip throughout Washington for years.

This was one of the senator's secrets. Only a few close friends had ever viewed the small state-of-the-art exercise room in the senator's luxurious residence. His seven day a week, thirty-minute morning ritual there was known to even less. Travel was the only time he reluctantly missed the ritual.

Rayburt was known to be in his office by six— or earlier—most mornings, and he seldom returned to his mansion in time to see it without the streetlamps.

The senator lived alone. There was no Mrs. Rayburt to share the rewards of being the second longest-serving current member in the U.S congress. Ann Rayburt, the senator's young wife, had been killed early in his first term when she lost control of her little Mercedes convertible on the Arlington Memorial Bridge. The news had reached the senator at 4 o'clock in the morning. He was on a short trip back to his home state.

Devastated at the loss, Senator Rayburt never knew why Ann was out and crossing the bridge in the dead of night. Their home, a Washington apartment at the time, was located several miles from the scene of the accident.

The senator never remarried though he often attended events in the presence of three different female friends. These women, fashionable and socially prominent, each accompanied him to parties and other functions around the Capital at various times.

There were even occasional late evening dinners but never a suggestion of matrimony. Despite news articles to the contrary, the three individuals appeared only to be friends of the senator.

Gossip columnists loved speculating about his close female friends. The senator and the three ladies appeared to enjoy providing fresh reporting ideas. It was a bit of a game to them.

Margery Newberry was the senator's long-time tennis partner. They were a fearsome duo on the courts. Newberry was tall, six-two without heels, and pretty with blonde curls and soft blue eyes. The couple often made sports news, winning matches locally and occasionally in other cities. They always had separate sleeping arrangements when they traveled; the press had checked. Speculation over the years had often questioned whether both accommodations were used.

At less formal parties and functions, the senator was usually accompanied by Gwendolyn Huntington. The little brunette with the dark eyes was thought to be the senator's favorite of the three. She was from a small town in Kansas near southern Oklahoma and northern Texas and worked for a supreme court justice.

Gwen, as she was called by friends, spoke with a charming bit of a midwestern twang. Funny in conversation, she was known to tell a good joke and usually had a new one for listeners. It was also mentioned that her jokes were always clean. Gwen prided herself in only telling stories she would be willing to tell her eighty-eight-year-old grandmother.

Kaylee Taylor enjoyed Broadway shows and formal dinners. She and the senator usually attended at least a half dozen shows annually. Kaylee had a favorite. The couple had attended *Phantom of the Opera* three times over a span of several years.

Other than Broadway, formal dinners for foreign dignitaries were her preferred functions for spending time with the senator. Few knew Kaylee kept a secret score card for those. She had shaken the hand of three U.S. presidents, two kings and a queen, eight foreign presidents, and nine prime ministers.

An asset on his arm, Senator Rayburt enjoyed Kaylee's conversation. She always did her homework, brushing up on current events and other information concerning those she might meet during the span of an evening. Several foreign dignitaries had commented to the senator on Kaylee's deep knowledge of their country.

Each of the women had a special place in the life of the senator. They knew each other personally and were often seen together in public. Quiet lunches and end of day cocktails as a group were not uncommon. Whether they were intimate with the senator had beena subject of conjecture for years. Questions regarding the subject always garnered the same response from the senator and the ladies: "No comment!"

Individually, each of them looked forward to her time with the senator. He made them feel special. The ladies were envied by friends and strangers alike.

With a chiseled face reminiscent of Michelangelo's David, Senator Rayburt turned heads—both women *and* men—wherever he went. There were those startling grey eyes and long silver hair and brows. And the senator was tall. His 6'5" frame put him a head above others at most venues.

The chosen women in his life considered themselves fortunate, and each loved their time at his side.

~~~

Senator Rayburt was particularly busy now. Recently, private planning meetings were being held one after another. This afternoon, the senator would be in conference with a lone individual. Though this general would accompany Rayburt to a scheduled weekend meeting, the senator had decided to talk with him in private before Saturday's gathering.

As he waited, Senator Rayburt picked up the TV remote and tuned in to his preferred news station. His own photo and those of two other senators were positioned across the bottom of the screen. A little surprised to see himself, Rayburt immediately knew the subject of the report.

On Thursday afternoon he and the other two senators had held a news conference. The subject dealt with current conflict in the Middle East.

The correspondent was near the end of her report.

"Senators Allen and Carrolton are solidly aligned with Senator Rayburt against the president in this latest disagreement regarding Iran and its dealings with Russia. Without Iran's active influence in Palestine, there will almost certainly be a new war in the region. The result leaves the Middle East on the brink with Israel and the Palestinians staring down gun barrels while prepared to pull the triggers." She took a breath. "More on the hour."
~~~

Senator Rayburt smiled and clicked off the news as his secretary knocked on the door, announcing his expected visitor.

~~~

Army General Paul Grant Farmington sat across the desk from Senator Rayburt. General Farmington's current position was Chairman of the Joint Chiefs of Staff. His many years in the military had placed a significant set of ribbons and medals on his chest. He was proud of them and what they represented. The general enjoyed his role as the top officer in the mightiest military force on Earth.

Close for many years, General Farmington and the senator had graduated West Point together, finishing first and second in their class. The general enjoyed his GPA bragging rights even though the difference had been only a tenth of a point.

Farmington was a confirmed bachelor. In conversation, he told others his role in the military had required too much time to involve another. A wife would not have fit into his plan for life.

Along the way, several wistful ladies had attempted to change his mind. Close friends reported a couple had come close but then it would be time for a change in station. One determined lady had followed the general to the next assignment, but after a few months, she had packed it in and returned home.

Early in his career while still a junior officer, the general had acquired an interesting nickname. In public and private circles, General Farmington was often referred to as the Bear. Farmington stood 6'2" and weighed in at 238 pounds. Narrow at the waist—thirty-four inches—he was broad shouldered with
~~~

arms and neck to match. The Bear looked as though he spent significant time in the Pentagon Athletic Center.

He didn't, choosing instead to lift weights and utilize a treadmill, all of which he had requisitioned and set up in a small room inside his office suite at the Pentagon. Farmington called the space his thinking room.

The Bear wore a short-cropped military haircut, practically shaved on the sides. He sported a nose that had remained a bit crooked after being broken while boxing at West Point. Eyes that were piercing and almost black had put the fear of God in many a young lieutenant during the general's long history in the military. The general was a law-and-order type of officer who treated his people with respect as long as they did their job.

The general's term as Chairman of the Joint Chiefs of Staff was in its last year. He had relished every day of the assignment and wanted to finish with a flourish. The situation involving Iran and the Middle East presented an ideal opportunity.

Finding himself in his present position, the Bear couldn't believe his own good fortune. Three years ago, it had been rumored that General Ellis Easton was number one on the president's list for appointment to Chairman of the Joint Chiefs post. A sudden heart attack had taken Easton out of consideration. With him out of the running, the Bear had been approved as Chairman without opposition.

Over his career, General Farmington's personal example had been George Patton. The general had studied Patton's life, including his WWI record, but especially his actions in Africa and Europe during

WWII. Patton, a no-nonsense general, believed he was predestined to some great action in life. He wanted to fight, and Patton wanted to win.

General Farmington believed he was of the same mold and material.

Looking forward to the next few weeks, the Bear couldn't wait to deal with Iran and Russia when the upcoming operation was in place.

~~~

Senator Rayburt poured them a shot of Old Pepper Straight Rye Whiskey, a favorite of both men. Taking a sip, Rayburt posed the same question he had asked before. "Are we absolutely on schedule for having the military we need in time for the operation?"

"Actually, we're already there, and that's for all branches of the military," General Farmington answered, adding, "but we're not letting that news out. I don't want to jeopardize present short-term funding under the old rules. Nor do I want to raise any suspicions across the aisle."

"Are you still planning to utilize the national guard instead of regular forces?"

"It makes the most sense," the Bear told him. "The guard will be less intrusive. I will have regular troops disbursed across the country, purportedly on maneuvers. They can handle any problems beyond the national guard's capability."

Rising from his desk, Rayburt glanced at his friend before walking to the window. "I'm relying on your advice and expertise in those areas." He turned, changing the subject to an important point of their meeting.
~~~

"Are all action codes set for release?" Rayburt hesitated, emphasizing the next question. "Are we prepared to act?" The senator's eyes stared deep into those of the general.

"Yes, and yes," Farmington stated matter-of-factly. "Along with General Avery and General Wisecroft, I carry my set of codes everywhere I go." He patted the breast of his coat. "The others do too." The Bear chuckled. "We even sleep with the codes."

Senator Rayburt nodded and grinned. "Good to know."

General Farmington spoke up. "There is still the problem we have with the congresswoman from New Orleans." The general glanced at Rayburt and shook his head. "The offer you made her could have done us in."

The senator's voice dropped a notch as he said grudgingly, "I take full responsibility." Senator Rayburt then looked at the general and said in a stilted voice, "I don't often make this kind of mistake. I misjudged the congresswoman. Thought I could control her. I was wrong. I should never have tried to bring her on board."

"Well, it can't be undone," General Farmington said. "The contract was implemented last night."

"Then it's handled?"

"Yes."

Changing the subject, the senator said, "The operation will be on us before we know it." He glanced at the general. "The coronavirus pandemic couldn't have come at a better time. For our purposes, there couldn't be better circumstances." Rayburt went on. "Few individuals—in or out of government—even suspect how their lives are going to be permanently changed. This country has never faced these conditions. Masks are everywhere you look, and stay-at-home precautions are keeping much of the population off the streets. Millions are working from home."

The Bear nodded.

"It's scary how the number of immunizations has dropped off," Rayburt said adding, "One of my recent reports indicated only 14 in 100 are now receiving the inoculations. People are getting complacent." He added, "This thing isn't over."

The senator dropped into his big chair, elbows on the desk, and changed the subject again. "We're almost there, Paul."

"Yes." The general nodded as he picked up his service cap and started to leave. With a hand on the door, he turned back. "Have all the details concerning the special contractor been handled? We can't afford any mistakes there, either."

Rayburt gave the Bear a chilling look. "Yes, I took care of that several hours ago. I have hunting connections in Louisiana."

The senator didn't like being second-guessed, even by friends.

# Chapter Four

Mid-morning on Saturday, the Cessna 310Q approached from west to east, touching down lightly on the tarmac. Using less than a third of the 7,000-foot runway, the aircraft slowed and turned back toward the terminal, braking to a stop sixty yards out. Near the building, there was a sign proclaiming, "Welcome to Gulf Shores, Alabama." The twin engines were cut to idle, and the door on the right side of the aircraft opened.

Dressed in shorts, two men climbed out onto the wing of the 4-seater, and one hopped to the ground. Taking a moment, both slipped a covid mask over their face. The second passenger passed golf clubs and two overnight bags out to one on the ground.

Before closing the door, the tall one told the pilot, "Pick us up at 11:00 a.m. tomorrow."

"I'll be here."

As the aircraft taxied away, the two men gathered the clubs and bags and walked into the terminal.

Inside, the tall one stopped at the counter and asked about a rental car.

"I'll make a call, honey," the attendant told him. "We'll have one before you can get settled."

"Thanks," he told her.

Stacking their baggage aside, the men found seats in the lounge area to wait for their transportation.

As they were making themselves comfortable, the lady at the counter called out. "Got one on the way."

Without looking up, the tall one waved andsaid, "Thanks." His friend glanced her way  andwaved.

Watching them, she wondered where she'd seen that tall one before, that he looked familiar, even in the mask. She nibbled at a fingernail, not having an idea where, but just knew she'd seen him.

It bothered her to not remember.

Still unable to make a connection, she glanced back at the men a couple of times.

Before they could get comfortable, a car pulled up outside and the driver tooted the horn.

"That's your  rental." The woman pointed outside.

Thirty minutes later, they had dropped the driver at his office, signed for the car, and made their way to the Cuban Towers on West Beach Boulevard. After parking, they unloaded the clubs and bags and made their way to a rented condo on the fourteenth floor.

On the way upstairs, the tall one noticed there was no thirteenth-floor choice for the elevator. *Hmm...that makes the fourteenth floor really the thirteenth floor.* He grinned. *Glad I'm not superstitious.*

He didn't mention his observation to his traveling partner or to any of the others when they arrived.

~~~

They dropped the luggage near the door and the golf clubs were tossed into a closet. The masks came off and were left beside the TV.

"Kind of a worthless effort to carry the clubs around knowing we are not going to use them." General Farmington was shaking his head but had a grin on his face.

"Need the props if we want to look like golfers having a fun weekend," Senator Rayburt said. "We don't need anyone recognizing us. It would be a problem if the press knew we're here for a group meeting."

The senator walked over to the balcony doors. He could look across the highway and scattered beach houses to the Gulf of Mexico. "I've often wanted to come down here and see what everyone was talking about." Glancing at the shore, he said, "It's the off season, but look at those people walking on the beach. They're there without a problem in the world. I don't see a single mask."

The pristine white sand stretched as far as he could see.

Quickly back on task, Rayburt turned to General Farmington. "What time are we expecting the others?"

"Any minute now."

As if on cue, there was a knock on the door. The general opened it and ushered two masked individuals inside. These men were also dressed for golf. General
~~~

Charles L. Avery and General George P. Wisecroft said friendly hello's and shook hands with Farmington and the senator. General Avery had been in his position as Army Chief of Staff for almost a year; General Wisecroft had been Commandant of the Marine Corps slightly longer.

Before they could be seated, there was another knock at the door, more of a tapping sound this time.

"That'll be Elena," Senator Rayburt commented.

General Farmington walked over and opened the door a second time. The woman standing there was dressed in a tennis outfit and sweater. She was wearing a color-coordinated mask and holding a racket. "May I come in?"

The Bear still had his eye on her attire, surprise apparent on his face. She answered his unspoken question.

"My cover for the meeting," she said. "My husband's playing golf. We told everyone this was our getaway weekend."

At first glance, Elena Springer-Preston, Deputy Director of CIA for Operations, looked in her early forties. Tiny lines around the eyes suggested she was probably older. The sweater came off. Her arms and legs, showing amply in the tennis outfit, were toned and tan. Obviously, she hit the courts as often as a woman of her status and responsibilities could arrange.

Farmington stepped aside, a slight smile now showing. He gestured for the Deputy Director to enter.

"Just like a woman," the Bear commented as she passed him. "Always late." He made the comment with a grin.

She glanced at him, flashing a disarming smile, and said, "I choose to think of my arrival as saving the best 'til last."

Everyone chuckled including General Farmington.

She looked the general in the eye. "Trueché?" she said smiling and then removed her mask and reached to bump elbows.

The general nodded. He knew when to move on. "You know everyone, I believe."

The other attending generals each acknowledged the CIA Deputy Director.

"Welcome Elena," Senator Rayburt said when it was his turn.

"Good morning, Senator."

With greetings made, Senator Rayburt opened his overnight bag. Glancing at the others, he set out two bottles of his favored rye whiskey. "I thought a drink might be in order given the gravity of the decision we're making."

Five glasses were rounded up and each soon held two fingers of whiskey.

"Toast, everyone." The senator held his drink out and touched it to each of the others.

Everyone seated themselves, leaving only the senator standing. Rayburt moved directly into the agenda. "Fellow planners, we all know why we're here."

The Bear nodded; the others sat silent and still.

Senator Rayburt walked over to the windows facing the shoreline. He stood watching waves lapping lazily in the distance. The others waited.

After several seconds, Rayburt turned, walking back to the others. Resting his hands on the back of a chair, the senator remained standing.

"Gentleman, Deputy Director Preston." The senator hesitated for a moment.

Then, "This is the last decision point. Too much of our plan will have already been set in motion. After today there can be no turning back though Implementation Day is still weeks away." He looked into the eyes of each of them, finding determination on every face, even the Marine Commandant.

George Wisecroft was the only individual giving Senator Rayburt any concerns at all. There was nothing specific the senator could pinpoint. The Marine Commandant, having come from a military family, had served his country faithfully for thirty-six years. The senator was also aware that Wisecroft's great-grandfather had died a hero's death at Gettysburg.

Senator Rayburt had worked closely with General Wisecroft on numerous occasions concerning military legislation and funding. He had no reason to doubt Wisecroft's patriotism or his willingness to act—just a nagging uncertainty inside Rayburt's own mind.

Glancing at the general, he thought, *I'll digdeeper tomorrow during our one-on-one.* Rayburt pondered. *I don't want to lose George, but at less than onehundred percent, he's dangerous.*

At that very moment, the senator noticed General Wisecroft watching him. Rayburt stared back. After a moment, the general looked away.

*Yes, tomorrow.* Rayburt thought.

The senator turned his attention and his thoughts back to the other officers and Deputy Director Preston. "Any last-minute suggestions or subjects we've overlooked?"

Surprising him, the first to speak was Wisecroft. "Based on your latest information, is the pandemic going to be a problem?"

The others glanced at Wisecroft and then turned their attention back to Senator Rayburt for his answer.

"That question came up yesterday afternoon," the senator said. He didn't comment on the circumstances but did tell them what had been discussed in conversation with General Farmington.

Finishing, he said, "If anything, I think the pandemic will be to our advantage."

Glances passed around the room, each of the individuals looking at the others. Still, no one spoke.

Finally, the senator settled into a chair, elbows on his knees. "Last, last chance," Rayburt said as he waved an arm across the group. There were no smiles or comments as each of them shook their head.

The senator moved the agenda forward by referring to General Wisecroft's last question.

"Everything I've heard and read leads me to believe the pandemic will make our task easier." Rayburt glanced at the others before continuing. Then, "Even a voluntary stay-at-home proclamation will reduce the number of people ready and willing to join an uprising. People won't want to get involved."

A couple of the generals nodded a yes. The others were quiet.

Rayburt suggested they have another small drink while finishing off the specifics. He poured one for himself and passed the bottle to the Deputy Director.

"Now, let's go over the details one last time." The senator took a sip from his glass and leaned toward General Farmington. "Paul, are you satisfied with the Navy and Air Force?"

"I am," Farmington answered. "Admiral Patron and General Bloodworth are on board. These critical commanders will follow my orders even if they might question our methods."

"What about the National Guard?" This question was from General Avery.

"It's handled," the Bear said with authority. He went on to give them the appropriate points of his and Senator Rayburt's conversation from the previous afternoon.

When Farmington finished, General Wisecroft asked, "What about the Vice President and Speaker of the House? Have any of the previous arrangements changed?" He turned to the Deputy Director, adding, "Interrupting the chain of command is critical."

Preston, who had been listening closely, answered in a sharp tone. "I'll repeat what you've all been told." The former teacher stared at General Wisecroft as she would a sixth grader who had not listened to instructions. "The CIA is responsible for both parties. Under the pretext of a possible breakthrough with Iran regarding Russia, the Vice President and the Speaker of the House will be traveling together to Tehran during the critical period. They will be expecting to attend a secret meeting with Iranian President Rouhani. The groundwork has all been laid."

"Isn't it unusual for the Vice President and the Speaker to be traveling together?" asked General Avery. He added, "Presidential chain of command and all that."

"It is," the Deputy Director said, "but these are unusual circumstances. It took some doing."

"Is an actual meeting scheduled?" General Wisecroft asked.

"Yes," the Deputy Director assured him, "but for our purposes and by prior arrangements, the VP and Speaker will be on a refueling stopover in Paris when the Memorial Day Parade begins." She went on. "Taking them out of the chain of command is crucial to our plan and that operation is my responsibility."

Her expression had become hard, dark eyes now focused on Wisecroft. "I know my job," she said, "and you…" She took time to look at each of the others. "All of you can be assured I will handle the situation."

"And?" General Wisecroft was pressing her.

Deputy Director Preston had not attained her present post by being shy or easily broken with words.

"Paris," she snapped to Wisecroft in a sharp and raised tone of voice.

General Avery, who had been watching and listening attentively, was startled, flinching slightly.

Senator Rayburt was watching the exchange with interest. The generals were watching too. Farmington appeared to be enjoying the exchange.

The senator recalled his conversation with Farmington on Friday afternoon.

The Deputy Director continued, her eyes narrowed and focused on Wisecroft. The voice was low but still commanding. "A potential problem with their aircraft will be discovered, and the two of them along with staff will be escorted to the American Embassy to wait while repairs are made. Once there, everyone on the flight will be detained by people who are sympathetic to our cause."

General Wisecroft wasn't satisfied. "One more thing," he said. "I understand the specifics, but how do we justify our overall operation within the constitution?"

Preston's face was red, and her hostility was directed solely at General Wisecroft. She was ready to set him straight, but before she could answer, General Farmington stood up, interrupting an accelerating conflict.

The Bear's action allowed a certain calm to return to the room. A couple of deep breaths could be heard.

"Again," he said, "as Deputy Director Preston reported, the Vice President and the Speaker are handled." The general was an imposing figure as he took command.

The Bear quickly moved to a new subject. "The president's request for the Memorial Day parade to be a military show is a major stroke of luck," Farmington said, a cryptic half-smile on his lips. "The fact that it's the president's own idea is priceless. He's effectively ordered us to have military forces out in Washington and across the entire country. The operation only requires moving troops and equipment a few blocks to encompass the White House."

Senator Rayburt still had questions. "We appear to be adequately covered in the continental U.S." Then he said, "Give me details outside the states." Thesenator had walked over near the balcony door again as he posed the question. Senator Rayburt turned and waited.

The Bear was prepared. "Outside the continental U.S., combat exercises are scheduled in Korea and for Europe. Otherwise, U.S. and Japan Maritime Forces will conduct navigational maneuvers in the East China Sea. Our naval command will oversee those efforts."

"What about China and Russia?" the senator asked. "Won't they see the operation as a somewhat chaotic situation and want to act on perceived advantages?"

"We don't think so," the general said. "Besides, neither of those countries are really prepared for a large-scale military action at this time." The general added, "Our military satellites are watching for significant movement, and neither country is doing anything unusual at the present time."

"What about the Middle East?" General Avery asked.

The CIA's Deputy Director answered the general. Her voice had calmed. "Israel will be informed through our embassy immediately after the operation is secure—same with Russia and China. This will be true also for the UK and Europe too. Other Middle Eastern nations will be informed within two hours of the actual operation. Friend and foe across the globe will know within the same two hours.

The general returned his summary to the home front.

"Here in the states, the Army and Marines will move into major cities across the country in the days immediately leading up to the operation. The presumption is that these maneuvers are a part of the military show for Memorial Day. We will use the pretext of practicing to defend against possible land-based military invasion."

The two men stared at each other for a moment before Senator Rayburt spoke. "So, we are sufficiently prepared to take command of this country."

"Yes sir, Senator," General Farmington said direct and forcefully. "We're ready."

Spoken as they were, the general's words could have as easily been directed to the Commander-in-Chief.

"To a new day," General Farmington said as he took a sip of the whiskey.

Preston raised her cup saying, "To a better day."

"To the future," a couple of the others said in unison.

"Then it's done," Rayburt said as he reached for his glass. Raising it again in a toast, he saluted them.

The Deputy Director and each of the generals stood and returned the gesture.

The senator capped it off. "We're in. It's a go."

~~~

The Deputy Director left the others late in the afternoon, returning to her condo to join her husband for dinner. The senator and his military leaders
~~~

enjoyed a splendid seafood feast early that evening. A very good white wine accompanied the fare. The restaurant, small and private, was located on the top floor of the Cuban Towers. Their private dining room presented a majestic view of the sunset with its rays reflecting off low clouds and the waters on Little Lagoon and Mobile Bay.

Later, over drinks in the condo, the four men spoke casually of golf. Stories were told and laughter was contagious.

Early on Sunday, donuts and coffee got them through last-minute thoughts. Elena Springer-Preston rejoined them. Each of the individuals had comments, and there were a few general questions.

After an open session, Senator Rayburt pulled Preston and each of the generals aside individually. He wanted last minute personal assurances from everyone that they were totally onboard with the extreme and sweeping steps they were taking. The senator also wanted to hear—one last time—that the preparations by each individual and his or her area of command would be complete by the execution date. They were down to a few weeks now and moving forward. They were now past the point of no return.

General Avery was first. The senator led the way out onto the balcony.

"Are we ready, General?" Rayburt asked.

"In my opinion, yes," General Avery answered. "Every area under my command has fulfilled the requirements set for them. Only a select few are privy to the underlying reasons for the actions we've taken up to this point."

They discussed specifics with Senator Rayburt asking questions and the general supplying the answers. The list was short. There was not much left that needed to be discussed. A short fifteen minutes later, they returned inside.

The Marine Commandant was next.

"The marines are ready," Wisecroft told the senator when asked. "The commanders in the field have gone beyond what I expected of them."

"I've read your reports, but what about you, George?" the senator asked. "Are you ready?"

The commandant glanced toward the incoming waves on the horizon, hesitating before answering. Not unlike the general himself, the Gulf of Mexico appeared turbulent this morning.

Senator Rayburt waited.

When he turned back to the senator, General Wisecroft said, "I have reservations, Wayne." He continued to look the senator in the eye as he added, "I would hope we all have reservations."

The senator remained silent, listening.

General Wisecroft shifted his weight from one foot to the other, turning slightly toward the Gulf before continuing.

Without looking back, he said, "Though I agree with the reasoning behind our operation, I deplore the fact that it's so against the constitution."

His gaze returned to the senator. "We have to do it," General Wisecroft said. "I wish we didn't, but…"

"Then I can depend on you," Senator Rayburt said. It was a statement, not a question.

"Yes," the general responded, "I'm in." He added, "All the way."

They bumped elbows and headed back to join the others.

~~~

Deputy Director Preston was the last to join the senator on the balcony. He could tell she was still disturbed by Saturday's clash with Wisecroft. Rather than brushing the confrontation aside, Senator Rayburt met it head on.

"Can you work with General Wisecroft?"

She stared at Senator Rayburt for a moment before answering. "I can deal with him," she said, "but...?"

Preston glanced away.

"But?" the senator prompted.

She looked back, her eyes locked on the senator's. "I may be speaking out of turn," Preston said, "but I don't trust him." She remained focused on the senator's eyes for a moment, then looked away.

Glancing out at the gulf, Preston appeared to be organizing her thoughts.

"Wisecroft wouldn't go to President Carrigan, would he?" She wasn't exactly asking a question of the senator. Preston was presenting a fearsome possibility.

She waited for a response.

"No. He's on board," Senator Rayburt told her. "George is a constitutionalist, but he understands the present situation requires extreme measures. He's given his word that he is with us. I trust him," the senator said.
~~~

"I hope you're right," she said. Preston leanedher head to the side, her face drawn in an expression of doubt.

The senator moved on. "As we've discussed, I will want you to go to the Middle East immediately after we're in control. Our decision on dealing with Iran will need to be communicated to the Supreme Leader and to other interested parties. This would normally be handled by the Secretary of State, but I want all parties to realize the importance of our actions. By having you, the new Vice President, deliver the message, I think we will have made our point."

She nodded.

# Chapter Five

Late Saturday afternoon, Rage flew to Knoxville where he was met by friends. The couple returned him to Coker Creek and his car, leaving Rage to drive the remaining five miles to his mountain cabin.

Back home, he unpacked, fell into bed, and slept for eleven hours until the break of dawn on Sunday. Waking, Rage stretched, listened, and then smiled. Off in the distance, he heard the call of a whippoorwill that frequented the forests around the cabin.

Rolling out of bed, he hurried up to the loft and his computer. Fifteen minutes later, he had what he wanted.

Downstairs and still in his robe, Rage made coffee and took a cup of the dark brew out to his easterly-facing deck. He picked up the portable phone on the way out. The sun was just peeking over the mountains as he settled into one of the chairs.

With another sip of coffee, Rage dialed a number and listened as a sleepy voice answered.

Mike Webster perked up when Rage identified himself. "How was your trip to Prague?"

They had talked beforehand; Mike knew where his mentor had gone.

"It was interesting," Rage told him. "I'll tell you about it sometime." Then, "Where are you?"

"Atlanta? Why?" Mike sensed something was coming.

"Can you meet me in Chattanooga this afternoon?"

An extended hesitation this time. "…Sure."

"There's a Cracker Barrel just off I-75 before you get into south Chattanooga." Rage gave the directions he had pulled off Google Maps. "Two o'clock, okay?"

"Two o'clock." The phone went dead. The Author smiled and took another sip of his coffee. Mike was picking up Rage's own habits.

~~~

They both drove into the parking lot five minutes early. A warm handshake and then they walked into the restaurant. Seated, they each ordered water and a sandwich.

"I guess you're wondering why the rush to meet," Rage said softly.

"It did cross my mind."

"I have a proposition."

The younger man leaned in.

"How would you like to come to work with me?" There was a slight grin on Rage's face.

Mike edged closer, saying, "I'm not unhappy at the U.S. Marshals Service, but I'll listen."

"What I'm going to tell you must be held in strictest confidence."

"No problem."
~~~

When Rage had finished detailing his meetings in Washington, Mike relaxed back into his chair and took a deep breath. Rage named the organizations but not the individuals he'd met with in D.C. His younger friend was only a little surprised that Rage could get quick meetings with such high-level people.

Their food came, giving them each a few moments to think.

When the waitress left, Mike asked, "Where would I stand in this organization?"

"With me. I would want you to help run the day-to-day operations." Rage took a bite of hissandwich.

"What about money? It will cost a chunk to do what you are suggesting." Mike pulled his plate closer and picked up a French fry.

"Funds won't be a problem," Rage said, adding, "I have it covered." He didn't elaborate.

"How many people?" Mike was back to details.

"A dozen, maybe fifteen ultimately," Rage said. "That's total. Eventually, some will be in Europe. The total number includes the two of us."

"Would I have input on the people we use?" Mike asked as he touched the corner of his mouth with a napkin.

Nodding, Rage had obviously given this some thought. "If either of us votes no on a particular individual, they're out. No discussion." Rage pulled at his collar before continuing. "Our people would be free to live anywhere and do whatever they want when they're not on assignment for us. We'll pay top dollar, and they can use their free time as they wish." He paused. "Benefits too. We can deal with the details later."

Smiling, Mike rubbed his fingers together indicating money. "You must really be flush."

"I'm okay." The look Rage gave Mike indicated that subject was closed.

"When do you need my decision?" Mike asked.

"As soon as you can."

"A couple of days?"

"Fine." Rage reached across the table for a handshake.

# Chapter Six

The senator arrived back at his home in Washington at 6:05 on Sunday evening and was greeted by one of the cooks.

"Everyone else is gone," she told him. "I stayed to make dinner in case you hadn't eaten."

"Thank you, Edith, but I'm not very hungry." He realized he probably shouldn't rush her out. "On second thought, maybe a bowl of soup and some crackers."

She smiled. "I'll have it on the table in ten minutes."

"Set it on the island," he told her. "You can bring me up to date while I eat."

There was a short stack of mail at the end of the expansive island. "I'll check this while I wait." Glancing at the large stove where Edith was warminghis light supper, the senator checked his watch. He'd have to rush the soup to be at his computer by seven.

Rayburt glanced at his cook again. Busy, her back was to him.

Edith ran the big house for the senator. She had been with him since he moved to Lanier Heights. All 4'9" of the woman spelled boss—both voice and demeanor. She oversaw operations both inside and outside, hiring and firing as necessary. Everyone reported to Edith. Senator Rayburt couldn't imagine the house without her.

The senator finished the soup a few minutes later under Edith's watchful eye. Wiping at a corner of his mouth, Rayburt said, "Now toss the bowl in the sink and get out of here." He wanted the house to himself.

"But...?" Edith tried to argue, but he delicately eased her out the door and watched as she walked to her car.

Glancing at his watch, Rayburt breathed a sigh of relief. He should be okay timewise. Then out of the corner of his eye, the senator saw Edith pause, then turn and take determined steps back toward the house. Nearing the door, she glanced up and lightly slapped the side of her head. "Forgot my book," she said. "Can't make it through the evening without it."

Inside for only seconds, she was back at the door, waving the book, and headed to her car a second time. "Night," she called back without turning.

With the house finally empty, Senator Rayburt hurried upstairs to his third-floor suite. Walking into the large bath, he glanced at his watch. He only had a few minutes to access the hidden space and log onto his computer.

The procedure for opening the concealed door required three one-minute pauses in the process. Senator Rayburt caught himself glancing at his watch several times as he waited for the time to pass. Seven o'clock was almost on him.

Finally in, the senator sat down and turned to the external monitor. A laptop was connected to the monitor. He turned on the computer, and an innocuous appearing software sign-in screen appeared.

Using a code committed to memory years ago, the senator opened the ultra-secure video conferencing program, an encrypted tool used solely for private interaction with this group. Immediately, he could see the familiar setting on the monitor. There were five black screens showing only last names at the bottom, nothing otherwise. Four men and the woman from Switzerland.

As usual, the sixth screen *was* there along with the others. The camera on his computer was projecting an image on the sixth screen—the senator's. The other five *could* see him.

Ms. Keller was the first to acknowledge him. The black screen with her name at the bottom flashed yellow. "Good evening, Wayne." She always used his given name.

"Good evening," the senator answered.

Now Mr. Holden's screen blinked yellow, and Keller's turned black.

"How did the Gulf Shores meeting go, Senator?" Holden asked.

Rayburt hesitated, thinking, *He never wastes words or time.*

"It was a good meeting, Mr. Holden. I believe we have the best team available for this operation."

Mr. Nkosi asked, "Are all of the Joint Chiefs on board?" He spoke perfect English but with a slight South African accent.

"Two are not," the senator answered. Anticipating the next question, Rayburt continued. "Admiral Riverdale, the Vice Chairman, and General Smith, Chief of Space Operations, are not included."

"Is there an important reason?" Nkosi again.

Senator Rayburt answered. "Based on conversations and past actions, General Farmington and I believe Admiral Riverdale would side with President Carrigan in any action taken to unseat the president." He continued, "General Smith is close friends with the Admiral and appears to share his views."

"I understand," Mr. Nkosi said.

"Do you see the two of them presenting a problem?" Another of the men, Mr. Peeters, asked this question.

"Yes, I was going to ask that also." Ms. Keller again, her screen momentarily flashing yellow.

Senator Rayburt answered. "I don't see a problem. General Farmington and I have discussed the situation. We have no reason to believe Riverdale or Smith have any knowledge of the takeover plans. They will learn along with the rest of the world."

Then one of the others, Mr. Weston, the U.S. expatriate, asked the question Senator Rayburt had hoped would not surface. "Is the problem with the Louisiana congresswoman handled?"

The senator took a breath. Rayburt had hoped they didn't know. "The problem is under control," he said. "General Farmington and I discussed the congresswoman recently. The general has assured me the situation has been handled."

There was a significant pause, and then Mr. Weston said in a low intimidating voice, "I hope you are right."

Mr. Holden spoke a harsh reminder. "Senator Rayburt, there is no room here for error. A slip could expose our board to public scrutiny. That *cannot* happen." He paused. "You do understand, don't you?"

The senator could almost hear the others sit up, listening for his answer.

Rayburt nodded. "I do understand."

The senator realized he was sweating. He dared to glance at his image on the monitor. There were tiny beads of perspiration on his forehead. Reaching for a tissue and wiping his brow, Rayburt could only wish his obvious stress had not been so visible to the other board members.

After another few minutes of minor questions, the meeting adjourned. Rayburt exited the chat session, deleted tonight's history, and leaning back, relaxed slightly.

Closing his computer and monitor, Rayburt had an uneasy feeling in the pit of his stomach. He was very uncomfortable with the implied threat voiced by Zack Holden.

~~~

Senator Rayburt had been a member of the strange six-person Board of Director's since the beginning of his second term in the senate. Still, after all the ensuing years, at times Senator Rayburt felt ill- at-ease in these meetings—the outsider—the one who doesn't really belong.
~~~

Only here did this emotion manifest itself. It made no sense.

~~~

In all the years he'd been a member, the senator had met his fellow board members in person on only one occasion. All other times had been by phone or at these electronic sessions. In most of the meetings, the senator assumed the other board members were separated, each joining the conversation from wherever they happened to be. At a few, though, the five were obviously in one location, Rayburt guessed, based on the exchange of conversation between them.

The senator had never shaken their hands nor clinked glasses except for the one occasion. Rayburt also had no idea where they were located during the meetings. They could have been in New York or Paris, Hong Kong, Dubai, or even Washington. Senator Rayburt never knew, nor did he ask.

The senator glanced around his own special location for the video sessions. The space was relatively small but well laid out.

A few years after joining the board, Senator Rayburt had purchased his house in Lanier Heights, a small urban neighborhood located in the northwest section of Washington, D.C. The senator's new home was the exception in his neighborhood. Most of the dwellings were on small tracts of land and packed close to each other.

A friend had divulged that one of the few large homes with land would be coming on the market. The three-story house had been built in the late 1800s and was luxurious—polished wood, brass, and marble at every turn. The house was set back from the street at
~~~

the end of a long circular drive protected by an electronic gate.

Rayburt had bought the home after only one visit.

The Belgian, Mr. Peeters, suggested Rayburt have a hidden location within his new home where he could take their meetings in a very private setting. The other board members quickly agreed, and funds were allocated for the project.

A contractor from the Midwest was hired andpaid by the board. Work on the project was done in secret and under the cover of darkness. No permits were requested. When completed, the new space was known to only the senator, the contractor, and the board.

A computer was installed along with other equipment and wiring to give the senator complete privacy for the board's meetings.

Included with other construction, Zack Holden suggested the senator allow the contractor to add a way to leave the house in case of a sudden emergency. After all, the senator's bedroom suite would be on the third floor. This made sense to Rayburt, and an emergency exit was added to the construction.

Residing on the third floor led to complications. An escape had to be designed and constructed allowing an individual—the senator in this case—to leave his suite and secretly make his way downstairs to a tunnel entrance at or below the ground floor. Once there, the tunnel would lead to a camouflaged exit at the edge of the property.

The contractor and an architect employed by the board put their heads together and came up with a solution. It was a huge task, especially the tunnel. Special equipment was required and delivered in secret.

Construction began. Materials and equipment were purchased or rented and delivered by four different out-of-town suppliers over a five-day period. Supplies were housed in the senator's large four-bay garage until needed. Once construction began, workers were transported to the Lanier Heights location each evening in an enclosed van. They never knew the address or had an outside view of the project where they were working.

One of the most challenging aspects of the undertaking was a way to move someone from the third-floor secret office to the tunnel entrance downstairs. The senator himself offered up a solution—a spiral staircase.

The architect glanced at the contractor, saying, "Yeah! That would do it."

The staircase, because of its size requirements, would be a special order. It would need to be narrow and come in relatively short sections. An order was submitted.

Every step was taken to keep the concealed office, stairway, and tunnel secret. Soundproofing was a major consideration. Though very expensive, special insulation of a type used in sound studios, and deep carpets were used to excess.

Finally, the project was ready for the senator's approval.

Construction from start to finish had been completed in three weeks.

The senator's secret office and escape became a reality, and he was quite satisfied with the results.

Once the overall project was complete, Senator Rayburt attended all the board's meetings from the concealed space inside his home.

~~~

No new members had been added since the senator joined the board. Twenty-three years in this strange relationship, and he was still the junior associate.

Yet, Rayburt couldn't complain. Being on the board and taking advantage of the available global information had made the senator wealthy beyond any dream he might have had as a younger man. His financial situation briefly tugged at Senator Rayburt's thoughts.

He owned nice cars, flew private or first-class anywhere he chose, took several vacations to exotic locations each year, and was the owner of secret accounts in six different names spread across seven foreign countries and a dozen cities. Assets included just under nine hundred million dollars in those hidden accounts the last time he had reason to check. And back in his home state, there was a small operating ranch where he headed for occasional R & R. Finally, there was the estate with its mansion here in Lanier Heights. The last valuation for insurance purposes had come in at just under forty million.

Being on the covert board had been good for him.

It had been good for others too.
~~~

During the years Senator Rayburt had been a member of the board, they had given advice and answered questions for leaders around the globe.

There were others, though, that they refused to aid. Colonel Gaddafi of Libya was one of those.

Gaddafi, near the end of his rule, sought information concerning neighboring countries. The Libyan leader had offered twenty million U.S. dollars for their aid. The Board discussed the request, agreeing he was searching for a way to escape his own country. They unanimously decided against dealing with Gaddafi. Years earlier, the members had informally agreed to refuse requests that were individually motivated.

During the last twenty years, other countries across the globe had paid much less and received the board's help in various areas.

Well placed information and precise advice coming from the board had started and ended wars. Likewise, they had made it possible to feed and house millions in underdeveloped countries. Friends had been made of enemies and likewise, enemies of friends in their long-term goal of a one-world government.

The members had watched their goal inch closer. Another five years of strategic manipulation of the world's power countries such as the U.S., Russia, China, and Western Europe would be critical.

~~~

Smiling, Senator Rayburt recalled the beginning.

A few months into his second term, an envelope was squeezed under his apartment door in the dead of night. Already retired for the evening, the young
~~~

senator heard the noise and climbed out of bed to investigate. He walked through the apartment searching for the source of the sound until he reached his front door.

There it was.

The envelope contained an address, a key, and ownership papers for a condo in Washington, D.C. The deed was in the senator's name.

"Huh?" was his first reaction, a sense of suspicion sweeping across his mind.

Bordering on a state of shock, Senator Rayburt sat down on his sofa. *There's gotta' be a mistake. Who would give me a condo?*

Scanning the papers, they appeared in order and really did name him as the new owner. Checking dates, Rayburt saw the papers were dated two days earlier and indicated Wayne W. Rayburt had purchased the condo himself. There were a couple of pages requiring signatures and an envelope to send those back to an attorney in Georgetown.

*This is some elaborate joke*, Rayburt thought back then. *It* had *to be a prank.*

He was tired. He'd check it out tomorrow. Tossing the envelope and its contents on the coffee table, the senator returned to his warm bed where, for the rest of the night, he had trouble sleeping. *A condo...*

Senator Rayburt left his apartment at 6:00 the following morning and drove to the address given in the envelope. It was a good-looking building in a desired area of the Capital, and there was a doorman.

The senator identified himself and was directed to the elevator. Walking down the hall on the third floor, the whole experience felt surreal. He knocked at the door and then entered using the key from the envelope.

The condo was way above his present accommodations. It had three bedrooms and three and a half baths. There was a living room, a dining area, a den, and an office/study, all fully furnished.

The senator walked about almost in a daze. There was a balcony; that was furnished too. Walking back to the kitchen, Rayburt, on impulse, opened the refrigerator. He stood staring for several seconds. The fridge was stocked. Everything one could need for the next several days.

He had been carrying the original envelope as he scrutinized the condo. Dropping into a chair, the deed was examined again. Everything looked official. It appeared he was the owner. He would certainly call the attorney in Georgetown when he reached the office.

The senator was ready to get out of there, but there was one more surprise.

At the front door, there was something he hadn't noticed on arriving—another envelope. It was taped on the inside near the lock. He pulled it loose and returned to a chair.

Inside was a handwritten letter addressed to Senator Wayne Washington Rayburt. It was unsealed. Opening it brought some apprehension.

Curiously, the letter didn't mention the condo. Instead, the senator was requested to call a phone number in Chicago. He was given a time for the call— 10:00 a.m., Washington time. Today.

The letter made a request. The senator was not to discuss any part of the situation with anyone before the call.

Really curious now, Senator Rayburt could see no harm in granting that request. He would discuss the matter later with the lawyer in Georgetown.

He glanced at his watch. 8:17 a.m. Plenty of time.

~~~

Back at his office, Senator Rayburt told his secretary he had an important call to make and to hold all others. The senator also told her he was not to be disturbed before he finished the call.

At ten o'clock, the senator followed the letter's instructions. Using a secure line, he dialed the number he had been given. A male voice answered.

"Hello, Senator Rayburt."

"Good morning." He wasn't going to get excited until he knew the situation.

"Senator," the voice said, "I have a request. I and my associates would like you to join us for dinner tomorrow evening."

When Rayburt hesitated, the voice said, "We would like to meet you in Washington." Then the man said, "We believe you will find the time well spent."

"Where?"

"The Inn at Little Washington. Nine, tomorrow evening. Ask for Mr. Holden's party."

Senator Rayburt was familiar with the restaurant, though he had never dined there. *If nothing else, a nice dinner.*
~~~

The Senator wasn't sure the time would be well spent, but he did want to clear up the matter of the condo. "I can meet you there."

"Thank you, Senator Rayburt. Have a pleasant day." The phone clicked, and the line went dead.

# Chapter Seven

Arriving at the restaurant the next evening, Senator Rayburt, following instructions, was shown to a private dining room, and seated at the end of a table set for six. Five other individuals were there and waiting.

Introductions were made by Zack Holden.

A woman, Jolanda Keller from Switzerland, was seated at the senator's left with Nicolas Peeters, originally from Belgium, seated beside her. Frank Weston was on the right side of the table opposite Peeters. Weston, a U.S. expatriate, now called Spain his home. Bandile Nkosi, a South African, was seated on the senator's right. Johannesburg was home to Nkosi. Zack Holden, apparently the group's leader, sat facing the senator at the opposite end of the table. Holden told Senator Rayburt his boyhood home was Canada. Holden didn't say where he resided currently.

As they chatted, the senator warily observed the five individuals. Judging by conversation and questions, all were highly intelligent, which he expected. Also, by the senator's judgment, each of them probably brought a different field of knowledge to the table.

As a group, they were a few years older than the senator, ten or twelve at the most. Zack Holden was probably the senior member of the board—maybe late forties. Jolanda Keller, the senator suspected, was probably the youngest and closest in age to himself. She was fortyish. The others fell in between, somewhere in their forties.

Drink orders were taken, and they were left for a few minutes of general conversation.

Ms. Keller asked about the senator's early years and his family.

Those were not subjects Senator Rayburt often talked about. Some things were better forgotten. The senator's family fit that mold.

The household had been a disaster.

His only sister, a year younger than himself, had been killed along with her boyfriend in a car crash during high school. Their older brother had been sent to prison for dealing drugs and had been stabbed to death in his cell. The mother disappeared when her children were little more than toddlers. Rayburt couldn't even remember her face. He hadn't yet started school when she vanished. Finally, the senator's father had died of cancer during Rayburt's first year in college.

Happiness during those years had been hard to come by.

The senator was a survivor though, and the exception in his family even as a youngster. He was bright, outgoing, and popular. From the time he was twelve, Rayburt could never remember a time when he didn't have a job to earn money. And he could never remember not loving football. The sport had been the tool he used to attain success.

Tall with a filled-out body at fifteen, young Wayne Rayburt ran roughshod over his school's opponents. Three years of the same had college football scouts sitting in the stands every Friday night by his senior season. His state university initially made the best offer for an education, and young Rayburt was ready to put his name on the dotted line.

Then a miracle happened.

On the evening before the signing ceremony, one of his state's U.S. senators called. There was an excellent possibility young Rayburt would be invited to be a member of the following year's freshman class at West Point.

The invitation, along with application forms and medical requirements, arrived only days later. Wayne Washington Rayburt signed on the dotted line and became one of several hundred plebes in the following fall's beginning class at the military academy.

Four years later at age twenty-two, Rayburt tossed his hat into the sky along with nearly one thousand of his close friends. He was now a second lieutenant in the U.S. Army.

He had been voted second team all-American in his senior year and MVP in the Army-Navy game. Rayburt had also carried a 3.92 GPA for his time at West Point.

Rayburt then went on to proudly serve his required eight years.

While gaining an education, he had become interested in debating and politics. With his education and service behind him, Rayburt—backed by old money—ran for mayor of his hometown and won.

Three years later, he was elected to the U.S. senate in a special election after the sudden death of the incumbent. Once he reached Washington, early family memories and his young life prompted the senator to return to his home state only when duty demanded.

With seven years in the senate now, he was on several important committees. Senator Wayne Washington Rayburt had clawed his way to the top.

There was much that could have been said, but his answer to Ms. Keller had been brief.

"I was a normal kid," he told her. "Went to school in my hometown, got an invitation to attend West Point, played football, and then went into politics after college and my required term in the military." He finished with, "I'm the last member of my family. I had a sister and a brother, one younger and one older." Finally, "My father died while I was in college."

She listened and then said, "I'm sorry for your loss."

If anyone bothered to check, they would find his comments scarce, but accurate.

Nkosi wanted to know if his race for the senate had been difficult.

The South African had been involved in politics. "I was a mayor for a short time in my early adult years before I formed my business and became a counsellor." He hadn't elaborated.

Finally, Weston and Nkosi each had asked about bills presently before the U.S. Senate.

The young senator told them a $217 billion dollar highway bill had recently passed and would be signed by the president, but without a much sought-after Drunk-Driving Rule.

Weston wondered aloud if Clinton, the current president, would be impeached by the House of Representatives. The second term senator thought the impeachment was a forgone conclusion and said so.

Drinks came; conversation turned to current events.

Zack Holden asked the young senator his opinion on the long-term situation in the Middle East. Senator Rayburt was able to state his thoughts in only a few remarks.

"The Israeli's are too restricted," the senator said. "They need help. Given recent bombings and terrorism, they're forced to defend themselves against the Palestinians and others." Leaning forward, he added, "The Jews may be a minority in the region, but they're a significant and uncompromising force. They must be dealt with, and it needs to be done at the negotiating table rather than on the battlefield."

The senator was quiet for a moment, glancing at each of the others. Then he said, "By word and deed, they're in their homeland to stay."

Holden smiled. "Yes." Senator Rayburt's answer had satisfied him.

"One other comment on the Middle East," the senator said. "The entire area is a hotbed of conflict, much of it directed against the Jews." Rayburt glanced at each of the five around the table before continuing.

"A list of those involved could be compiled on that subject. Any one of several countries including

Iran, Iraq, Turkey, or Egypt could be included on the list."

There were several nods around the table.

After dinner, they ordered another round of drinks and got down to the matters at hand.

"We are five members of what we loosely call a board of directors," Holden told the senator, and then added, "Actually, we are more of a committee than a board, and we casually call ourselves 'The Committee.'"

The senator listened.

Holden continued. "We watch and study activities around the globe and offer advice to government and business leaders who seek our input. On occasion, we make the first contact if we think our studies and discoveries are important to an individual country or to a region. Often, our global studies point to solutions that are long-term and affect an area rather than a single country."

Mr. Holden paused for a moment.

"Still," he said, his eyes focused on the young senator, "Long-term solutions for an area or even the world, begin with the actions of one country."

Senator Rayburt raised a hand indicating a question.

Holden nodded.

"You haven't mentioned China or Russia," the senator said. "These are the active power nations along with the U.S. Do these countries ever seek your guidance?"

Nicolas Peeters of Belgium glanced at Holden too. He appeared interested in Mr. Holden's answer.

"There are forward thinking leaders in all power countries, North Korea being the exception," Holden said. He added, "We expect to add them in the future. Kim Jong-il will not always be their leader."

"You haven't answered my question," the senator said. "China and Russia…"

"There are people there who seek our information and advice," Holden said. "Those countries will be major players in the world of the future. Present leadership may or may not be a part of that future."

With a sweeping gesture, Mr. Holden said, "Let's get specific with Senator Rayburt. He must be tiring of our questions."

The senator breathed an inner sigh of relief. At times, the evening had felt more like an inquiry than dinner with new acquaintances.

Mr. Holden said, "Since we are independent and not responsible to corporate stockholders or anyone else, we're free to disclose the truth as we see it to all interested parties. In return, our friends are inclined to pay handsomely for our advice."

"Then you must have established a good track record," the senator said. "In what areas do you offer assistance?"

Glancing at the others for a moment, Holden then returned his attention to Senator Rayburt. "We are most often interested in political implications, but on occasion, we advise our clients concerning critical supply and demand. It is good to know if a required item is going to be available or in short supply, and when. This would apply to domestic commodities and supplies as well as military munitions and equipment.

"As an unencumbered committee, we are also free to explore world politics as they may affect the future and issue advice accordingly."

Holden glanced around the table again and then back at the senator. "You understand these are general comments," he said. "Being more specific at this point could threaten client confidentiality."

Ms. Keller interjected a comment. "Our track record, as you put it, is exemplary. Those who have followed our recommendations and utilized our information and input have never regretted their decisions. Not even one time."

The senator glanced back at Holden and had a suspicion the man's eyes had never left his own. *He's evaluating me. They all are.*

Nkosi spoke up. "We operate in complete secrecy which allows us to make decisions without scrutiny." He added, "Our recommendations are seldom questioned."

"Where do you concentrate your efforts?" Senator Rayburt asked.

Weston answered the senator's question this time. "Anywhere our advice is requested or required. As was said earlier, at times, depending on circumstances, we may make the first contact."

Questions flowed over dinner and for the next two hours. The senator asked several, gaining a better understanding of the board's operations.

A most interesting piece of information came when the senator asked for specifics on how they were paid for their advice.

The South African answered. "You will find us unique in that respect," Mr. Nkosi said. "We never discuss fees with our clients, and we always bill $1,000 for our services."

This surprised the senator.

Mr. Nkosi continued. "Our clients are free to pay the amount we've billed them."

Zack Holden smiled. "They're also free to pay as much as they wish. Our advice is much sought after, and fortunately, most of our clients fall into this last category. They are happy to pay us well."

His elbows on the table, Senator Rayburt said finally, "Changing the subject, there is one last matter I would like to question."

All eyes were on him.

"The condo," Rayburt said.

Everyone around the table smiled.

Mr. Holden answered. "We set wagers on when you would ask."

"It's been on my mind," Rayburt said.

Holden glanced at his watch and then at Ms. Keller. "You win, Jolanda."

"I'll collect after drinks," she said, smiling.

There were chuckles all around.

"Senator Rayburt," Holden was addressing him again, "we traveled to Washington to ask you to become the sixth member of our board. Your position as a U.S. senator could be very valuable to us. We came believing you would agree to take the sixth seat."

The senator leaned forward even further in his chair. His expression didn't change. "I'm listening."

Holden leaned in, too, his elbows on the table, one hand under his chin. "Let me preface my invitation with these comments."

The group's leader had turned very serious.

"We," he gestured to include his fellow committee members, "find it most efficient to operate in total secrecy. The sources of our information do not go beyond these individuals. You will appreciate that factor better if you come on board. If you should decide not to join us, you should understand there will be no proof that this dinner ever took place. You go your way. We go ours. We will have never spoken."

Holden stared at the senator. "Do we understand each other?"

The senator took a moment before nodding.

Holden took a moment too, then smiled. "Now, back to the invitation."

He explained, "You would be expected to observe world events with a critical eye. As you travel, talk to leaders *and* people on the street." He glanced at his fellow members and then back at the senator. "Listen to what is said and always search for hidden meanings. Attitude is important too, yours and your contacts. Read people as you never have before."

Holden leaned forward again. "Every contact is an opportunity."

"What happens with our discoveries?" the senator wanted to know.

"Write a report on anything you feel warrants it. Forward a copy to each of your fellow board members."

Holden was on a roll.

"We meet as a group in some electronic form at the beginning of each month. Final reports and client advice summaries will be written by one or more of our members. Information and advice details due the client is delivered in person by our member in charge of the analysis."

"I see." Leaning back, the senator was truly impressed.

"We share client fees after expenses. Knowledge you gain from our endeavors may be used for self-gain in any way you see fit. Buy or sell stock." He hesitated. "Buy businesses if you are so inclined. Whatever you consider appropriate for yourself. Enjoy life."

"Back to my earlier—"

"The condo," Holden chuckled. We thought a U.S. senator should own, *not* rent. The condo is free and clear and in your name. If you consider it necessary, Senator, you may sign a note to the board. The cost of the condo would be deducted from your share of future payments from our clients."

"I *would* want to sign a note," Rayburt told them.

Frank Weston pulled a form from his coat pocket and shoved it across the table to the senator.

Rayburt glanced down, reading for a moment, and then pulled a pen and paused, glancing at each of the others.

"Does this mean you accept our job offer?" Ms. Keller asked.

"I do," the senator said, "if it doesn't conflict with my senatorial duties."

"We all hold positions," Holden said, gesturing toward the others. "Your duties with the senate are an asset, not a liability."

"I understand," Rayburt told him, looking at the note.

"There is one other factor you should also understand," Holden said, his voice and tone quite serious. "Yours will be the only public face on our board," Holden told the senator. "As such, you will be expected to apply great care in all your dealings, both as a senator and as a board member. A significant miscue in either could have dire consequences affecting our board *and* you as an individual."

It was a serious moment.

"Do we understand each other?" Holden asked.

Senator Rayburt leaned back, thoughtful for several seconds. Then, "We do, but on these conditions. I will have forty-eight hours to make any private inquiries I may believe appropriate regarding the five of you." He looked at each of them individually. "Assuming I am satisfied, this," Rayburt held up the note, "will be forwarded to an address you will give me. If I am not satisfied, a cashier's check will be sent."

He signed the form and placed it in his coat pocket.

Holden stood up. Rayburt too.

Everyone stood as Holden walked around the table to the senator. Holden brought his drink with him. They clinked glasses and shook hands.

The others followed Holden, each of them clinking glasses with the senator.

Senator Rayburt slept well that night. His last thoughts were of Holden's suggestions of a New World Order.

# Chapter Eight

The twenty-three years since that initial meeting passed much faster than the senator would have believed possible. He had made initial inquiries regarding the five individuals. Satisfied with the response, he forwarded the note and became the sixth member of the elite Board.

Senator Rayburt had participated with his newfound colleagues in numerous intelligence recommendations across the globe during the ensuing years. His reputation, like that of the board, had flourished with time, both in the U.S. and abroad. The senator's proposals were always well thought out and his advice rock solid.

A year and a half prior to the most recent U.S. presidential election, Zack Holden and Nicolas Peeters had approached Senator Rayburt with an alarm. Various board members had developed intelligence regarding significant dissatisfaction with presidential candidate Allen Carrigan. These concerns were widespread, both in the U.S. and across the globe. Not at all surprised, Senator Rayburt had encountered similar fears in private conferences with American and foreign dignitaries.

It was believed that if Carrigan should win the presidential election, his goals for dealing with Middle Eastern countries and Russia could undermine world peace. China, with its two-million-man army, would likely involve themselves in any destabilization. The result could potentially bring down the United States as a world power.

A few weeks into discussions, a plan was floated concerning a coup to unseat Carrigan if he was elected to the presidency. The plan quickly grew in favor. When Carrigan won the very close election, steps were already in place for his removal.

Senator Rayburt, in off-the-record surveys of strategically important world leaders, was considered the best candidate to head a replacement government.

He was also the choice of the clandestine board of directors on which he served. Though Rayburt didn't initially promote the notion, the senator himself secretly believed he was the only acceptable individual capable of leading an effort to overthrow the president.

What had its beginning as an idea nearly two years ago was now a full-fledged plan in motion. If successful, in a very short time the country would see a dramatic change in leadership in Washington, D.C.

~~~

April came, bringing the operation a week closer. As usual, early morning found Senator Rayburt at his desk in the senate office building. The senator was leaning back in his large and impressive leather chair, a gift from George H. W. Bush on Rayburt's long-ago election to the senate. The two men had become close when the young senator arrived in
~~~

Washington and had remained friends until the former president's death.

Thinking of the week ahead, the senator was contemplating the details he expected would come to fruition.

Then the phone rang.

The senator glanced at the wall clock opposite his desk. 5:17 a.m. Someone else was up early.

On the second ring, Senator Rayburt glanced at the caller ID. He smiled, doubting it really was the president's office on the line. Still, since he was the only one in at this hour, the senator picked up the receiver and said hello.

An easily recognized voice announced, "Wayne, this is the President." Without waiting for a reply, Allen Carrigan skipped to the point of his call. "Can you come over to the White House? I need to talkto you."

The senator thought of the ongoing plans to unseat the president.

The friendship of the two men stretched back three decades. They had run for senator in their respective states at the same time. Rayburt won; Carrigan had not. Six years later though, Carrigan had run again and won against the one-term incumbent. He had served in the senate until his successful race for president.

"When do you want to see me, Mr. President?"

"My car is waiting out front for you now." There was a chuckle. "I knew you would be in your office," Carrigan said. "You and I are the only ones dumb enough to be at our desks this early in the morning."

Rayburt chuckled too. "How can I refuse such an invitation when the King's chariot awaits?" The senator realized there was more than a touch of irony in his voice. Rayburt's ongoing disagreement with the president's Middle Eastern policy negotiations was no secret.

"Then I'll see you in a few minutes," Carrigan said. The call was over.

The senator glanced outside. Darkness still held claim to the Capital.

~~~

An aid, familiar to the senator, was waiting when the president's limo and security cars stopped under the portico at the White House. The woman opened the vehicle's door and stepped back allowing the senator to gain his footing.

"Good morning, Senator Rayburt. Follow me, please."

"Good morning, Aileen." Following her, he said, "How are things in Ireland and Falcarragh these days?" The senator had asked about her home on a past visit when they had a few moments to talk. He had picked up on her name and the slight Irish accent. He had also googled Falcarragh, Aileen's home. The small town was on Ireland's northern coast.

She smiled at his remembering. "It is quiet," Aileen told him, adding, "as always."

She turned, leading him directly through to the Oval Office and the president.

As the door opened, she said, "It's always nice to see you, Senator."

He nodded, watching as she closed the door behind him. Senator Rayburt was always stunned at
~~~

the striking resemblance between the president's aid and the first lady.

Rayburt strolled forward as Carrigan rose and walked from behind his desk. The president shook hands warmly, his free hand gripping Rayburt's arm in a friendly gesture. Carrigan was not wearing a mask, so the senator removed his and stuck it into a pocket.

"Good morning, Wayne. How are you?"Carrigan sounded genuine and unpretentious. Thatwas one of his known traits.

Then the president commented on the handshake. "You know we'll probably have to stop that. It spreads the germs, they say."

"Good morning, Mr. President. I hope you're well." Senator Rayburt was known for his down-to-earth demeanor with others, the president included. "I've grown tired of wearing a mask."

"I hate them," the president said, "but what are you going to do?"

Senator Rayburt commented on the vaccine. "Reports crossing my desk indicate the population as a whole is buying into the covid inoculations. That should save some lives. Congratulations."

"Let's hope it really does slow the virus."

Although Allen Carrigan was not a short man at six feet, he found himself looking up to the senator.

Coffee awaited them on a small table adjacent to the sofas and chairs. The president waved Rayburt to one of the chairs, taking a seat himself at the end of a sofa. Each of them reached for the coffee.

A sip, his smile gone, Carrigan set his cup aside. Then the president put it all out front. "I need your support, Wayne."

The senator set his cup down too. "My thoughts haven't changed."

Though he had no intention of backing Carrigan, Rayburt was interested in hearing the president's most recent argument.

"Hear me through," the president said. "I know your earlier position, and this isn't new, but we need Iran's help. Otherwise, there's going to be a major war in the Middle East."

The president's argument hadn't changed either.

Carrigan continued. "Palestinian forces are grouped across the Golan Heights. They're prepared to cross into Israel any day now." The president stood and began pacing slowly in front of his desk. His eyes on the floor in front of him, the president was silent for a few moments before turning back.

Rayburt waited.

Still without looking at the senator, Carrigan began to lay out his points.

"Syria will back the Palestinians if they cross. If not with troops, then certainly with intelligence, equipment, and supplies. Other countries surrounding Israel could potentially do the same." The president took a long breath and turned to face Rayburt. "Wayne, as you know, the Kremlin is backing Syria." Carrigan returned to his place on the sofa. He sat forward, turning directly to the senator, his knees almost touching Rayburt's.

Gesturing with his hand, the president stated his case. "Wayne, I know you don't agree with my current policy regarding Iran, but we need Tehran's Supreme Leader on our side." Carrigan scooted even closer. "Otherwise, I've been told to expect an all-out war. My security people and many other Middle Eastern experts agree on this." He tapped Rayburt's knee with a finger as he made his point.

Glancing down and a bit uneasy at the touching, Senator Rayburt stood and walked behind the sofa requiring the president to turn, following Rayburt with his eyes.

"I don't think I can do it, Mr. President." Rayburt hesitated. "You know the reasons behind my stand on Iran. They haven't changed. I believe if we continue to mollycoddle those people, we're sending the wrong message to everyone." He locked eyes with Carrigan as he said, "That would include our enemies in the Middle East as well as our friends everywhere."

Not surprising Rayburt, the president was prepared for a fight.

"Are you ready to tell the American people that you would rather isolate Iran than halt a major war in the region involving the Jewish state?" Carrigan went further. "A lot of your base is Jewish, isn't it?"

The president knew that it was. But Senator Rayburt knew he could appease his Jewish base once he was in the Oval Office.

The senator paused again. *I can buy some time if he thinks I'll consider helping.*

Senator Rayburt knew the chances were quitelow that the Palestinians would act before the coming coup. Information gained through the contacts of the board of directors indicated just the opposite. The Palestinians did not feel they were ready to take on the Israeli army. The fact was that a possible war in the Middle East was probably several weeks, maybe even several months, away.

The board of directors had reliable informants on the ground on both sides of the conflict. Rayburt knew he would have plenty of advance notice if action on either side was imminent. Inwardly, the senator was satisfied. There would be action in the U.S. long before anything took place in the Middle East.

Rayburt walked back and placed a hand on the back of his chair. He asked the president, "Do you require an answer today?" Seating himself and leaning forward he added, "If you do, I'll be forced to be against you."

"But why?" the president asked. "What will be different tomorrow, even next week for that matter?"

"I have inquiries out," Rayburt said, "and I would require that information before I even consider switching my position."

The president watched him closely. An ability to read body language and vocal hidden meanings in the voices of others were also traits attributed to the president.

Rayburt remained quiet, not letting expression or posture betray him.

Carrigan asked in a resigned voice, "How much time do you need?"

"Several days at least. Maybe more."

Senator Rayburt knew he had the president now.

But President Carrigan wasn't quite finished.

"I need you on this," the president said without breaking eye contact, "but if you stand firm, I'll make it work without you."

Senator Rayburt stared back at the president before nodding and turning to leave.

The president remained where he stood as the door closed behind Senator Rayburt. He mused that it was almost as if the senator had a different goal, one of his own makings. Carrigan had a bad feeling about his old friend.

The president wondered...*What could be gained by his reluctance to act in a way to gain peace in the Middle East?*

~~~

Back in his office before most of Washington's weekday staff had arrived for work, Senator Rayburt phoned the Pentagon after taking his chair. Though they conferred daily—sometimes hourly, given the president's latest push on Iran—the senator wanted a face-to-face with General Farmington. The Chairman of the Joint Chiefs of Staff was an early riser too.

Arrangements were made. The general said he would be in Rayburt's office at 9:00 a.m.

Though curious, Farmington asked no questions as to the purpose of the meeting. He would find out soon enough.

~~~

"Sorry about the short notice," Senator Rayburt told him when the general arrived.

"It's a busy day as they all are," Farmington said. "I made a few calls on the way over."

Senator Rayburt waved toward a seat.

The Bear placed his cap on the opposing chair and sat down.

"Utilizing every minute," Rayburt said. "I do the same."

Changing the subject, the senator told General Farmington about his unexpected early morning visit with the president.

"Carrigan's worried," Rayburt said, "but my sources are convinced the Palestinians won't act immediately. Probably not for several months." Smiling, he said, "By that time, you and I will be operating out of new office space and will have the situation in hand."

The general gave him a thumbs-up.

"Are all your people on alert?" Senator Rayburt asked.

"Everyone, everywhere," the general answered. "We'll be staging maneuvers as practice for a large-scale foreign backed attack with no advance notice."

The senator stood and walked around the desk. He moved Farmington's cap to the desktop and sat down in the chair. "Will the services follow commands once they realize future maneuvers aren't practice actions?"

"My people are trained to follow commands," General Farmington said. "I have prepared operational orders for distribution along with feasible explanations. The officers will follow my command."

"I don't doubt you," the senator said as he glanced toward the window. "You understand I'm trying to not miss anything." He stood and returned to his desk.

Once there, he turned back to the general. "Carrigan is still concerned about covid. That's good. It gives him something to worry about besides the Middle East." The senator eased into his chair.

The meeting was over. Without further comment, General Farmington reached for his hat.

# Chapter Nine

At 3:00 a.m. on a morning in early April, a large military convoy rolled out of the main gate at Camp Lejeune in North Carolina. The 2nd Marine Division had its orders. Trucks, trailered tanks, mobile missile launchers, various other equipment, supplies, and personnel were on the move.

An hour later, the Marine Expeditionary Force and its non-combat support teams departed the base and headed north.

Before dawn, local police and sheriff's officers in North Carolina and other states were taken by surprise upon finding their interstates and other highways occupied by United States fighting units. Local law enforcement had not been informed and had no reason to expect the military to be out in force. Early risers along the routes of the two separate units stared in surprise at the unusual movement of equipment and troops.

Questions were flying. In one small town a man asked his neighbor, "Has something happened that they haven't told us?" He was sincerely worried. "Maybe we're being invaded?"

Officials who were contacted didn't think so. "It's only maneuvers," a public announcement said. "Maneuvers and practice for the Memorial Day parade."

Local news shows speculated that perhaps the military was preparing to enforce a mandatory Covid- 19 stay-at-home order.

Grocery stores were busy, and service stations were dealing with lines that extended into the streets.

Arguments remained the norm regarding masking with physical altercations the result in many cases. Some only wanted to wear them when they were out in public; others didn't want to wear them at all.

Covid-19 cases were still crowding hospitals.

~~~

The Marine land convoy made its way to the Army base at Fort Jackson, South Carolina—coincidentally, about the same distance and difficulty as if they had traveled to the U.S. capital. A three-day exercise combining the Marine unit with the Army's 193rd Infantry Brigade gave each a chance to practice exercises of all types.

Crowd control was high on the agenda. New recruits doing basic training at Jackson were pressed into service for the practice.

Otherwise, a significant portion of available time was used to keep the troops' basic skills at a peak. Fort Jackson's rifle ranges were busy for the entire three days.

The separate Expeditionary Force traveled north for a day before returning to Camp Lejeune. The final exercise required the unit, along with air cover, to
~~~

storm ashore in targeted landings along Lejeune's fourteen miles of beaches.

Marine Commandant, General Wisecroft, boarded a helicopter on the second day for a two-hour flyover of the beach landings. Observing closely, he asked questions and occasionally offered advice.

Overall, the force gave every appearance of being combat-ready. General Wisecroft told his officers to inform the troops he was proud of them. They would appreciate those words. Wisecroft was known as an officer who took care of the rank and file. In return, the unit's officers, non-commissioned officers, and the men they commanded would follow their general's orders without question.

~~~

Airborne units were active during the same period. The 82nd Airborne Division stationed at Fort Bragg in North Carolina boarded aircraft in the deadof night. The 101st Airborne Division at Fort Campbell, Kentucky, was involved in a similar exercise. Theaircraft flew airborne units to an undisclosed locationin the western United States. There, a combat practice exercise was held, combining both divisions. Two days later— fully prepared for action—they returned to their home bases.

Military maneuvers were taking place across the entire continental U.S. that week. Large cities saw a significant influx of military traffic. New York, Philadelphia, Chicago, San Francisco, Los Angeles, and Seattle were among them. Hawaii and Alaska sawtheir own share.

Sightings of the military were initially reported in headlines by national and local news but rapidly
~~~

became commonplace and lost appeal. The average man on the street felt safer knowing the military was protecting the country, but he didn't feel the need for continuously talking about it. This was especially true given that the conspicuous show of force had lasted only a few days.

Interestingly, little had been mentioned about the fact that few of the military forces encountered had been wearing masks of any sort. Yet, the Covid-19 coronavirus was leading in the news with new cases, ICU admissions, and death counts rising every day. This was a real and present danger to every individual. The public appeared more concerned with the ill and dying among them than with the military and their maneuvers.

~~~

A day later at the Pentagon, General Farmington met with Army General Charles Averyand Marine General George Wisecroft. There wereonly a few weeks left until their subversive plans were to come to fruition.

Avery and Wisecroft were sitting across the desk from the Bear.

"Were you satisfied with the exercises?" Farmington asked. He glanced back and forth between the two.

Wisecroft answered first. "I was down at Lejeune observing the II Marine Expeditionary Force," he said. "Based on what I saw and the reports of my commanders, the Marines are combat ready." The general was proud of the force he commanded.
~~~

"I'm not surprised, George," General Farmington said. "You've done a fine job in your time as Commandant."

He shifted his attention to General Avery. "Charlie, what about your people?"

"We're ready too," the general said. "In addition to normal units on station throughout the continental forty-eight, I'm holding three unassigned Corps in reserve. Those units are strategically placed for movement to wherever they're needed." He looked General Farmington in the eye. "We're ready, Paul."

Rising and walking around the desk, Farmington placed a hand on Avery's shoulder,saying, "I knew we could count on you, Charlie."

~~~

In the outer office, a colonel known to the generals stood to say hello. Colonel Rederton, an aid to General Farmington, had met both generals on numerous occasions, and they were familiar with his background.

Kyle Weston Rederton was a Marine full colonel. He had been the youngest member of his 2001 graduating class at West Point and at the young age of 39 was on the short list to wear his first star.

General Avery had been poised to grab the colonel for his own staff when the Chairman of the Joint Chiefs claimed Rederton. Likewise, General Wisecroft was very familiar with the young colonel. They had discussed theoretical battle strategy on several occasions at informal meetings chaired by General Farmington. Wisecroft had been pleasantly impressed by Colonel Rederton.
~~~

Acting as an aid to General Farmington for the last seventeen months, the colonel had been asked to sit in on several of the casual get-togethers presided over by the general. General Wisecroft had attended most of those gatherings. The meetings were held in Farmington's conference room at the Pentagon and usually concentrated on conflicts, ongoing or expected, around the globe. The most recent discussion had focused specifically on Iran and its sale of oil to the Russians.

General Wisecroft had listened closely to Rederton's infrequent comments. Though there was nothing he could specifically point to, Wisecroft came away with a deep feeling that the colonel harbored different convictions regarding the Middle East than those of General Farmington.

~~~

Back in his own office, General Wisecroft left his hat on the rack and settled into his chair. Turning to the window, he sat still for a few moments. Colonel Rederton had continued to be on his mind since the earlier chance meeting. Picking up the phone, the general asked his secretary to chase down the colonel and ask him to drop by at some convenient time.

A few minutes later, Wisecroft was informed that Colonel Rederton would be in the area early that afternoon. At 1:15, they were seated across from each other.

"I've watched and listened to you in General Farmington's meetings," the general said, "and I come away with the feeling that you are not in total agreement with the general's concerns regarding
~~~

Iran." General Wisecroft paused. He watched the colonel, wanting to see how he would respond.

Colonel Rederton took his time. After a glance over the general's shoulder, he turned his eyes back. "May I speak frankly, sir?"

"I hoped you would," General Wisecroft said. "That's why I asked you to drop by." The general added a leading statement calculated to open the colonel's defenses, "I'm guessing you and I have some of the same misgivings."

The colonel looked into General Wisecroft's eyes for a long moment before speaking. He wanted to choose his words carefully. Finally, Wisecroft leaned forward in his chair.

"This has to be off the record, sir." The colonel's eyes were pinched, his forehead showing deep wrinkles beyond his years. "I'm putting my career on the line even thinking these thoughts."

"Go on," Wisecroft prompted. "This is only the two of us having an exchange of ideas."

The colonel appeared to relax a little. "It isn't so much General Farmington's disagreement with the president. It's that I've come away with the feeling that there are others with him who would consider taking up arms against the present administration." He paused again, then said, "For lack of a better way of stating my impression, I wonder if there are those who would consider forcefully replacing our elected leaders." Colonel Rederton breathed a long sigh. He had stated his case. His thoughts were out in the open with one of the top leaders of the United States military. General Wisecroft was also a man he respected and trusted.

It was the general's moment to turn to the window.

General Wisecroft thought about his own leanings. He didn't like what they were planning: Senator Rayburt, the generals, and others, himself included. Now it was evident that a few well-positioned and well-informed individuals could see through to the action that was to be executed in a few weeks. General Wisecroft had feared this would happen. He had even expressed his fears to General Farmington.

Now the officer sitting in front of him verbalized those same concerns. This could not be overlooked.

*I will have to pass this on,* he thought. *There may very well be others who suspect a coup is in the making. The whole operation may be in jeopardy.*

He tried to put himself in the colonel's place. Rederton's concern was obviously for the country. Wisecroft thought about the implications for the colonel.

*I'll ask for Farmington's guarantee that the colonel not be reprimanded for his concerns. I'll try to protect him.*

"I'm sure I would know if there were ongoing plans for a coup," General Wisecroft said. He hoped he was convincing. "Have you expressed these thoughts to anyone else? I hope not. That could be dangerous for the Marine Corps and for you."

"Oh, no sir," Colonel Rederton stated emphatically. "I care too much for this country and for the Marines." He added, "I only confided in you because you also indicated misgivings. Perhaps I misunderstood."

General Wisecroft was ready to close the conversation. He stood, saying, "I do worry about the discord between General Farmington and the President, but we in the military are obligated to follow the orders of the president. I can't imagine General Farmington would do otherwise."

Colonel Rederton left shortly thereafter.

General Wisecroft immediately picked up the phone, calling the Chairman of the Joint Chiefs. General Farmington suggested he come right over when Wisecroft stated his fears about an unnamed officer.

General Farmington waved Wisecroft to a chair when he arrived. "Tell me about your conversation."

Seated, General Wisecroft talked Farmington through Colonel Rederton's concerns using the colonel's exact words in several instances. When he finished, the Chairman of the Joint Chiefs sat quietly for almost a minute before speaking. Then, his words spoken quietly, Farmington said, "We'll have to find a way to keep the colonel busy until the operation is behind us."

"He's a good officer," General Wisecroft said. "I have no doubt that Rederton's concerns are for the country."

The Bear nodded. "Still, we can't take the chance that he would discuss his concerns with others before the operation is executed."

General Wisecroft had an uneasy feeling. "I don't want the colonel's career to end because he expressed concerns for the country."

"Don't worry, George," Farmington assured him. He was quiet, thinking for several seconds. Then,

"I'll send Rederton down to Eglin Air Force Base on a mission that will keep him busy until the operation is in place." Seeing empathy in Wisecroft's expression, Farmington stood and walked around to take his place at the large desk.

"I promise to keep him occupied." The Bear smiled at his long-time friend.

The meeting was over.

~~~

In a maintenance hangar near the flight line, the mechanic was hurrying to finish his work for the day and get out of there on time. A phone call brought one more chore.

This order was unorthodox in nature but would only take a few minutes. *And the extra pay is very good,* he thought, carrying his toolbox as he walked out to the parked aircraft. The job was off the books too—no paperwork.

He had finished and was back in the hangar before quitting time and walked out to the parking lot with his buddies. He looked forward to dinner with his wife, and later, he would see the guys again at the bowling alley.

Life was good.

~~~

Early that evening at Joint Base Andrews outside Washington, D.C., a Piper Seneca V twin-engine six-seater aircraft taxied up short of Runway 01 Left. The pilot was waiting for take-off permission as he and his passenger talked about the weather.

"It's beautiful tonight," the pilot said. "You picked a great evening to fly."

Without smiling, his passenger replied, "I didn't pick it. Someone else did."

The pilot glanced at the Marine colonel in theright seat, then along the tarmac and back to the southern approach. The sky was clear. Holding the brake, the pilot then revved the engines, testing them one last time as he waited for clearance.

Moments later the tower called their number, giving permission to roll.

Without further conversation, the pilot turned the aircraft onto the runway and pushed the throttles forward. Under his control and gaining speed rapidly, the aircraft's nose soon tilted upward and lifted into the night. Immediately, the lights from traffic on the Capital Beltway Outer Loop loomed off in the distance.

Suddenly, there was a loud tearing sound. The aircraft immediately rolled into a severe left turn and dipped its nose. Though he tried desperately, there was not enough time nor altitude for the pilot to keep them aloft even if the controls had functioned properly.

"We're going in," were the last words he transmitted to the tower.

A stand of pines stood between the aircraft and the cars on the highway ahead. The aircraft's tanks, topped off for the flight, ignited as the craft tore into the woods. Wings separated, spreading fuel and fire in their wake. An explosion erupted, followed by silence except for the sound of crackling flames among the wreckage in the trees.

# Chapter Ten

One of the fishermen saw the big white egret when they rounded the bend. He pointed it out to his brother-in-law. The first impression was that the big bird was perched on a bag of trash. The garbage was resting on a limb in the bushes near a stand of cypress trees. It probably wouldn't have noticed if they hadn't slowed for a floating log.

Watching since the boat came into view, the egret suddenly took flight and landed a hundred yards inland on a moss-draped limb of a mammoth oak tree. The sound of its wings echoed across the swamp for several seconds.

"Why would some fool bring his trash out here to dump it?" The man was sitting in the bow of the boat. He had been preparing his rod for the big largemouth bass he expected to be reeling in soon. "Let's pick it up and drop it in the dumpster back at the landing." He motioned to his brother-in-law who was running the motor.

Without comment, the boat veered toward the litter. The man in the bow put a hand on the side and leaned over to grab the trash. Suddenly scrambling back and screaming something unintelligible, he turned, his face pale and fearful.

He managed to utter, "Holy Mother of God…"

"What's wrong?" The operator couldn't see the problem. "What?"

"It's not trash," his companion uttered. "It…it's a body!"

The operator glanced over the side. Then the engine roared as water churned around the propeller. The boat backed away. What they had thought was trash had suddenly materialized into a human body—an obviously very dead human body.

The engine idled and then died after a few seconds. The two fishermen sat staring at the dead man. With their craft drifting slowly away, they glanced at each other. Both were struggling to control emotions. The brothers-in-law had been fishing Lake Martin for years. This was a first.

Speechless, they sat gawking at the corpse. Dressed in dark clothes, it was hung on tree limbs only a few feet away. Face down, its arms and legs spread below the surface, the body was rising and falling with ripples on the water.

"Holy Mother of God." The man in the bow said it again.

The one in the back crossed himself. Then, "We can't leave him here."

Shaking his head, the one in the bow glanced toward the body and stated emphatically, "I ain't riding with no dead man in the boat." Then he looked at his relative.

With a frown pinching his forehead, the operator looked his relative in the eye. "We can't leave him," he said. "The 'gators'll get him for sure if we don't take him out of here." Glancing at the body again he added, "I'm surprised they ain't already taken him to the bottom."

Nodding slowly, his brother-in-law unenthusiastically agreed. "Yeah, I guess you're right. We gotta do it."

Neither of them wanted to touch the dead man, but there was no alternative if they were going to keep him from the alligators. Dragging the body up and out of the water was difficult though the man was relatively thin. Finally, still face down, the body was secure at the middle of the small boat, arms and head hanging off on one side, his lower legs and feet off the other. The brothers-in-law watched as though the body might suddenly awaken and threaten them.

It didn't. It just lay there—dead and decaying—all promises of life gone.

~~~

Back at the Lake Martin Road boat launch, a crowd gathered quickly. Fishing boats didn't normally return from the swamps with a human body stretched across their midsection. Three sheriffs' department cars arrived within minutes. They came from BreauxBridge with sirens blaring. A 911 call had been madeas soon as the brothers-in-law slid their craft up to the wharf.

Arriving deputies were as curious as the onlookers. Everyone was asking questions.

The owner of the little bait shop back in town had been watching the action, his hands shoved deep in his back pockets. "Where'd you find 'em?"
~~~

The relative from the bow answered. "Down south in the edge of the swamp." He glanced at his brother-in-law for confirmation.

"Yeah, two or three miles." They both were nodding.

"Can you take us back there?" a deputy asked.

"Sure," the man on the engine said. "Thought the law would want to know where we found him, so we tossed a tarp on a tree limb."

The deputies unloaded the dead man from the boat and onto the old, weathered wharf. They carefully turned him face-up. "Anyone know him?"

Several onlookers shook their heads while others just stared. A deputy turned the body enough to reach his back pockets. Finding nothing there, hepatted the coat and checked the man's shirt. In a pocket, there was a wet, folded sheet of paper and aroll of cash. Nothing else.

"Bring one of the cars up close and put this on the hood to dry." The older deputy was taking charge.

A few minutes and some speculative conversation later, everyone watched as the coroner's wagon backed in near the body. Then they waited as more questions were asked. Two hours would pass before the dead man was moved.

By then, the sheet of paper taken from the dead man's pocket had dried. The only thing written there was the partial name and address of a convenience store in New Orleans. It meant nothing to the deputy, but he slipped the tattered sheet into a plastic cover to accompany the body to the morgue.

~~~
~~~

One hundred and thirty miles east in the Orleans Parish Coroner's office, another body lay on an autopsy table. The forensic examination into a young woman's death was only minutes away.

"I wish we had a name," the masked Medical Examiner said aloud as he walked to the side of the table.

An assistant looked a bit startled. "We don't have an ID?" she asked.

He looked her way, asking, "You know her?"

"Sure," the assistant told him matter-of-factly. "That's Congresswoman Kato. I recognize her from the news on TV. I've read that she keeps an apartment down in the Garden District."

"Hmm..." The examiner reached for a scalpel. "Not anymore, she doesn't."

~~~

General Farmington called the senator on a secure phone and immediately stated the subject. "A potential problem is developing down south."

The senator's voice was hard, probing. "What sort of problem?"

"Your contractor has been found."

Senator Rayburt was quiet for a moment. Then, "I didn't think finding him was a possibility. As I remember he was going away forever. 'Gator grub,'" he added. "You gave explicit instructions."

"I thought that too," General Farmington said.

"What happened?"

"Two fishermen found him in a swamp," Farmington said.

The senator thought for a moment and then asked, "Have they tied him back to New Orleans?"
~~~

"I'm not aware that they have."

"Good," Senator Rayburt said. "Let's hope they don't. At least for a couple of weeks. No way to move him now."

"Yeah."

# Chapter Eleven

Cary Warren picked up her phone immediately upon seeing the news flash on TV. The article had identified the mystery woman killed in a New Orleans convenience store as U.S. Congresswoman Josette Kato. Identification had not been announced until forty-eight hours after the shooting.

*Landie had to be heartbroken.*

Cary thought of her elderly friend and the anguish she must be feeling.

Having met the young congresswoman several times before and after her election to congress, Cary had been very impressed. Seeing her with Landie, it was obvious the young woman felt a special attachment to her elderly grandmother.

Cary reached for her phone.

When Landie answered, Cary said, "I just heard. I'm so sorry."

A sob on the other end was the only response.

"Would you like for me to come and stay with you for a couple of nights? I know the family will be in and out, but I thought you might need someone to talk with outside the family."

There was no hesitation in Landie's voice when she replied. "That's such a thoughtful idea. Yes, please. When can you come?" The elderly woman sounded relieved, as though she'd been waiting for Cary's call.

"It's early. I'll try to get a flight out of Knoxville this afternoon. My crew can handle things for a couple of days."

"Thank you."

Cary heard another sob.

~~~

A grandson picked her up at the airport and drove Cary to Landie's house.

Barry could only talk about his Grand MaMa. "I've never seen her so upset," he said as he dropped Cary off. "She was proud of Josette, and they were close."

Landie met her at the door. A hug and then, as usual, Cary was offered coffee and a cookie at the kitchen counter. After an hour, the two women went into the living room. Cary took the sofa while Landie eased into a chair facing her. With her long legs tucked under, Cary asked, "Have Josette's parents been given details."

"No, not really. The police told Bert and Susan it appeared the shooting was connected to a robbery. The cash drawer was empty except for the change." Landie took a breath and continued. "The store clerk was clubbed unconscious. Then Josette was shot at the back of the store." She hesitated and looked at Cary. "It seemed strange...to shoot a customer, but not the clerk."

"Were there details? Was anything caught on security cameras?" Cary asked.
~~~

"I don't know," Landie said, her words soft and slow. "No one has really told me anything."

Cary thought she should change the subject. Landie was obviously uncomfortable talking about the shooting.

"Did you see Josette often?"

"I did. She came to visit me every time she was in N'awlins."

Cary smiled at her friend's local pronunciation of her city.

Landie continued. "In a way, I was her sounding board. Josette told me things she wasn'tcomfortable telling others."

"Boyfriends and things like that?" Cary asked. *Every girl needs that kind of confidant.*

"Oh, no." Landie shook her head and a finger, too, for emphasis. "She didn't have time for boyfriends." Landie eyed Cary, hesitating for a moment. Then, "Josette...talked about concerns with duties and allegiances involving her office."

Before Cary could ask questions, there was a knock at the door. A neighbor was introduced; the woman was bringing a cake for Landie. Cary took the dessert into the kitchen as Landie thanked the woman. Glancing back, she couldn't help taking a finger swipe of the icing. Her eyes fluttered as she smacked her lips.

After a few words of condolence, the neighbor said goodbye and hurried away.

Cary had been intrigued with Landie's earlier comment about duties and allegiances. She wanted to ask for more, but Greg was walking up the sidewalk as the neighbor was leaving. Landie's eldest son stayed for an hour, and then others were in and out during the remainder of the day.

Cary lost the thought until several days after she'd returned home to Tennessee. By then, Landie's granddaughter had been laid to rest, and the moment had slipped away. Cary didn't want to disturb her elderly friend with odd questions about Josette's private comments.

~~~

Several evenings later, Cary was alone in her apartment. Josette's untimely death and her visit with Landie were fading into the past. Turning off the evening news, Cary sat in near darkness contemplating her own future.

She was living the good life—a great job, friends, more money than she needed, and...Mike. Life was pleasant in so many ways.

Cary was aware that for many, this was not true. The coronavirus was now killing people across the globe as the health community tried to keep up. Vaccinations were being touted as one of best alternatives for avoiding Covid. Masks were still high on the list of preventive measures. A bright spot was that although masks were still suggested at inside venues, they were suggested but not required outside. This was especially true if the individual had been vaccinated.

Shaking her head, Cary tried to push the virus to the back of her mind. Though she was sympathetic to those who were dealing with the illness, Cary had other, more personal matters to consider.

She and Mike were growing closer.
~~~

For the last several months, they had been spending as much of their free time together as possible. Over that same period, an occasional kiss atthe door had turned into a breathless embrace on her sofa.

The next step had been inevitable.

~~~

Often, on weekends, Mike would have a free day and come to Knoxville where they would spend time with each other. A single night together was a luxury.

Cary had gone to Atlanta on a couple of occasions, but both preferred the smaller city.

Occasionally, they would both fly to an agreed upon destination where no one knew them. Not that they minded others knowing their closeness, the two of them simply enjoyed being alone with each other.

Cary had grown very fond of Mike and was pretty sure he felt the same. She had tried but couldn't quite put her finger on the reason for their being drawn to each other. Perhaps it was because each was alone in the world. Cary's adoptive parents had been killed in the automobile crash during her last months at University of Tennessee. Mike's elderly uncle, the last in his family, had died of a heart attack two years earlier. Now they only had each other.

Neither had used the word "love," though Cary had wanted to on several occasions. They had even discussed it.

That was one of the things they enjoyed about their relationship—they each felt free to talk about anything.
~~~

Turning to stretch her long legs on the sofa, Cary was letting her thoughts run wild, secretly afraid she felt more for Mike than he did for her.

*I'm setting myself up for a fall.* Doubt had moved in. *I can't imagine he feels the way I do.*

Still on the sofa, she awoke at one o'clock in the morning, tears on her cheeks and a longing in her heart. *Circumstances won't let us be together, and I don't want to be apart.* Cary walked down the hall and, pushing the covers aside, fell into her bed.

When she awoke in the morning, Mike was immediately on her mind.

*So, what's new?* She smiled and threw her feet off the side of the bed.

There was much in each of their lives to keep them busy. Quite often, Mike found himself ordered to a new situation and location by the U.S. Marshals Service, often with only a short notice. Too often, he couldn't tell Cary where he was going, and she'd have no word from him for days, occasionally even weeks on end.

Cary was busy too. Trebeck Corporation was growing and needed more and more from the marketing department. To meet new requirements, Cary had added several people to her staff and often found herself working weekends. That had helped defer her loneliness, but still, her erratic workload made it difficult to have a private life.

On a rare recent weekend morning off, she was sitting at the kitchen bar having her obligatory cup of coffee. Cary was thinking of a recent situation.

Mike's obligations with the Marshals Service weren't the only obstacles making it difficult for them to have anything resembling a normal relationship. Cary's work situation fashioned its own complications.

Recently, they'd had plans to meet in Memphis and take a short river cruise. Three hours before she was to catch a flight, a message came down requiring all department managers to attend an important meeting on Saturday morning.

*Not again.*

Cary considered the possibilities, realizing quickly that there was no way to avoid the meeting.

She had called Mike immediately, breaking the news with a choked voice. He understood. At least, he said he did. He made it easier by reminding Cary that he was usually the one breaking their engagements. That didn't really help. It was her this time, and she didn't like the way it was making her feel.

"Another time," he'd said in parting.

Yet, because each cared, they managed to find time to be together. And they had talked about their pasts. They'd even gotten into discussions about the future. Cary told Mike everything she knew about her birth mother, where Janice Talmer came from and her early death—things he hadn't learned while they were combining efforts to find her mother's killer. Mike already knew about her birth father and his fall from political glory in New Orleans.

Surprising her, Mike talked about his mother and the way she'd caught a bus one night and never returned when he was a youngster. He also told her about leaving south Alabama on the night he graduated from high school and never going back.

Mike spoke warmly of the special people he met in Washington in those early years. In many ways, several of them—Rage Doyle and others—had become his family.

Cary and Mike each had their own stories and emotional scars. They speculated that those wounds were a part of the binding that had brought them together and kept them that way.

Just thinking about him gave Cary a warm feeling.

# Chapter Twelve

Mike Webster had made his decision. He would be joining Rage's new enterprise. Dreading to tell Jack Robbins, Webster flew to Washington for a face-to-face with his current boss.

"I'll be helping to start a new company," he told Jack.

"What kind of work will you be doing?" he was asked. "Can you be specific?"

"We plan to take behind-the-scenes jobs where others don't want to be connected," Webster said, holding his hands out and open. "That's about all I can say for now."

"Who will you work for?" Jack asked. "Private companies or the government?"

"Whoever needs us." Then Webster added, "I'll tell you more as soon as I can."

Jack was listening closely and leaned forward in his chair. "Any openings? I might be interested. "

"You?" Webster was surprised. Jack's entire career had been with the Marshals Service.

Webster's boss nodded, saying, "Keep me in mind."

"I'll do that."

Since he was not on assignment for the Marshals at the present, Robbins told Webster he was free to go home and make the new arrangements. He decided to go to Knoxville instead. Calling ahead, he cleared the timing with Cary.

By the time his plane landed, Webster had written several pages of notes to discuss with Rage when they met again.

~~~

Cary was excited when he called her from the airport.

"How long can you stay?" she asked.

"A couple of days," he said. "I'll need to go to Atlanta early Thursday."

"I'll see you at the apartment," Cary told him.

The evening began with Mike telling her about his decision to leave the U.S. Marshals to work with Rage.

Later as they sat drinking iced tea, she asked, "Will this job be less risky?" That was her first question. Cary was generally aware of his undercover work with the U.S. Marshals Service. She knew it was a dangerous profession.

"There's danger everywhere," Mike told her. "I could get hit by a bus as I cross the street."

"You know that isn't what I mean." She shook a finger at him.

He relaxed, hoping she would too. "Sure, there could be danger, but I'm careful, and I'll have you around to keep me in line."

"Where will you live?" she probed.

"I haven't thought about that," Mike told her. He really hadn't.
~~~

"Maybe here in Knoxville?" She asked hopefully. "You can have a real home. A real home in one place."

With a gleam in her eyes, she went one step further. "If you lived here, it could be good for our relationship."

Mike leaned forward, a slightly sinister grin on his face. "We have a relationship?"

She threw a sofa pillow at him.

~~~

"I'm on board and ready to work," Webster told Rage in an evening phone call. "When and where do you want me?"

"Great," was Rage's initial response. Then, "How about coming to the mountains for a planning meeting?"

"I'm in Knoxville now," Webster said, "but I'm headed home tomorrow. I could drive up to your place from Atlanta on Saturday morning." He didn't elaborate, and Rage didn't ask. He was aware that Webster and Cary had been spending significant time together.

"Plan on staying a couple of days," Rage suggested. "I'll put you up at the cabin. We should be able to get the basics together for an organization."

~~~

The letter was unexpected.

Cary and Landie did their communicating by phone. In the time they had known each other, Landie had never once mailed a letter to her, not even a Christmas card. Yet, there was an envelope in her box on Friday evening. Cary was tearing it open even as she unlocked the door to her apartment. Tossing her handbag on the sofa and settling into a chair, she unfolded the single page and began to read.

> *Dear Cary,*
> *You must be very surprised to receive this short letter. Let me explain.*
> *I need to talk to you, but I don't want others to know my concerns. As you are aware, I do not use the computer, so my only ways of reaching you are the phone and writing. I am afraid to phone for reasons I will tell you in person. Therefore, I'm sending this note. When you were here recently, I mentioned that Josette was concerned about a situation in her office. There is more I should tell you. And I have questions only you can answer.*

Cary leaned back in her chair. She immediately remembered the uneasiness she felt when Landie had used the words 'duties and allegiances' in their conversation about Josette. Now Landie wanted to tell her more...and ask questions.

*I can't imagine how I can help or what answers I can give.*

She turned back to the letter.

> *Could you come to New Orleans so we can visit and talk? I know it's an*

*imposition, but I would be forever in your debt. Some things are better discussed with special friends and not relatives.*
*Hoping to hear from you soon.*
*Sincerely,*
*Landie*

Dropping the letter on the table beside her, Cary reached for her phone. In the next five minutes, she arranged to fly to New Orleans early on Saturday. A second call let Landie know she would arrive there a little after eight o'clock in the morning.

~~~

With the taxi disappearing in an early morning fog, Cary stood on Landie's porch and rang the bell. The door opened and the two women shared a hug.

After the hug, Landie leaned back. Her eyes were red, and Cary immediately realized something new had happened.

"What is it?" Cary asked. "Have you had more bad news?"

"It's Susan," Landie said as she stepped aside for Cary to enter. "An ambulance has just taken her to the emergency room at Ochsner Medical Center."

"Susan?" Cary, at a momentary loss, walked inside.

"Josette's mother," Landie exclaimed. "Bert's wife. My daughter-in-law."

"Oh!" It finally clicked. "Susan. What happened? When?"
~~~

"During the night," Landie told her. "Susan's been dealing with what she thought was a bad cold or maybe the flu."

"They hadn't considered covid?" Cary asked.

"Not until now. When she lost consciousness, Bert called 911. When he described the symptoms to the dispatcher, an ambulance was sent out." Landie wiped her eyes. "Bert called as he was following them to the hospital."

When Cary suggested they sit, Landie said, "No, let's eat."

Breakfast was almost ready. Bacon had been fried, grits were boiling, eggs were ready to fry, biscuits were warming, and coffee was made. A genuinely southern breakfast.

Cary was ready for it. She'd only had an orange juice on the plane. She'd been hungry when she left home and remembered her disappointment when the flight attendants said they were restricted on food services because of covid.

O.J. was the best they could do.

When they were seated, Landie asked about the flight to New Orleans. "Did you have any problems at the airports?"

"No trouble at all," Cary said. "Everyone's wearing masks now. It's mandatory on all the airlines."

There was no mention of Josette nor any of the other subjects Cary expected until the kitchen had been cleared. Now, they settled in the living room and talked while they were waiting for a call from Bert.

The phone rang a few minutes later, but it was Greg. He wanted to know if Bert had been in touch since he reached the hospital. When his mother told him no, Greg said he'd call again later.

Finally, Cary and her elderly friend had a few minutes to talk.

"You must have wondered why all the secrecy?" Landie said.

Cary nodded, preferring to let her elderly friend move at her own pace.

"I don't think Josette felt safe to express her worries to anyone else," Landie said. "With me, she expected her words and thoughts would go no further. Who would…who *could* I tell? I think it helped Josette to verbalize her thoughts." Landie hesitated for a moment, then added, "She could do that with me."

Cary nodded again.

"Then that man murdered Josette." The elderly grandmother's voice had softened to a harsh whisper.

"But wasn't Josette shot during a robbery?" Cary said. "That couldn't have been because of her work."

"Was she really killed in a robbery? Or was she eliminated?"

Landie stared at Cary.

Then, after a moment, she asked, "I've wondered why that man would shoot Josette but not the clerk…if it *was* a robbery?"

Cary was stunned for a moment. "But aren't the police calling it a robbery?"

"They are, but I believe that man came looking for Josette." Landie's voice was strong again. She was fighting for her granddaughter. "There are other details."

Cary listened closely.

Landie peered at Cary. "Josette thought something bad was being planned inside the government, and she thought a senator she was working with was behind it."

*A senator?* Cary was surprised. "Who was he?"

"I don't know," Landie told her. "She never used his name. Josette always referred to him as 'the senator.' And she worked with several different senators over the years, so knowing names wouldn't clarify this one."

"Did she say the senator was a man?"

Landie thought for a moment. "I don't think she ever said exactly. She just referred to 'the senator.' I think she would have said if the senator had been a woman. I just assumed..."

Cary needed a moment. She excused herself and went into the kitchen, returning shortly with a glass of water.

*Josette was working with a senator. And she thought he was planning something sinister? 'Something bad.'*

Cary took a sip of the water and pondered. *Landie thinks Josette was murdered, that her death had nothing to do with a convenience store robbery. And a senator may be involved...but which one?*

Recovered, she asked, "Exactly what did Josette say that made you think the senator was doing something wrong?"

Landie gazed at Cary for a moment before answering. Looking away, she said, "That was the strange part. Josette didn't try to convince me." She hesitated. "It was like she was reasoning with herself."

Landie stared past Cary for several seconds as if she wasn't there. Then the grandmother said, "She told me the senator said something in confidence and then wished he hadn't."

"What did he say?"

"He said that when he was in the Oval Office, things would be different."

"So, the senator was planning to run for president?"

"That isn't what he said." She glanced at Cary. "And Josette was sure that was not what he meant."

"Did Josette tell you that?" Cary asked.

"Yes. I asked her specifically."

"When?"

"Just an hour before she was killed. She had stopped by on her way from the airport. I walked out on the porch as she was leaving for her apartment."

Cary watched her elderly friend carefully as she asked the question. "Did Josette say why she thought the senator was serious?"

Landie hesitated for several seconds. "He asked her to go with him, to be on his staff and act as one of his top advisors."

Cary was surprised again. "Why did he ask Josette?"

"I questioned her about that too. She said he needed her education and experience."

"She was qualified?"

"Oh, yes," Landie said. "Josette had a master's degree in International Relations concentrating on the Middle East. Besides that, she spoke five languages and was writing a dissertation on foreign politics for her Ph.D."

"Did she have practical experience?"

Landie had obviously been keeping up with her granddaughter since Josette left New Orleans. "Before she ran for congress, Josette had worked as an aid for two senators on the Foreign Relations committee."

Cary listened, stunned at Landie's knowledge regarding the situation.

They talked on, Cary with questions, Landie giving answers. Their conversation, with breaks, lasted into the afternoon. It was all about Josette.

Finally, the phone rang again. It was Bert.

"They have her in the ER." Landie was telling Cary what Bert was telling her. "He'll call when he has more information." End of conversation.

They went back to Josette.

Landie summed up her thoughts about her granddaughter's death as she led Cary back to the kitchen. Cookies and milk were placed on the counter; they had skipped lunch.

"I don't believe she died in that robbery," Landie said. "When Josette turned down the senator's offer, I think they decided she had to be eliminated. Josette knew too much." Landie glanced at Cary. "The senator had given up too much information for her to be outside his control."

"Was she given any time to make up her mind?" Cary asked.

"She was," Landie answered, "but she had already sort of given her answer." She stared at Cary. "Josette thanked the senator for the opportunity but told him she thought she wanted to continue as a congresswoman."

"That should have ended it," Cary said.

"He was angry when she turned him down. The senator told Josette she would regret that decision."

"Did she think he was threatening her?"

"She didn't take it that way. The senator's words concerned her, but Josette thought he meant she was missing an opportunity."

To Cary, it seemed Landie's assumption was like a grandmother's grief. Too much like Landie couldn't get her mind around the shooting being a simple senseless act.

Cary's thoughts were still running wild. *But if Landie's facts are accurate, it's possible that Josette was told something that could be dangerous to the senator. In that case, Landie could be right. The senator's words may have been a threat. Josette might really have been in danger. But from a United States senator?*

This was way too deep for Cary. She needed help.

"Would you mind if I talk with Mike about this?" Cary asked. She reminded Landie about him.

As Landie pondered, Cary's mind swept back to her earlier conversation with him. Maybe Mike and Rage could help.

"I want to know the truth about my granddaughter's death. That's all I'm looking for."

There was a tear on Landie's cheek as Cary walked out on the back porch. She dialed Mike's cell number.

# Chapter Thirteen

Arriving at Rage's mountain cabin at just after ten on Saturday morning, Webster was not surprised that his friend was at the desk in the cabin's loft. Waiting as his new boss descended the stairs, Webster strolled across the deck looking out at the mountains.

Rage swung open the French doors and stepped back after shaking hands. "Come make yourself a cup of coffee. We'll sit outside and talk."

Comfortable on the deck and with a sip of coffee still on his lips, Webster asked, "Do you spend much time out here?"

"Too much, probably." Rage was holding his cup with both hands and gazing at the far-off view.

"I can't imagine getting too much of this," Webster said, sweeping his hand toward the valley off to the east.

"I thought that, too, when I first bought the land and asked the Smith brothers to build this cabin," Rage said, "but, as strange as it sounds, you get used to the view being there." He took another sip of his coffee. "When I'm at home, I come out most mornings and watch the sunrise." He looked at Webster, a slight grin on his face as though he was about to divulge a secret.

"I come out during the night too, usually around two o'clock in the morning. On a clear night, the stars are indescribable. I'll wake you if you want to see them."

"I would," Webster told him.

Setting the coffee aside, they turned to the business at hand. Rage went inside and returned with clipboards, pencils, and a legal pad for each of them.

Webster pulled his own list of notes from his pocket, asking, "What kind of assignments do you anticipate?"

"No way to know," Rage said, adding, "Investigations certainly, individuals and situations. Beyond that, I'd be guessing. We'll have to see what comes our way."

"What about personnel? Do you have some people in mind besides you and me?"

Rage chuckled. "We'd have to be content with small assignments with only the two of us to handle everything." His casual mood disappeared. Rage leaned forward and said, "I've talked with a friend who is with the military. He's eligible to retire, and he's looking for something interesting to do."

"What does he do for the service?"

Rage stood and leaned on the rail. "Herbie is with the Criminal Investigation Division of the Army—the CID. He's a Chief Warrant Officer."

Webster was interested. "Sounds like the kind of experience we'll need."

"Good man too. I've known Herbie since 9/11. We both spent time in New York after the Towers came down."

"Married?" Webster asked.

"Widowed. His wife died several years ago. No children."

Webster nodded and made a couple of notations on his pad before turning back and suggesting they also talk to Webster's boss, Jack Robbins. He described the family. "His wife is Monica. Two youngsters: a girl and a boy. He would fit in. Jack's a no-nonsense type of guy. Smart and a good sense of humor too."

"Talk to him," Rage said. "See if this situation would suit him. I trust your judgment. I suggest you have him meet you somewhere to talk details."

"Right, I'll call him. When I told him I'd be leaving the Marshals, he was interested." Webster glanced at his notes. "We need to be careful of our communications—phone, emails, everything. There may even be times when we'll need burner phones."

Rage told him about the encrypted phone and added, "Compliments of the CIA." Then he asked, "Do you have anyone else in mind?"

A moment of thought and then a big smile brightened Webster's face. "Yeah. Yeah, I do."

"Let's have it," Rage said. "This must be a good one."

"It is, if he's interested." Webster hesitated and then said, "In fact, I may have two."

Rage rolled an arm, gesturing for him to continue.

"When I was recovering at the Charlotte facility, I became friends with a guy on the staff." Webster stood and walked across the deck. Turning back, he said, "Bob Ramsey is his name. Bob's about 6'3", and he's a nurse. Pretty capable with a gun too. He helped when the drug people came for me." Webster sat down again. "Bob might be interested. He works directly for the government and might be close to qualifying for retirement."

Nodding his agreement on the nurse, Rage then reminded him, "You mentioned another possibility."

"A woman," Webster said, a slight grin on his face. "Amy Hogan—also a U.S. Deputy Marshal."

"The Marshals could get ticked off if we take several of their people," Rage suggested. "Hogan would be the third."

"You're right." Webster said. "Let's talk to the people we've already mentioned and see how it goes? Besides, we don't have a job yet."

Deciding they could start their organization with just the two of them, Rage suggested others might be able to help on a part-time basis. "Each of them has particular talents," he said. "Equally interesting, each of them obviously has an ability to adapt to new circumstances. That's not something you can teach."

"True," Webster agreed.

A few minutes after twelve, they made sandwiches and continued with plans as they sat on the deck. Things were coming together.

At mid-afternoon, the cabin's landline phone rang. Rage went inside to answer. Gone for only a couple of minutes, he returned and handed the phone to Webster.

"It's a woman." He winked.

~~~

Knowing there would be no cell service in the mountains, Mike had forwarded his mobile phone to the cabin's landline. He recognized Cary's number and was smiling when he said hello.
~~~

The smile didn't last. He walked out the main door and into the yard to listen.

He had heard about the death of the congresswoman from New Orleans but had no idea she was Landie's granddaughter. "I'm sorry," Mike said, also recalling Bert and Susan, the congresswoman's parents. Nice people.

Cary brought him up to date. Then she summarized Landie's concerns regarding the shooting. Wondering aloud, she asked if this would be something the new organization could investigate.

"I'll pass it by Rage," Mike told her.

After discussing additional details about the shooting, they agreed to talk again on Sunday.

~~~

Bert called again while Cary was on the phone.

"Susan is on a ventilator," Landie said as the door closed behind Cary. "They've given her drugs to fight organ failure, and they're monitoring her in the ER. Bert's going to call if anything changes."

Nothing to do now but wait.

~~~

"We may have our first job," Webster announced as he stepped back onto the porch.

"Tell me," Rage said, looking up from his clipboard. It turned out he was not familiar with the congresswoman, and although Rage was aware of Landie, he had never met her.

Webster talked for thirty minutes, giving him basic details Cary had furnished and answering Rage's questions. He began with Landie's assertion that her granddaughter had been murdered.

"Wasn't she shot during a robbery in New Orleans?" Rage asked. "That's what I read," he said.

"Landie doesn't think the granddaughter was killed in a robbery," Webster said. "She believes her granddaughter was killed because of connections in Washington."

"Really? What connections?" Rage asked. "She was only a second term congresswoman. What could she possibly know that would get her shot?"

"Josette was working with a senator," Webster said. "As such, Landie thinks the granddaughter was privy to important information. Possibly something secret."

Rage smiled. This was a little hard to accept. "What qualifications could she have that a senator would need?" he asked.

Webster explained Josette's education and experience to Rage.

When he finished, Rage released a deep breath. "Wow. So, who's the senator?"

"We don't know," Webster said. "Josette never named him to her grandmother. She always referred to him as 'the senator.'"

"Why did the congresswoman tell all these things to her grandmother?" Rage asked. "Seems an unlikely conversation," he added.

"I asked that of Cary," Webster said. "It appears Landie was the granddaughter's unofficial confidant. They often talked when Josette flew home to New Orleans. The congresswoman told her grandmother things she didn't discuss with others."

"Hmm…" Rage stared out at the mountains for a few moments before asking, "What else did Cary tell you?"

Webster, standing since he returned from the yard and Cary's phone call, now slipped into a chair. "The grandmother poses some interesting questions."

"Like what?"

"I'm quoting here. Cary said Landie asked, 'Was Josette really killed in a robbery, or was she eliminated?'"

"That's pretty far-fetched," Rage said.

"I'm not finished. Then Landie posed this question. 'Why would that man shoot Josette but not the clerk if it was only a robbery?'"

Rage didn't have an immediate answer for that one, but he asked, "Aren't the police all over the robbery and shooting? I mean with the victim being a U.S. congresswoman, wouldn't they be pretty sure?"

"There's more," Webster said.

Rage nodded.

"Josette thought something was being planned inside the government."

"By this unnamed senator?" Rage asked. "Again,

Landie's words," Webster said. "Josette thought the senator was planning something sinister. Something bad."

Rage was quiet for a moment and then asked, "Exactly what did Josette say that made Landie think the senator was doing something wrong?"

"That's the strange part. Landie said her granddaughter didn't try to persuade her about the senator." Cary hesitated. "She said it was like Josette was trying to convince herself."

"That was all?" Rage questioned.

Webster stood and paced toward the end of the deck. Turning finally and facing back to Rage, he said, "Josette indicated the senator told her something in confidence and then wished he hadn't."

This caused Rage to sit up. "What?"

"The senator said that when he was in the Oval Office, things would be different."

Standing now, Rage asked if Josette thought the senator was planning to run for president.

"That wasn't what he said, and Josette was sure that was not what he meant."

"Is that what Josette told Landie?"

"Yes. I asked Cary specifically."

"When did this conversation take place?"

"The last time Josette and her grandmother were together according to Cary."

"When was that?"

"An hour before she was killed," Webster toldhim. "Josette had stopped by on the way to her apartment from the airport."

"Did Josette say why she thought the senator was serious about the White House?"

"That's the final nail," Webster said. "He asked the congresswoman to go with him, to be one of his close advisers. The senator said he would need people he could trust, loyal advisers with Josette's education and personal experience."

"Did she give him an answer?"

"Not exactly, she had told Landie. Josette indicated she'd think about the offer but didn't think she wanted to leave the House of Representatives."

"That should have been the end of it," Rage said.

"But it wasn't," Webster said as he returned to his chair. "Landie still had her questions and opinion. Landie thinks Josette was murdered when she refused the senator's offer. Maybe she knew too much and suddenly became a liability."

"Hmm…"

"Cary said she must have had a skeptical expression on her face because that's when Landie made her accusation. 'Was Josette really killed in a robbery, or was she eliminated?'"

~~~

The congresswoman had been shot and killed during a robbery. She had recently refused a job with an admired senator. Cary said that there were other details that would be made available if Mike and Rage decided to pursue the matter.

Rage was interested. "Experience," he said. "We can start with a small project. I'll reach out to Herbie and see if he's serious about wanting a change. He's the detective among us."

"What's his full name? Herbie can't be all of it."

Rage grinned. "Heber Kean O'Connor." Thenhe chuckled. "Irish. Like I said, he goes by Herbie."

"You'll call him?"

"I'll do it now. Speed should be one of our assets." Rage stood up to go inside. Looking back at Webster, he said, "Call and get us on a flight out of Knoxville to New Orleans."

As Rage turned to the door, Webster posed a final question.
~~~

"What are we calling ourselves? We need a name."

Rage smiled. "SPI." He spelled it.

"S-P-I?" Webster waited, eyebrows raised, appearing confused.

"Strategic Private Investigations," Rage told him.

Webster thought for a moment. "I like it," he said as Rage was closing the door behind him.

# Chapter Fourteen

Mike was unable to get them a flight until late Saturday evening. It would be deep in the night before they arrived in New Orleans.

Rage called Herbie and explained the situation. His friend was interested and available. Agreeing to meet them in New Orleans, Herbie flew in from CID headquarters at Quantico, Virginia. It was well into the night before they were settled in their hotel.

After a short rest, the three men were up early on Sunday to listen to Landie's story. A short phone conversation between Cary and Mike confirmed the women would come directly to his hotel room.

~~~

The women dressed as if going to church hoping questions wouldn't be asked if family members dropped by. Landie still didn't want anyone, including family, to know about her conversations with Josette. Their discussions had always been in confidence. Now Josette was dead, and Landie hoped some sense could be made of the mystery surrounding her granddaughter's passing.
~~~

They had already called a taxi when Greg came through the back door. Seeing them dressed, Landie's son immediately said he'd drive them to church.

"We have a taxi on the way," Landie told him.

"Call and cancel it," he said.

They argued with Landie winning. "We'll be going out to eat after church," she added. "Don't expect us back until you see us." She winked at Cary. Greg threw up his hands as a horn beeped outside.

"See you later." Landie waved as Greg started along the sidewalk toward his house. Her son was shaking his head as he walked.

~~~

Mike Webster, Rage Doyle, and Herbie O'Conner were waiting. They stood and shook hands when the women arrived. Introductions were made and coffee and breakfast pastries were ordered.

Two chairs were left for the women, and the men sat on the edge of the beds.

Cary offered to brief them.

Glancing at Josette's grandmother and receiving a nod, Cary began an attempt to convince the men that the young congresswoman had been assassinated.

"There were only two people in the store, Josette and the store clerk." Cary looked at each of the men. "Then the shooter arrived. The clerk said it was as though he had followed Josette."

She gave the thought a moment to settle.

"All this was in the police report Bert was given.

Then, the shooter clubs the clerk."

Cary hesitates, glancing at each of the men again.
~~~

"This clerk has seen him, eye to eye, and can potentially give details, but the shooter leaves him alive and kills Josette. That's strange."

At that moment there was a knock at the door interrupting Cary. Their breakfast order has arrived. It took a few minutes for calm to settle again

Everyone had their coffee and a roll as Cary continued.

"As I was starting to say, it's strange that the shooter left a witness alive. Then he kills someone who probably wasn't even aware he had entered the store until she was confronted."

She looked for a moment at Rage and Herbie. "You've probably talked and already know parts of what I'm telling you, so I'll make it brief."

She looked at Landie, then turned back to the others.

With the focus on Rage, she said, "Josette's grandmother was her sounding board. She told Landie things she wouldn't tell anyone else. She also talked about subjects she wanted to get straight in her own mind."

Peeking at Landie again, Cary moved on.

"The congresswoman had been working with a U.S. senator. We don't know all the details, but Josette had seen and heard enough to believe the senator and others were plotting a takeover of the government."

Herbie gestured for Cary's attention. "Was she sure that was the senator's intent?"

"Josette was sure," Cary said, looking first to Herbie and then Rage and Mike. "He asked her to go with him." She let that settle. Then, "We don't know the identity of the senator. Josette never named him to her grandmother."

"But she was sure about a takeover?" Herbie was still digging.

"He told Josette things would be different when he was in the Oval Office." Cary hesitated again before going on.

Herbie took the pause as an opportunity to ask another question.

"Did she give the senator a definite answer about joining him?"

Obviously, neither Rage nor Mike had mentioned Josette's vague refusal of the senator's offer. She hadn't exactly told him no.

Cary explained that. "Perhaps anything other than an emphatic 'yes' would have scared him. Josette wasn't yet a part of an inner circle. As such, perhaps the senator didn't believe he could afford to have her outside his control."

Rage glanced at Mike, then at Herbie.

After another ten minutes, Cary took a breath and leaned back in her chair. Everything Landie had told her—everything Cary knew or suspected—was up for scrutiny.

Herbie voiced the first question to Landie. "What are the police saying?"

Responding immediately, the grandmother told him, "They think it was nothing more than a robbery."

"I'm assuming the man returned to the cash register after he shot your granddaughter," Herbie said.

Landie nodded.

"Is that right?" Herbie asked, "Because if it's as you say, he would have wanted it to look like a robbery."

"Yes," Landie answered. "He had ordered the clerk to open the register when he entered the store. Then he struck the clerk with his gun." Still looking Herbie in the eye, Landie added, "Josette's parents were told security cameras showed the man snatching money from the drawer before hurrying out the door."

"Did he have a car?" Mike's question this time.

"The police said he ran along the sidewalk." She held Mike's attention. "He might have had someone waiting to pick him up."

Rage cleared his throat. "Did there appear to be any conversation between your granddaughter and the gunman before Josette was shot?"

"Yes," Landie said, "there was." She continued, giving Rage the details. "It happened when he confronted Josette at the back of the store. The shooter was facing my granddaughter with his back to the security camera. The detectives said he appeared to ask her something. The camera couldn't see her answer, or they'd have had a professional lip reader look at the video. They did say she appeared surprised at whatever the shooter said."

"How did they know he asked your granddaughter a question?" Herbie this time.

Landie had the answer. "Josette hesitated before nodding her head as she answered."

"Was there more than one security camera?" Mike again.

Landie turned toward him. "I asked Josette's mom and dad that same question. Bert and Susan talked to the police. They were told there was one camera inside the building and another outside at the front." She added, "It's an older store."

Mike nodded.

Across the table, Herbie had been listening quietly. He spoke up now. "I know the New Orleans Police Department Commander. I'll give him a call and see if we can look at the file."

"It's too bad we can only go on what Josette told her grandmother," Rage said.

Landie waved a hand. "Oh, there's more information somewhere."

All eyes turned.

"Josette kept a journal."

She immediately had everyone's attention, even Cary's. A journal had not been mentioned in their conversations.

"I'm sorry. I forgot about it." Obviously embarrassed, Landie touched a finger to the edge of her chair as though removing a speck of dust. "My old brain just remembered," she said as she met their eyes again.

"Where is the journal now?" Cary asked. "Did she carry it with her?"

"I have no idea," Landie said. "Journal is my word." She glanced at four stunned faces. "Josette said she was keeping memos about important conversations and other information. She never told me where she kept them."

Mike locked eyes with Rage, an understanding passing between them. They needed whatever notes Josette had been keeping.

Reaching for the coffee, Mike topped off their cups. With a fresh sip, Rage said, "I think we have enough to get started. Herbie, you talk to the police.

Mike and I will work on a strategy approach." He looked at the women, politely giving them orders too.

"You ladies need to contact Bert. We need permission to search Josette's apartment. If any new ideas come to mind, give Mike a call."

Rage had an afterthought, his focus on Landie, "Tell Bert we're all thinking of Susan."

Coffee and conversation were over. Time to work.

~~~

On the way back to Landie's house, Cary was quiet, looking out the window and deep in thought.

"Is something bothering you?" Landie was observant.

"Oh...no, nothing." Cary realized her lack of attention had been noticed by her elderly friend.

"I saw you watching Mike," Landie said. "Does he know how you feel?"

Cary studied her friend for a moment. It hadn't occurred to her that anyone noticed.

"I don't think he knows," she said after a moment. "He's so into this new work with Rage. And especially now with Josette's death." Cary smiled, adding, "Like so many males, he can only process one thing at a time. Right now, that's the search for the senator."

She touched Landie's arm. "Maybe when this is over, he'll think of me."

~~~

Newly appointed Police Department Commander, Wendall Johnson, was happy to hear from Herbie, even during the weekend.

Herbie got right to the point. "Can you see me on short notice? Today, if possible. It's important, and I'm in New Orleans,"

"Sure," Johnson laughed. "Everything I do is on short notice, and it's all important." Then he said the words Herbie needed to hear. "Come on down. You'll give me an excuse to get away from all the politicos pounding on my door."

When he arrived, Herbie was immediately led into Johnson's office. "The Commander is waiting for you."

After friendly greetings, Herbie told his friend he was interested in the recent shooting of Congresswoman Kato.

"That happened the day I was sworn in," Johnson said. With a curious look, he asked, "Why are you interested?"

"The congresswoman's grandmother has asked me and some other friends to inquire," Herbie told him.

"It appears to be a straight-forward robbery and shooting," the commander said.

When Herbie didn't respond immediately, Johnson added, "Well, isn't it just a robbery?" He paused. "Or do you and your friends know something I don't? Or does the grandmother just have doubts?"

"You're probably right about it being a robbery," Herbie told him, "but the grandmother had been Congresswoman Kato's confidant." He hesitated for a moment and then said, "They've had some interesting conversations."

Commander Johnson listened as Herbie told him about Josette's work in Washington. "Sometimes enemies are made without meaning to. That's a part of being in congress," Herbie said. "We just want to follow up on a few things and make the grandmother happy."

"If that's all this is, I'll see that you get a copy of the file," Johnson told him. He added, "Don't upset my people if you can help it." Then he told Herbie, "We have the congresswoman's computer too, but we haven't found anything important there. We've made a copy of her hard disk drive, so...so I guess we can release the laptop too. Maybe your people can find something we've missed."

"Do you think we could take a look at the store's security camera information?" Herbie asked.

"I'll see that you get a URL link for the company's website and the security camera's pickup. You'll find two sets of videos, one inside and another outside the store."

"Thanks, Wendall."

The chief said the file and Josette's laptop would be delivered to the hotel by 6:00 p.m. "Sorry about the timing, but we have nearly two dozen officers out sick. This covid thing is overwhelming us," he explained.

Sunday had been a busy day.

~~~

That same weekend, an autopsy was in progress at the St. Martin Parish coroner's facility in Breaux Bridge, Louisiana. The body on the examination table was an unidentified male, 5'9" tall, 158 pounds, dark
~~~

hair, and mustache with a sprinkling of gray, dark complexion, possibly Cajun, and an estimated age of 40–45.

Basic autopsy notes were being recorded. Two small gunshot entry wounds, probably .22 caliber. One to right rear of the head. A second one above right ear. No exit wounds. Estimated time in water, four hours. Subject was deceased prior to encountering the swamp, no water in lungs.

Conversation between the medical examiner and his assistant centered on the fact that the body had been found on the surface of the lake.

"Check the police report again. I believe it indicated the body was hung up on tree limbs?"

"That's what it says." She had turned to papers spread on another table.

"Hmm...lucky the fishermen happened along," the examiner said. "If a gator had beat 'um to him, this poor soul would have never been found."

Photos and dental imprints were made, and fingerprints and DNA samples taken. Two .22 caliber slugs recovered from cranium. Normal items in pockets; everything but identification. With the autopsy completed and photos made, the man's body was moved to temporary storage awaiting someone to identify and claim him.

The wrinkled sheet of paper with the New Orleans address found on the body was copied and the original dropped into the file. The copy made its way to the police file. A connection to the New Orleans case had been made based on the address.

~~~
~~~

Rage, Webster, and Herbie gathered to examine the copy of the congresswoman's file when it arrived at the hotel Sunday evening. Josette's laptop was temporarily set aside as the men zeroed in on the robbery investigation file.

Assorted pages, photos, documents, and other details were quickly scattered about on the extra bed in Webster's room. Rage pulled a chair close and was flipping through the congresswoman's Summary Autopsy Report. Herbie walked to the window as he studied photos of the store's interior. There were several showing the area where the congresswoman was shot. There were several, too, of Josette's sprawled body.

Webster was working at the small desk where he had set up his own computer. Using the IP address, URL links and other information they'd been given, he quickly connected to the company's website and tapped into the security camera pickups.

"Got it," the others heard Webster say. They quickly pulled chairs close and leaned in toward the screen.

Webster explained what they were seeing. "Someone has set up a video file for the robbery and shooting footage." They watched as he clicked on the file.

~~~

**A silent video began running showing the inside of the store. The camera was near the checkout. The clerk was busy stocking cigarettes on a rack behind the counter. He finished and turned a few seconds before a young woman pushed through the front door. As she passed the checkout, each could be**
~~~

seen appearing to smile though masks blocked their faces.

The woman raised a hand, waving and saying, "Hi."

It was easy to imagine her one-word greeting.

Rage pulled his chair closer. The video continued holding the complete attention of all three men.

As the woman turned the corner at the coolers, a scruffy-appearing man entered the store wearing a covid mask and holding a pistol in his right hand. Pointing at the clerk, he obviously ordered the register opened and the clerk to raise his hands and turn away. The clerk obeyed. Moving quickly, the unkempt man stepped forward, stretched across the counter, and struck the employee in the back of the head with the gun.

Leaving the checkout area, the man hurried to the back of the store where the woman, partially hidden by shelves, could just be seen starting to close a cooler door. She turned back into part view of the camera, a half-carton of eggs in her hand. A wide-eyed expression claimed her face when she saw the pistol. The woman had obviously not noticed the commotion at the front of the store.

Partly blocked from view by shelves and with his back to the security camera, the shooter said something to the woman. Though mostly obscured from view, she appeared to nod as she answered him. Already at close range, the man then raised the pistol and fired a shot into her chest leaving the cooler door to swing closed on its own.

**The woman's body fell almost entirely in view of the security camera.**

"What did she say?" Rage couldn't wait. Webster ran the video back and they watched the short sequence several times.

At last, Webster stopped the video and looked up. "I have no idea. Maybe 'yes'?"

"I couldn't tell either." Herbie was as lost as the others.

Rage motioned for Webster to continue as they each leaned forward. Their eyes returned to the computer's screen.

**The gunman shot the woman again, this time as she lay sprawled on the tile floor. The broken egg carton lay beside her, egg whites seeping out at the edges. Leaning over, he watched her closely for a few moments. Nodding then, the man stood and hurried to the front of the store where he emptied the open cash drawer and rushed toward the exit.**

**The 180-degree security camera on the wall behind the register picked up something new.**

**A teenage boy dressed in a dark hoodie had his head down and was focused on entering the store. He stepped quickly out of the man's way. The youngster, obviously startled, then stood in the doorway for a few seconds watching as the man sprinted into the darkness along the street.**

The video ran on for a few seconds with no changes except the teenager walking to the register, looking over the counter, and then making a call on his cellphone.

The front door had closed aided by the wind.

"Play the outside footage," Herbie said.

Webster clicked on another file and started the video.

Running from the moment he stepped outside, the shooter fled along the sidewalk leading out St. Charles Avenue. Neighboring bushes quickly obscured his flight. The video ended a few seconds later with an empty sidewalk and a sparsely filledstreetcar passing along the tracks.

With questioning eyes, the three of them glanced at each other.

Rage was the first to speak. "Wish we knew what he said to her."

Webster and Herbie nodded.

"Only the two cameras, huh?" Rage was thinking out loud.

Webster was busy on the computer.

"What are you looking for?" Rage asked.

"Just curious," was his response. Webster didn't look up as Rage and Herbie began a general discussion of the shooting.

A couple of minutes later, Webster waved their attention back to the computer screen. He glanced over, directing a question to Herbie. "I thought Commander Johnson told you there were only two security cameras?"

"He did," Herbie said. "One inside and another outside."

Rage pulled closer. "What have you found?"

"Another camera," Webster said. "The file name for this one was 'Cooler,' and it wasn't with the others." He glanced at Rage and Herbie. "It wasn't called a video. That's probably the reason the police missed it."

After locating the date and time of the robbery on the video, he said, "Let's take a look."

Judging from the view, this third security camera was in a back corner of the store's walk-in cooler. From its position, the footage was probably meant to discourage employees who might use the cooler to smoke weed or whatever else they didn't want management to observe.

Immediately, it became apparent that the camera's visibility into the store was limited. Without comment, they watched still footage of supplies stored in the cooler, the seconds ticking by.

Then, surprising all of them, the murder victim appeared, opening the cooler door, and reaching for a small carton of eggs. Shelves were spaced just right to allow them an excellent view.

**Almost immediately, the man from the earlier videos—the shooter—could be seen through the open cooler door as he approached the woman. Eggs in hand, she turned, still holding the door. The man spoke to her. Apparently, surprised, she took a step back.**

**In full view of the cooler's security camera, the man appeared to ask her a question. She apparently answered, nodding.**

**He nodded too. Then in a quick motion, the man raised the pistol and fired a single shot into her chest. She fell, the eggs crashing to the floor beside her.**

**The cooler door slammed shut.**

**Though the glass doors were partially fogged, the shooter could be seen firing a second shot at the woman as she lay on the floor.**

The three men exchanged knowing glances as Webster exited out of the shooting video. Even with the masks, it didn't take a professional to know what the shooter had asked Josette.

Rage spoke the words out loud. "Are you Congresswoman Kato?" He glanced at Webster and Herbie; they both were nodding.

Everyone was quiet for a moment. Then Rage said what they were all thinking. The Congresswoman had nodded "Yes" to the shooter's question.

Webster finished their thoughts. "He shot her again when she was down. Then he took the money from the register and ran." Webster hesitated and then tacked on the exclamation point. "Somebody wanted it to look like a robbery."

Herbie summarized everything they had watched. "He didn't come to rob the store. This guy came to kill the congresswoman."

"Yeah," Rage said, "he did."

"But why?" Webster was asking the question.

Herbie answered. "When we know that, we'll know who we're dealing with."

Rage stood then and took charge. "Herbie, your friend, and his people obviously don't know about the cooler video. I think we should keep it that way for now."

Turning to Webster, he asked, "Can you make it difficult to find that file?"

"I can, but is it necessary?" Webster asked. "Aren't the police wrapping up their investigation? They certainly kept a copy of the store's hard drive, but they've already searched it." He looked at Herbie. "Haven't they concluded the murder was a result of the robbery?"

"True," Herbie said. "If they haven't already found the cooler video, they're probably not going to."

Rage listened, knowing his friend was familiar with the investigative process.

Herbie continued. "The detective in charge told Commander Johnson they're looking for the shooter to close their case. That tells me they won't be going through these computer files again."

"What else do we have?" Rage asked.

Webster had turned and was reading eyewitness reports. He looked up, asking, "Whywould he shoot her at all if it wasn't a targeted hit?" He pondered for a moment. "And why didn't he shoot the clerk?"

"Both good questions," Rage said. "We need answers."

Webster pointed toward Josette's laptop on the bed. "If we don't find what we want on her computer, we'll have to look elsewhere. The next logical starting point is the congresswoman's New Orleans apartment," Webster said. "We need to find her private notes wherever they are."

# Chapter Fifteen

Sunday night's meeting at the hotel concluded with an agreement that they should go through Congresswoman Kato's New Orleans apartment the following morning. Mike called, and Josette's father gave them permission.

Since Herbie was friends with the new police commander, he would stop by headquarters on his way to the apartment to see if there were any new developments. They had decided a visit would gain more than a phone call. Rage and Webster would go directly to the apartment.

~~~

When Herbie was shown into the commander's office, Johnson looked up from papers he was reading. A half-smile came to his face.

"I have good news and some bad," Johnson said. He pointed to one of his side chairs. "We found the man who shot the congresswoman. That's the good news." He continued.  "The bad is that we found him in the St. Martin Parish morgue."

Herbie frowned. His friend was right; this *is* bad news. "Do you have an ID?"
~~~

"That's the other bad news," Commander Johnson said, shaking his head. "We still don't know who he is."

"How did you find him?"

"Sent out a law enforcement query with a still photo from the robbery's security video." He handed Herbie a copy of the notice. "The coroner over at St. Martin Parish matched it to an unidentified male pulled out of Lake Martin on Friday. Two fishermen found the body in a swamp on the south end of the lake."

"Drowning?"

"Nope. A shooting at close range," Johnson said. "Two .22 caliber hollow-points to the head."

"Wow!" Herbie exclaimed. "Someone really meant to get rid of this guy."

"Yeah. Then they dumped him out in the swamp. We think whoever shot him expected the alligators to get him. The fishermen got there first."

"You're sure it's the same guy?" Herbie questioned. "No doubt?"

"Oh, it's him," Johnson said. "Only difference was the hair. He had a crew cut when they pulled him out of the swamp, long hair when he shot the congresswoman in New Orleans. That must have been a wig."

Johnson reached to the corner of his desk and shuffled through a stack of papers. "Just got this a few minutes ago." He found what he was looking for and handed the single sheet to Herbie. Wrinkled and somewhat water stained; an address was still readable: a St Charles Avenue convenience store in NewOrleans.

Glancing back at Johnson, Herbie had a questioning expression on his face. "Is this what I think it is?"

"Probably," Johnson said. "It's the location where the congresswoman was shot. The paper along with a roll of money was found on the shooter's body when he was fished out of Lake Martin."

Herbie was satisfied; the congresswoman's killer had been found. Now they needed an ID.

"I expect you're working on a name now," Herbie said.

"My lead team will be running photos through police facial-recognition databases," Johnson told him. "We're hoping for an ID there."

Herbie understood. He had used the recognition databases on numerous occasions.

~~~

Rage and Webster were already in the congresswoman's apartment when Herbie called. Rage told Webster the news as soon as the call was over. Herbie had said he would take a taxi to the apartment.

Rage put his phone away, telling Webster they should start the search. "For the moment, we'll leave it with Herbie's friend to come up with the shooter's identity."

Rage and Webster took a slow walk through the small apartment before getting down to specifics. Each of them made notes for an in-depth search. Then a detailed quest began. Rage started by checking out the living room and eat-in kitchen. Webster worked his way through the sparingly furnished bedroom. Josette's bath would be next.
~~~

Standing near the bedroom's single window, Webster purposefully looked about the space. A small mirror hung near the door into the living room. There was a double bed, a chest of drawers, and a straight back chair. A table beside the bed held a small lamp, a digital clock, and a recent *Vogue* magazine. He opened the chest, drawer by drawer, going through them one at a time. Bras, panties, tops, sweaters, shorts, nothing out of the ordinary. He pulled things back in each drawer, searching all the way to the bottom and the edges. Still nothing.

As an afterthought, Webster ran his hand underneath each drawer thinking Josette might have taped something there. She hadn't.

Finished, he stood near the door and studied the room. *Other than sleeping here, she obviously didn't spend much time in the bedroom.* Webster lifted the edge of the mattress all around—searching—still finding nothing.

Standing at the door to the bathroom and looking back, Webster let his mind wonder. *What would Congresswoman Kato be thinking about when she was alone here in this tiny bedroom? Maybe, what have I gotten myself into?* He wondered, *Was she afraid for her life in recent weeks?* Letting the mood sink in, he stood still for a few moments. *Did she have reason for fear?*

Finally turning, he stepped into the bathroom, visually examining it inch by inch. Touching nothing until he reached the tub, then Webster pulled back the shower curtain. There were a couple of shelves of supplies. The top one held body wash, liquid hand soap, shampoo, and conditioner. A skin brush and shower cap hung on plastic hooks near the shower head.

A second shelf held her cleaning supplies. There were brushes, a squeegee, a container of Mr. Clean Magic Eraser Pads, and a large bottle of Shine cleaning vinegar.

Pulling the curtain back in place, Webster then turned to the drawers beneath the sink. Nothing strange there either. In fact, he realized, *she didn't even stock any sleep aids.* And there were no prescriptions or over-the-counter medications. *She must have been a goodsleeper and not prone to minor illnesses.*

A frown wrinkled his forehead. *It's too clean. Landie said she kept a journal of some sort. If it isn't here, where?*

Moving on to Josette's closet, Webster touched each garment. Each pocket of every item was checked. Shoes were systematically searched too. He found five twenty-dollar bills in a shoe and wondered if she'd put the money there and forgotten it. *Maybe something for a rainy day.*

Finished in the closet, he glanced back. Satisfied he hadn't missed anything, Webster moved on. Turning, he took one last look around the closet and the bath.

Something bothered him, but he couldn't put a finger on it.

"Webster?" Rage was calling.

"Coming." He glanced back at the bath one last time.

Walking out of the kitchen, Rage met him, spreading his arms, palms up. "Nothing. Kitchen or living room. How about you?"

"Nothing for me either, in the bedroom or the bath," Webster said. Almost forgotten now, he didn't mention the strange feeling he'd had only minutes earlier.

Rage was ready to move on. "We'll check her computer; there may be something on it."

Josette's laptop was on a table in a corner of the living room. They had brought it with them from Webster's hotel room.

The doorbell rang. Herbie.

He provided a review of what he'd learned at Police Headquarters. "Still no identity on the shooter," he said.

Rage brought him up to date on the apartment, basically saying they'd done a search but hadn't found anything—certainly no journal.

Herbie suggested they do a more thorough search. Said he had some ideas. "The grandmother was emphatic about a journal." Herbie waved an arm, taking in the entire apartment.

"If it isn't here," he said, "we'll have to consider her apartment in Washington."

Rage spoke up. "If we don't find a written journal here, then her notes or whatever must be on thelaptop."

Webster and Herbie both agreed.

"Landie said the congresswoman carried the laptop with her everywhere," Webster said.

Rage and Herbie glanced at each other, then both nodded.

"I think we should finish what we've started first." Webster gestured to the apartment.

Once they agreed, Webster suggested he and Rage switch locations and renew the search. New eyes might find something the other had missed. Herbie could bounce between them with suggestions.

By noon, they had exhausted possibilities. Every drawer, cabinet, nook, and cranny had been thoroughly searched—no journal.

Without an immediate plan for continuing, the three men locked the congresswoman's apartment and went out looking for something to eat. Rage suggested a local sidewalk restaurant out on Carrollton Avenue where they could get a muffuletta.

"A what?" Herbie asked.

Webster leaned in, obviously curious too.

"About the best sandwich you'll ever eat. There's a Sicilian bun and marinated olive salad." He moved his hands as though making the sandwich himself. "It has layers of mortadella, salami, Swiss cheese, ham, and provolone. Pickled olives too."

Webster caught himself watching Rage's hands as he prepared the imaginary muffuletta. He smiled. *I can almost taste the olives.*

Rage had obviously watched the meal being prepared more than once.

"That's just one of their sandwiches," Rage told them. "There are others too."

At the restaurant, they were seated outside. Rage ordered the muffuletta.

Herbie threw up his hands and said, "I'm in for the muffuletta."

Webster grinned and made the waiter's work easy. "Me, too."

As they were eating, Webster suggested, "A woman might see something in the apartment or have an idea we've not considered.

"Good thought," Rage said, agreeing. "Women are good at hiding things. Do you have someone in mind?" He grinned, knowing Mike and Cary were more than just friends.

Webster returned his grin saying, "I was thinking Landie and Cary could come down and walk through the apartment with us. They might find something we've missed. Who knows? It's a thought."

"It couldn't hurt," Rage said. He was quiet for a moment. Then looking at Webster, he got the ball moving. "Call and have them get a cab and meet us at Josette's apartment."

Mike was already punching Cary's number into his phone.

Both women liked the idea. They had finished lunch and were itching to help.

~~~

Forty-five minutes later the women were working their way through the apartment; the men were on their heels. Drawers and cabinets were being opened again. Female hands searched under drawers again for anything there.

Nothing stirred the women's attention as they made their way through the kitchen and living room. No one rushed them either. Their search needed to be thorough.

They reached Josette's bedroom.

"We're looking for her journal, right?" Cary asked the question, her voice a little muffled. She was down on her knees, an arm under Josette's dresser, fingers probing.

Mike answered her. "We're looking for anything that might help us understand a need to have
~~~

her killed." He glanced at Landie. Those were harsh words for the elderly grandmother to hear. Landie was tough, though; her expression didn't change.

Mike was starting to feel a letdown as the women entered Josette's bathroom. He had searched these rooms carefully. The bedroom and closet, like the kitchen and living room before them, had not produced any surprises.

Rage and Herbie had tired of following the women. They were concerned about getting in the way too. Both had expressed doubts as the women eliminated drawer after drawer and room after room.

Leaving Webster to assist the women, Rage and Herbie excused themselves and returned to the kitchen table. They began discussing other locations to search. Josette's Washington apartment was high on the list.

Cary was the first to go into the bathroom. She checked drawers and cabinets, still finding nothing out of the ordinary. Glancing back at Mike, she leaned her head to the side and whispered, "Sorry."

Finally, with him watching, Cary turned to the tub and shower. Mike knew that was a dead end. He was ready to join Rage and Herbie in the kitchen when he heard Cary utter, "Hmm..."

As he turned back, she went a step further, obviously interested in something she'd seen.

"That's strange," Cary said. She was standing by the tub, hands on hips, staring at the two shelves of bath and cleaning supplies.

Looking at her and not the shelves, Mike, his eyebrows lifted, asked, "What's strange?"

Landie was there too. She answered him.

"The cleaner."

"What?" he asked. "What about the cleaner?" Mike didn't understand at all. He hunched his shoulders thinking, *So there's cleaner on the lower shelf. So what?* Then he remembered the strange feeling he'd had earlier.

Cary spoke up. "There's no spray pump," she told him. "It's a refill container. You wouldn't keep that in the shower. It would be in a closet or a cabinet."

"But it's just cleaner," Mike argued. "Who cares where she kept it?"

"She cared," Cary told him. She was giving Mike the "men just don't understand" expression.

"Look around," she said. "Josette was neat and purposeful." Cary pointed toward the top of the counter. "Creams, lotions, makeup, a hairbrush, perfume. Everything she would need to prepare herself to go out and meet the public."

"So?" he said.

"It isn't normal to keep a large container of cleaner in the shower," Cary argued. "A smaller spray bottle is what I'd expect."

She reached for the bottle. It lifted easily. Cary shook it. The container was partially filled, but it sounded strange when she shook it. Something was striking the sides, something that wasn't liquid cleaner. When the large cap was removed, a small plastic storage bag was attached. There was a single folded sheet of paper inside. Three sets of eyes stared at it.

Mike opened the bag and removed the paper. Smoothing the page flat on the counter, he read it aloud.

*<u>Add to the file :</u>*
*Notes on Senator:*
*Monday, February 17– Something is being planned – something very secret.*
*Something bad?*
*Senator met with General F today. Meeting again on Thursday. To be joined by Army Chief of Staff and Marine Commandant.*

*Info is from a note on Senator's desk. Asked me to get a folder for him – note was near his phone. Only a moment to read but details are accurate.*
*Overheard comments have me thinking they're making their plans to coincide with a holiday – Memorial Day? July 4th? Labor Day? And will involve a parade.*
*I think senator is being guided by someone outside the Joint Chiefs, likely via secured online video conference meetings?*
*I believe whatever they're planning will happen soon. Too many meetings…*

In a lower corner, Josette had scrawled a reminder:

*Add to file, then destroy.*

Staring at the page, Mike wondered, *What file is she indicating? Her journal?*

He glanced at the Landie and Cary and then headed for the kitchen.

Herbie was the first to look up, Rage a moment later.

"You found something?" Rage's eyes were on the wrinkled sheet of paper in Webster's hand.

"Yeah…well, maybe. The women found this ina bottle of Shine cleaner."

Cary and Landie had followed Webster into the kitchen.

Sliding the page and the open container onto the table between the two men, Webster glanced at Landie before saying, "Josette was in a senator's office when plans were being discussed. She obviously didn't like what she was hearing or seeing, probably on more than one occasion. Her note practically has sparks flying off it."

Rage picked up the note and the cleaner, examining them both.

"Where was this?"

"Bottom shelf by the tub," Webster told him.

Quick to pick up on a potential problem, Rage held up a hand gaining everyone's attention. Glancing at the women, he said, "We should cut the conversation at this point." Then he added, "Going forward, discussions should be on a need-to-know basis. I can already see the congresswoman's journal may be loaded with dangerous information when we find it." Nodding at them, he added, "Sorry, ladies."

Herbie nodded. Webster exchanged a look with Cary but remained silent.

Rage again. "We've probably lost one soul already because of what she knew." He glanced at Landie and Cary, saying, "We don't need to lose others for the same reason."

Leaving the note on the table, Webster replaced the top on the bottle. "Let's put everything back as we found it." He turned to carry the cleaner back to the shower.

Rage looked up, telling Webster, "Drop the note in the evidence file. We may need it later."

Drawers were closed along with cabinet doors.

Finished, they started toward  the door. Thinking aloud, Rage said, "I'm surprised the police found her computer here in the apartment. They probably beat someone else to it."

Josette's grandmother stopped dead in her tracks. She looked at Rage, asking a question. "You thought her computer would be here?"

Again, all eyes were on Landie.

"It was at my house," she said. "A detective—I think his name was Belou—asked Josette's dad about her computer. I gave it to Bert, and he turned it over to the police."

She took a deep breath, looked down at nervous fingers, then continued. "Josette was afraid someone would break into her apartment and steal it," Landie told them. "There had been several burglaries in her neighborhood."

Both Rage and Webster leaned forward as she continued. "A couple of months ago, she moved the computer to one of my bedrooms. Since then, Josette has been coming directly to my house from the airport and stopping again as she's leaving N'awlins to fly back to Washington. Each time, she's been spending an hour or more on the computer with the door closed." Dabbing at a tear, Landie turned her face away, her head down. "At least she did before…"

Then, seeming to remember something new, Josette's grandmother raised a hand, index finger extended. "There was a small notebook with the computer," she said. "I also gave that to Bert to pass on to the police. It was mostly personal notes of Josette's—sizes, vacation dates, birthdays, bands she liked, even a bucket list." She looked at the men. "Did the police return the notebook too? I wouldn't want to lose it. It was…personal."

Herbie answered her. "The notebook wasn't returned with the file and her computer," he said. "I'll get it back for you. Don't worry. I can see it's important." He gave Landie a reassuring smile.

Everyone was listening intently to the grandmother as she shed further light on the reason the computer and the notebook hadn't been found in the apartment. The explanation detailed several of Josette's neighborhood break-ins.

Landie was finished, having given them all she knew.

The session was over. Rage suggested Webster drop him and Herbie at the hotel and then drive the women back to Landie's house.

~~~
~~~

When he returned, Webster suggested they order food and begin an effort to breach Josette's security. They set up at the desk in Webster's room, the congresswoman's laptop next to his own. Rage, Webster, and Herbie each prepared a to-do list for the computer. Rage would have first turn at the laptop. He settled down at the keyboard with Webster at his elbow.

Herbie ordered sandwiches from the restaurant downstairs and listened while trying to stay out of the way. He had told the others up front that he was no tech guy.

Following up on Josette's notebook, Herbie made a call to Commander Johnson.

"He's out of the office."

Herbie left a message regarding the missing notebook, asking for a callback.

Rage and Webster had pulled their chairs close and were keeping their heads together at the desk.

Logging onto the congresswoman's computer had been easy enough, but opening files was obviously going to be difficult. First tries were futile. They tried several different applications and files. Everything of interest required a password. Though Landie had given them basic details, even with Josette's common information—social security number, date of birth, addresses, etc.—nothing clicked. Combinations of her house number and street, nor anything else they tried opened any file.

Then a bit of luck came their way.

While searching through the Applications file again, Webster noticed 1Password, a storage application for passwords. Familiar with the app, he stared at the icon for a moment.

*Her passwords are in there.* Leaning back, Webster looked at the screen for a long moment. *Now, the simple question is what's the password for the 1Password app?*

A dark thought crossed his mind. *This may take a while.*

# Chapter Sixteen

At Police Headquarters, Commander Johnson glanced out the window behind his desk. He was thinking about the Congresswoman Kato's murder.

There was a knock at the door. Johnson's assistant stuck her head inside saying, "FBI Special Agent John Fordyce is here."

"Send him in." Johnson didn't recognize the name, although he knew several people in the local office.

Fordyce introduced himself, telling Johnson he was out of the Washington office. He wore a mask and didn't offer to shake hands. Taking a seat, the agent started the conversation. "We've identified the individual who shot your congresswoman."

Johnson leaned in. "Tell me." This was good news.

"His name's Radisson."

Special Agent Fordyce took a paper from the pocket of his coat. Unfolding and glancing at it, he gave the full name. "William Conrad Radisson." He added, "He's also referred to as Billy Conrad."

"The name's not familiar, "Johnson said. "Should it be?"

"Probably not."

Fordyce refolded the paper and put it away. "He *is* familiar to the FBI *and* to Interpol."

Surprise must have shown on his face before Johnson even asked the question. "Why Interpol?"

Continuing, Fordyce said, "Radisson has never been arrested, but he has been in places that got him noticed."

"What kind of places?"

"Security forces in a half dozen countries have him in the vicinity of several notable murders and assassinations," Fordyce said. "He's never been implicated, but he has been questioned. Air-tight alibis. He always seems to have one. That's why Interpol is interested."

"Are you sure it's the same individual?" Johnson asked.

"Police facial-recognition database comparisons gave us 99% assurance that it's Radisson." He added, "We've also compared fingerprints and dental records. It's him."

Holding Johnson's attention, the agent said, "On two occasions, Interpol had made inquiries as to Radisson's whereabouts after high profileassassinations in Europe, one in Spain and another in Belgium. Another time, Radisson was in Israel and staying at the same hotel where a ranking member of the Knesset died suddenly."

"Sounds like he's been busy," Commander Johnson observed.

"Obviously so," Fordyce said. "That's why it's so surprising finding him holding up a convenience store here in New Orleans."

"And killing a U.S. congresswoman." Johnson leaned forward, his elbows now on the desk.

"Yes, that too."

"An accident? Maybe she was just in the wrong place at the wrong time?"

Fordyce thought about Johnson's words before replying. "I doubt it. People in his business don't make those kinds of mistakes."

"I don't think so either," Johnson said. "What's next?"

"Following up all leads and going where they take us."

They parted company agreeing to share any new information regarding the congresswoman's murder or the shooter.

Johnson hadn't mentioned the local investigation involving his old friend Herbie O'Conner. The Commander didn't consider the local probe worth a discussion though he had agreed to pass on the shooter's ID.

~~~

Police Commander Johnson called Herbie, reaching him at the River Suites hotel.

Herbie listened for a few moments and then held his hand over the mouthpiece, saying, "The congresswoman's shooter has been identified."

Rage and Webster turned; their attention was now on the call.

"In Louisiana?" Herbie listened. "When?" More listening. "Where?"

When the call ended, Herbie relayed the information Johnson had given him. When he finished,
~~~

each of the three men relaxed back into their chairs. Silence filled the room.

Webster was the first to speak. "Assuming here. Why would a well-known suspected contract killer be called in to assassinate a second term congresswoman?"

He took a moment to glance at each of the others.

"It doesn't make sense," Webster stated. "On the surface, a second-term congresswoman wouldn't appear important enough for that sort of drastic action."

"Maybe Josette's note makes more sense now," Rage observed.

Webster and Herbie were listening, waiting.

"Something is being planned," Rage reminded them aloud. Remembering the note, he added, "Something secret...*Something bad?*" He emphasized Josette's question.

~~~

Cary hadn't slept well and not at all for long intervals. She had called the office on Tuesday morning, telling them she would be in New Orleans all week. She owed that to Landie. For now, helping to unravel the mystery behind Josette's death was the least she could do for her friend.

Back when Cary was searching for her birth mother's killer, Landie had taken her in and had even been kidnapped herself. Cary remembered like it was yesterday.

Greg had been staying with his mother, afraid something would happen. In the dead of night, two men had come for Cary's elderly friend. They disabled
~~~

Greg and took Landie. She had been held until Cary and Mike surrendered to them. Landie had acted as though there was nothing to it, but for Cary it had meant everything. To her, it had been an extreme selfless act.

*It's my turn now,* Cary thought. *I need to step up for my friend.*

Being close to Mike in Josette's apartment had brought back memories of an evening carriage ride with him in the French Quarter. More than that, it had stirred emotions she suspected were better left alone, at least for now. Being near him, sometimes even touching, had only served to confirm what she already knew—she was in love with Mike. That said, she had significant doubts about his feelings for her.

Even in their discussions, she didn't imagine that Mike was as serious as her. The last time they had been together at her apartment, Cary had challenged him for an answer of some sort.

"For just being friends, we're spending a lot of time together," she'd told him.

Mike had countered with that offhand humor of his. "But we're more than just friends," he had said. "We're *good* friends."

Cary could've slugged him. He had to understand she was being serious.

A thought had occurred. Mike might be that rare individual who would never commit to a serious relationship. If she decided that was their situation, it would be better to bail out now. Time would only make leaving more difficult.

"But for now," Cary said aloud, "there's work to be done."

Saying what she was thinking seemed to help somehow. For her own understanding, she summarized her thoughts aloud.

"I'm here for Landie and to help Mike and Rage find why Josette was killed."

She took a deep breath. *My own emotions willhave to wait.*

~~~

Cary spent most of the week with her elderly friend. Hours were consumed listening to stories of Josette. With thoughts expressed, Landie painted an image of her granddaughter, both as a member of the House, and as a young woman in Washington. According to Landie, in the beginning it had all been exciting to Josette.

To Josette, there was never enough time. There were hearings, conferences, and research taking up her daytime hours, and parties and receptions in the evenings. Landie didn't think her granddaughter enjoyed those.

"Why not?" Cary had asked.

"Josette didn't drink," Landie told her. "And too many of the parties and receptions were about drinking and gaining favor."

"A way to advance yourself..."

"Yes, and a way to get on the more important committees," Landie said.

Josette had been a good student and a serious adult. She took her oath and her job seriously. The opportunity to work on projects with the unnamed senator had been a break, Josette had told her grandmother. Then as time passed, she began to have doubts.
~~~

"Josette told you that?" Cary questioned.

"Not in those words," Landie said. "But I could tell. She talked less about her work with the senator and more about what she wanted to do on her own."

The two women enjoyed their time together. For a few days at least, Cary eased the loss of Josette for Landie. Though she could never take her place, Cary could understand losing someone; she had lost both her mother and father.

During her time with Landie, Cary thought often of Mike and wondered if he was getting closer to finding Josette's journal. She also wondered if he ever thought of her. Cary desperately wanted to call him, but she didn't.

Planning to join Mike on Thursday, Cary began a list of ideas and questions she would pass by him when they were together again.

One of her ideas involved a friend at Trebeck Corporation.

# Chapter Seventeen

Mike had reached the point of exhaustion. He had been attempting to break the password code for Josette's files since early in the week.

Glancing at his coffee cup, he saw that it was empty again. At ten-thirty on Wednesday evening, he'd ordered a BLT and a jug of coffee. Looking at the bedside clock now, he realized that was hours ago. The clock was indicating morning hours. Thursday morning!

Half of the sandwich lay undisturbed; the other half only had a couple of bites missing. This was the first notice he'd taken of the time since he ordered the food earlier in the evening. He reached for the coffee container—it was empty.

Massaging his head with fingers that felt almost numb, Mike gave in to the realization that he needed a break.

Clicking the sleep button on the laptop, Mike watched the screen fade to black. His mind was fading to darkness too, and it hadn't required a sleep button.

Standing and stretching, he leaned forward and shook himself like a dog scampering out of a cold creek. Feeling a bit more relaxed, if no less tired, he turned toward the bed and eyeballed the spread of papers and photographs scattered there.

Scooting Josette's file over, Mike made room for himself. Satisfied, he stripped to his shorts and crawled between the sheets, almost immediately dropping into a deep sleep.

Five minutes later—at least it felt like five minutes—there was a rapid impatient knocking at the door. Seeing morning light peeking between the curtains, he reasoned several hours had passed.

Climbing out of bed, he glanced at himself in a mirror, grimaced, and continued to the door. Rage and Herbie would just have to put up with the fact that he had been sleeping. He flipped the security latch, turned the deadbolt, and flung open the door. Mike had a grumbling word or two in mind for them.

But it wasn't Rage or Herbie.

A tall woman stood staring at him—eye to eye, toe to toe, in her stylish heels.

"Let me guess," Cary said. "You were sleeping." Flipping the long dark hair back over her shoulder, she walked—without invitation—past Mike and into his room.

"I've come to see if I can help."

"Ah..."

Cary glanced his way, eyebrows lifted, a questioning expression on her face.

"Honey, you'll have to be more articulate." She said it with a smile, adding, "You probably should get dressed too."

Mike looked around for his pants and shirt.

"Where are your co-conspirators?"

He was still trying to bring his brain up to speed. Only moments before, he had been passed outin bed. Now he was standing in the middle of his hotel room in his shorts and trying to react to a beautifulwoman who was asking questions and giving instructions faster than he could respond.

"I'm still asleep," he told her. "One thing at a time. Please."

Dragging his pants off the back of a chair, Mike hopped around on one foot and then the other until he captured both pant legs. Belted and zipped, he searched for his shirt.

"Looking for this?" Cary smiled and tossed it to him.

As he captured the first button, there was a new knock at the door, this one loud and insistent too.

"Want me to get it?" she asked, reaching for the handle before Mike could answer.

Rage was standing there. He was surprised judging from his expression but handled it nicely. Grinning and looking past Cary, he said, "I'm looking for Mike Webster. Is this his room?"

Mike was buttoning his shirt but stopped and glanced at his bare feet. That's where Rage was focused too.

"Cary just got here," Mike said sheepishly as he glanced at the two of them.

She grinned. Cary was loving this.

Looking at Rage but making sure Mike was watching, Cary batted her long lashes, and tucked her chin. "Now don't tell your boss a story like that." She gave Mike an exaggerated smile and continued. "Rage knows I spent the night here. You insisted."

Mike glanced at Rage, then back at her—then back and forth again.

"You didn't either," he said.

Mike looked at Rage while feeling a pink shade claiming his face, beginning at the neck and creeping upward. "She really didn't," he argued while shaking his head. "I didn't fall asleep until...what time is it? I worked late." He gestured toward Cary. "She woke me up five minutes ago."

When Mike looked back at them, Cary and Rage were both at the point of laughing out loud.

"Well, I was!" He finished buttoning the shirt only to discover he was off by one button. Muttering to himself and starting over, he turned, heading toward the bathroom.

"I was asleep," they heard him mumble, as he slammed the bathroom door.

~~~

That same Thursday morning, there was a knock on a door at the Pentagon. General George Wisecroft, Marine Corp Commandant, was sitting at his desk reading a report on the Middle Eastern conflict. He looked up. His military secretary, senior advisor, and task master, pushed the door back, announcing, "Sir, General Farmington would like a word with you." The Chairman of the Joint Chiefs brushed past and walked to a chair across the desk from Wisecroft.

The secretary exited, quietly closing the door behind him.

"Got a few minutes, George?" Farmington sat down and crossed his legs.

"Sure, Paul. What's on your mind?"
~~~

"You, George. You're on my mind, and you're also on the senator's mind."

Wisecroft leaned forward, his head tilted slightly, and eyebrows lifted, a surprised expression on his face. "I don't understand."

George Wisecroft's first exposure to the military had come in the form of his state college ROTC program and later, the Naval Academy. He loved the discipline and exactness of the military. With a Master's in Military Operations – National Security, Wisecroft turned to the Marines after graduation.

Young Wisecroft could have been the model for a marine recruiting poster. Trim, handsome, smart—spit-and-polished always—Wisecroft loved the Corps. And the leadership in the Corps loved him.

This was the first time in his thirty-six-year career that General Wisecroft had found himself on the wrong side of the military.

"We've been watching since you came to me regarding Colonel Rederton."

General Farmington paused, studying the Marine Commandant before continuing. Then he said, "You've been different since Rederton was killed." He was quiet for a moment. Then, "Colonel Rederton and his pilot died tragically. It's a loss to the Marine Corps and for everyone who knew them." He hesitated. "But they died in an accident. In war, there are casualties, and make no mistake, George, this is war."

He waited for his words to have their intended impact.

"I promised you I would keep the colonel busy, and he was on a mission for me. After all, he was on my staff. Something came up, and I sent Rederton to handle it."

"I understand," General Wisecroft said, "but I don't connect the colonel's death to a concern for my part in the ongoing operation."

"We get the feeling that you are not totally onboard with the Memorial Day operation."

"I'm confused, Paul." His eyes were locked with those of General Farmington. "You've known me for years. We came up through the ranks together." He stood up but remained behind the desk. "Why would you say I'm not fully committed?"

"All along, I've listened to your questions in the meetings I've held. Little things, innuendoes," Farmington said. Then he stated emphatically, "You have doubts, George."

Wisecroft's hesitation had been noted.

"I've learned to read people over the years," General Farmington told him. "I'm sure you do that too. Not just words but body language too."

He stood up now and walked to a window where he looked outside. Heavy traffic on distant highways around Washington was visible through the rain. Gazing out for a few moments, Farmington appeared in deep thought.

Turning finally, the Chairman of the Joint Chiefs studied General Wisecroft for a few seconds more before speaking. "This operation has to be done, George," he said decisively. "We've got to change the leadership. This is the only way available in a time period that can save us. We can't abide the remainder of this term for the president and his people and then possibly an additional four years. That must not be allowed to happen."

General Wisecroft couldn't disagree. "I know," he whispered finally, his head dipping forward. Looking up after a moment, he said, "But it's so against everything we've stood for all these years." He shook his head and turned to the window himself. Wisecroft's body sagged. "And people are already dying."

General Farmington's face had grown red as he listened. "George, Colonel Rederton couldn't keep his mouth shut. Think how easily you got him to talk."

"But that was because he trusted me," Wisecroft countered.

Farmington was pushing. "Rederton voiced doubts without even knowing details of our plans," Farmington said. His face had grown darker, his anger barely contained beneath the surface of his words. "I couldn't take a chance," Farmington said in a soft voice. His eyes bored into Wisecroft's. "I just couldn't take a chance."

After a few seconds, Farmington continued, "Again, George, this is war, and there are casualties in war. Most are a part of the action, some are not, but they're casualties, nonetheless."

Both men dropped into their chairs. General Wisecroft spoke first. "I do understand, Paul. It's an unusual time calling for extraordinary measures. The coup is meant to save our country."

"Then we can depend on you?" the Chairman of the Joint Chiefs was pushing for renewed commitment.

"Yes," Wisecroft said as he turned and looked at General Farmington. "I'm on board, Paul. I won't fight you."

The Bear left without further conversation.

~~~

Wisecroft leaned back in his chair thinking of the last several hours.

The previous night had been a restless one, the most recent of many over the last couple of months for the Marine Commandant. The coup and his recent encounter with Rederton had both been heavy on his mind.

Then today, General Farmington had made his appearance. The general's words regarding the colonel had confirmed Wisecroft's suspicions.

He had looked at General Farmington. "So Colonel Rederton had to die?" He gave the accusation a moment, then added, his eyes on Farmington, "And the pilot with him?"

Farmington didn't disagree.

General Wisecroft realized the conversation was over.

Farmington, a scrawl on his face, had picked up his cap and left with no further comments.

~~~

Involvement in this coup was not of General Wisecroft's liking. Although he agreed with most of the reasoning and need for what Senator Rayburt, General Farmington, General Avery, and himself were planning, he did not agree with the method. A military takeover of the United States government without impeachment of the president was not covered in the constitution, and General Wisecroft considered himself a constitutionalist.

During the night, Wisecroft had recalled a similar situation that occurred in Chile in 1973. With President Nixon's approval and with aid from the CIA,a military coup unseated Chilean President Salvador Allende. General Wisecroft remembered learning about the coup as it was happening. That one hadn't turned out well in the long-term.

*I was in my second year at State, before the academy,* he thought. *The Marine Corps was starting to look good to me.*

Wisecroft had joined the Marines after graduating. Through the ensuing years, he had climbed the ladder to four stars. The oath he had sworn meant everything to him. It was all about his country and its constitution. Being sworn to protect and defend that same constitution gave root to the all-encompassing, present-day conflict in the mind of the general.

Still, until and even after the action would take place, the general knew he would be questioning his choices—*and* those of the others.

All this had been rambling through his mind during the short conversation with General Farmington. His last conversation with Colonel Rederton had also been on his mind.

*It would have served no purpose to confront Paul with my suspicions,* General Wisecroft thought. *Whatever the reasons, Colonel Rederton is out of the picture now. Whether by accident or an intentional act, Rederton won't spread his doubts to anyone else.* General Wisecroftclosed his eyes for a moment. *I thought I was shielding him while at the same time protecting the operation. I almost certainly sent the colonel to his death.*

Finally, the enormity of it all became clear. *The colonel's death had not been an accident, but there was no going back.*

Standing, General Wisecroft glanced around his office. He was searching for something he knew he would not find at the Pentagon.

It had been raining since early morning, not hard, just steady. He had a thought and walked to his closet. A general's stars were not required where he was going. Civies would be better. For these walks, he enjoyed the anonymity of being just another solemn visitor strolling among the graves at Arlington Cemetery.

Wisecroft shed his uniform and dressed casually to include a raincoat and an umbrella. As an afterthought, he folded his Aussie Crushable hat and stuck it in a pocket of the coat.

Before leaving, the general stopped at a table near the door. He picked up the framed photograph of a woman sitting in a backyard swing under a large tree. Kissing his fingertips, Wisecroft touched them lightly to the face of the woman pictured there. A small tag at the bottom of the frame held a set of dates: *1957 – 2010.*

"I love you, darling," he said softly.

After quietly staring at the image for a few moments longer, the general set the photograph back in its place and left his office for the metro stop. *She died on Memorial Day, 2010,* he thought as he walked through the light rain. *The senator's plans are to be executed on the coming holiday.*

A short time later, Wisecroft stepped off the Blue Line Metro at Arlington Cemetery. His plans were to stroll to the Kennedy graves as he had countless times before. Wisecroft welcomed the rain knowing there would be few other individuals along the way.

Arriving at the gravesite, the general stood at the foot of the President and Jackie's graves. He was silent and still for several minutes. Finally, he strolled further into the cemetery. Some of the general's best thinking came on these solitary walks. There was a lot on his mind today as he wandered slowly through the fields and hills crowded with crosses.

The rain slowed. Glancing at the clouds, the general pulled the Aussie hat out, unfolded it, and put it on. The umbrella was stuffed inside his coat.

Hands in his pockets, Wisecroft's thoughts were swirling like fireworks at a celebration. *This is against everything I've believed and fought for all these years.* He stopped, standing still for a moment, and locking his focus on the name etched into a nearby cross: Private William S. Richards. The general thought, *Did this young man die for what we're planning? Had the private given his life for this? The plans of a senator and a few generals?*

*Is this what you died for, Billy?*

Wisecroft slowly shook his head. *I don't think so.*

He pushed on. The rain was still coming down.

Walking with his head down, the general's mind was in turmoil from his thoughts much more than the weather. *Yes, along with the others, he disagreedgreatly with the president on Middle Eastern policy, especially that involving Iran.*

The general glanced back toward JFK's grave. *How would John Kennedy have come down on this idea?*

*Would the young president, under any circumstances, have opted for a takeover of the government?* Wisecroft doubted it. He wanted to believe an illegal, unconstitutional seizure of the U.S. government should never be the answer.

The general was having great difficulty. The overall plot was fully in progress, and in Wisecroft's own mind, he was still attempting to justify their strategy.

Nodding finally, his eyes drawn and a determined expression on his face, the Marine Commandant began his long walk back to the metro station. He had made his decision and understood it would not be to the liking of the senator and the other generals.

So be it.

Without breaking stride, he walked on knowing what he must do.

Minutes later while still deep in the rolling hills of the cemetery, the general stopped and pulled out his phone. Keying in a number and waiting, he took a deep breath and brushed rain drops from the brim of his hat.

When the call was answered, Wisecroft gave a short set of instructions. Finished, he walked on.

With the station in sight, the general glanced at the clouds rolling across the horizon. Was it his imagination, Wisecroft wondered, or had the rain increased along with his anguish? He didn't break stride.

~~~

Rage and Herbie flew out of New Orleans at midday on Friday.
~~~

Business travelers were starting to return home for the weekend. Covid masks were a part of the uniform

Flights were full and stacked up around airports everywhere. Likewise, traffic on streets and expressways was bumper to bumper. Everything across the eastern U.S. was slowed by the rain.

The two men parted company in Atlanta.

Herbie was expected back in his office at Quantico, Virginia, later that afternoon. He told Rage there were phone contacts and a couple of meetings he would pursue over the weekend and then return to New Orleans on Monday. They needed to know more about Josette's shooter. Who had hired WilliamConrad Radisson and what specific purpose was served in bringing down the young congresswoman? Herbie would be searching for a thread among the people he knew.

For Rage, a face-to-face meeting in D.C. was on tap. Bernie Sladen had said he was extremely busy but agreed to dinner. After their meeting the previous week, the NSA Chief of Staff was interested when Rage said he had an important topic to discuss.

Sladen suggested a small out of the way neighborhood restaurant. His recommendation was, "Great Italian stuff."

That was enough for Rage.

Seated, Rage told his friend that he and others were working their first assignment. After they ordered, Rage carefully laid out the details. He said, "We've run into a situation in Louisiana that may concern you and others here in the Capital."

Sladen leaned in. "Tell me more."

"You've heard that a young congresswoman was killed in New Orleans. A convenience store robbery, according to police."

"Yes, I heard, but only what was on the news. I haven't had a briefing."

"We think there's more to the story."

"Who is *we?*" Sladen asked.

Rage told him about Mike and Herbie.

When he finished, Sladen asked, "Where is your headquarters?"

"Right now, we're working out of the River Suites hotel in New Orleans. Out near the airport."

Rage gave his personal mobile number to Sladen.

Then, over the next thirty minutes, he gave up the scant details they had discovered. Finally, he mentioned a connection concerning an unidentified U.S. senator. Congresswoman Kato was discussed, and her shooter. When Rage mentioned William Conrad Radisson as her killer, Sladen leaned forward in his chair, becoming even more focused.

"He's dead?"

"Yes."

"Are you sure of the name?" Sladen asked.

"Very sure," Rage told him. "The New Orleans FBI made the identification using facial-recognition database comparisons."

"Where was Radisson?" Sladen asked. "How did they locate him?"

"Two fishermen happened on his body in the swamps down in Louisiana." Rage told him the few facts Herbie and Mike had turned up.

Sladen remained quiet until Rage finished. Then, "This is all news to me. It hasn't reached my desk yet. Radisson has been on everyone's radar for years. He's been near too many actions to not be involved in some of them." Sladen paused. "I guess this was one too many."

Rage called his attention back to the present. "Now, about the unnamed U.S. senator…"

"I'm still thinking about Radisson," Sladen said. "Are the local authorities sure he was the shooter at the convenience store that killed the congresswoman?"

"We're sure," Rage told him and explained about the security camera in the cooler. "We found the third camera after the police had finished their investigation." Rage added, "We haven't told them about it."

Sladen appeared surprised…and a bit relieved? "Let's keep that piece of information between us for the moment," he said to Rage. "I want to run down particulars on the connection first. We need details if a senator is involved?"

Rage said, "My people are working to identify him."

He didn't elaborate.

# Chapter Eighteen

Working as a team, Cary and Mike bounced ideas back and forth regarding Josette's key password. Since they had not yet found a diary of any sort, nor any list of passwords, they decided everything depended on breaking the code for her 1Password app. Their faces were showing signs; mental and physical fatigue were setting in. Working together, they had been at it for three days. For Mike, a couple more.

Care had to be taken. They both were aware of the risks.

"Will the program lock us out if we try to open it too many times?" Cary asked.

"Nope, I checked it," Mike told her. "The software designers took that into consideration. They developed the program with automated methods for blocking hackers using big computers and special software to breech the program. We're okay."

"Obviously, Josette didn't make it easy," Cary said. Sitting back into one of the stuffed chairs, she was quiet for a few moments, a thoughtful expression on her face. Mike was still pecking away at the keyboard.

Then Cary announced a new idea. "What if Josette used a passphrase to construct her key password?" She added, "A mnemonic device?"

She was thinking aloud, but Mike was listening. He stopped what he was doing, a finger poised tostrike a key. Turning his face upward toward the ceiling, his eyes squinched.

He was quiet for a moment before turning slowly toward Cary. "Yeah, a really good idea." Standing and rubbing his back, Mike looked at her for a moment before wandering over to the window and pushing the curtains back.

The sunlight encircled him, almost a halo. Cary smiled at the thought. *Nah, I don't think so.*

Then he turned, staring at her, his arms clasped behind him. "Musical maybe. A song she liked."

Cary could imagine the difficulty involved in that. "Even if it is a favorite song, it could be anything." She emphasized the thought. "Absolutely anything.We have no idea what she liked."

Mike was quick with an answer. "Ask Landie. She might have heard some comment. Josette spent a lot of time with her."

"I'll call." Crossing to the bed, Cary fished her phone out of the handbag she'd tossed there hours ago.

Mike watched her as he took a sip of the cold and bitter coffee he'd brewed at midmorning. Cary had passed on having a cup with a "You couldn't *make* me drink that stuff" expression on her face.

"Landie? We've had a thought."

Mike noted that she was giving him credit for the idea too.

"Don't think we're crazy, but did Josette ever mention a favorite entertainer, perhaps a singer?" She listened for another few moments. Then, "Nothing, but that she didn't like most of the new stuff?" Cary listened some more and then asked Landie to call if anything more came to mind. Then she said, "Bye," and the musical idea was gone.

Needing a break, they walked outside to the porch and down to the end of the building. Standing at the rail and staring out toward a very busy Veteran's Boulevard, Mike expressed both their thoughts and frustrations. "Watching lunchtime traffic and starting at ground zero again," he said.

"Yeah," Cary agreed. Turning and leaning back, she glanced his way. "We're running out of ideas."

"I know." Mike's voice was low, sounding exhausted and in need of a victory.

*He looks down,* she thought.

Standing close already, Cary took a half-step, went to tiptoes, and with the front of his shirt grasped tightly, she kissed him lightly on the lips. After a moment, she released the shirt and settled back on her heels.

"What was that for?"

"I felt like doing it," she told him with a smile. "I may do it again sometime. Is that alright?"

He smiled. It was an alright kind of smile.

Cary's phone rang. She eyed it, then looked at Mike. "It's Landie." Cary turned on the speaker. She crossed her fingers, holding them up for him to see as she answered.

Landie's voice was strong, full of hope. "I remembered something."

"What?" Cary couldn't wait to hear.

"Josette liked inspirational stories and poems and music, anything that made you want to be better."

Mike could hear the old woman perfectly. They both listened as Landie told them what she'd recalled.

"Josette often mentioned things she admired," Landie said. "A few months ago, she told me about a song she'd recently discovered. I'm almost certain she said the singer was female and that she was European. I'm sure Josette told me the name, but I can't remember. I'm sorry."

"It's okay," Cary said. "Tell me what you do remember."

"There was a particular song," Landie said. "Something about 'time' and maybe the word 'moment' was mentioned. Remember, that conversation was several months ago."

"It's alright," Cary told her. "I doubt that it's important anyway." She was trying to ease Landie's mind. "We're following several ideas and had wondered about the entertainer possibility."

"If I think of anything else, I'll call." Landie sounded satisfied as she said goodbye.

Cary and Mike glanced at each other and then walked back to the hotel room, their pace increasing as they neared the door.

Mike broke the silence as he plopped down at the computer. "A female European singer? Huh?"

"Yeah, and a song involving time." Cary was thinking too.

Fingers on the keyboard and eyes glued to the monitor, Mike immediately began googling word combinations. Cary grabbed a clipboard and started jotting down ideas of her own.

Thinking out loud, Mike said, "Singer, European, Time." Then he hit the return key.

Several things popped up—European singers, mostly male, and songs like "Rock the Night," "The Final Countdown," and "Superstitious." Nothing about time or anything else that was close to the words Landie's remembered.

"Try minutes, time, and singer," Cary said as she made notes on the clipboard. She was pushed back against the headboard on one of the beds, pillows behind her and the clipboard on her knees.

Mike typed in the words and watched as two song titles appeared, but neither included the word time. Exasperated, he shoved his chair back hard enough for it to strike Cary's bed with force.

Startled, she watched him walk to the window. Deep shadows were showing around his eyes. Mike had rubbed at his head until the hair looked like he'd been sleeping for hours. She doubted if he even knew. He obviously didn't care.

Without speaking, Cary smoothed back her own hair and swung those long legs off the bed. Mike needed a spirit lift.

Deep in thought and standing still at the window, Mike didn't realize she had moved until Cary's arms gently encircled his waist. Then she pulled him to her.

When he looked over his shoulder, she was smiling, her lips close to his ear. "We'll find the journal," she whispered. "All this work has to pay off."

Clutching his shirt, she turned him then, ducked under his arm, and pulled his body to her.

"Kiss me," she told him. "Like you mean it."

He did as he was ordered. *Really* like he meant it.

The kiss took her breath away but only for a moment. Then she sent him back to work.

Her hands on his waist, Cary gently turned him back towards the computer. Mike, being Mike, his mind immediately returned to the job at hand.

Back in his chair, Mike said his idea aloud. "Popular European female singers and time."

Cary sat on the edge of the bed behind him, listening and watching.

"Maybe their popular songs will ring a bell." He input the words and leaned back, watching the monitor. His voice low, Mike murmured, "Nothing." That said it all.

Releasing a deep sigh, he muttered, "What we need is a Class A hacker."

Cary came off the bed like she'd been fired from a cannon.

"Rita," she hissed. "Rita!"

"What?" Mike looked at her. He wasn't quite sure what was going on.

"Rita, my assistant," Cary said.

"Rita's a hacker?"

"No," she clarified, "but she knows someone who is. It came up in conversation recently when we were working on a problem."

Cary was standing over him now and punching a number into her phone. Someone answered. "Put Rita on the phone."

A moment later, Cary went into detail. Finished, she listened. "So, can you have her call me?" Another moment of waiting. "Like now. It's important. Uh-huh... Okay, do it."

The call was over.

"Her name is Inessa," Cary said to Mike. "Rita's going to try to reach her. Cross your fingers."

"This Inessa's a hacker?"

"Rita swears by her."

"Strange name," Mike remarked.

"She's Russian," Cary said. "The family came to the U.S. when Inessa was only fourteen."

Her phone rang. She answered, "Hello. Yes, this is Cary." She listened for a moment and then began explaining their situation to the caller. Pointing to the phone, she whispered "Inessa" to Mike.

Cary answered several questions and then said, "Hold for a moment."

Turning to Mike, she asked if he would allow Inessa to Screen Share the computer.

"Sure, give her whatever she needs," he said. "We'll be able to see what she's doing."

Minutes later, Cary and Mike sat watching as the curser on Josette's laptop darted about the screen. On speaker, Inessa asked several questions as she went about attempting to break into the 1Password app.

Cary and Mike already had most of the information she wanted. Cary had also explained her theory involving mnemonic devices. Inessa asked background questions and was told about the European singer angle.

More questions. More of the darting curser.

The guessing went on for long periods, as Inessa tried numerous possibilities. Still no results.

Finally, they were quiet, each deep in their own thoughts, occasionally making notes only to cross most of them out. They could hear Inessa talking to herself. Occasionally, she could be heard making angry comments in her native language. They could only guess what she was saying.

At last, Cary jotted a couple of additional lines and then looked up. "Try this combination," she said. "Moment, time, song, European, and female."

Mike stood up and gestured for her to take his place. Grinning, he said, "You help her do it. I've got a blister on my finger."

Clipboard in hand, Cary took his chair and watched the screen for a few moments as Inessa manipulated the keyboard. But like Mike, she wastired of the disappointment and turned away from the computer. Rising, Cary stretched and started toward the bathroom to wash her face.

Mike walked to the window and stood gazing out into the night. He listened as Inessa clicked keys, hearing her words as she spelled them out—five in all. "M-o-m-e-n-t..." Then he heard, "Here goes."

Click!

Mike waited for the exasperation.

"You better look at this," they heard her say.

He turned. Cary was already leaning in; Inessa had found something.

Three videos were positioned on the screen— two featuring Whitney Houston and another by a Dana Winner. The song in each case was "One Moment in Time."

"Moment? Time? It had both." Cary stared at Mike. "Landie's exact words."

"Who is Dana Winner?" Mike asked. Cary glanced his way, her head turned to the side and palms up.

"Google her on my computer," he instructed. "Maybe she's our elusive European female singer." He didn't sound hopeful.

Cary was glued to the screen. The result she'd googled read that Dana Winner was a stage name, giving the woman's legal name and other information including the fact that Dana Winner was Belgian.

"This is it," Cary exclaimed.

"Now google the lyrics to the song," he ordered in a harsh voice.

Looking back over her shoulder with a stern glance, she suggested, "Say please?"

"Please?" he said, subdued but with a wink.

A few additional stabs at the keyboard, and the words to the song appeared.

They both stared at the screen. Cary broke the silence this time. "Could there be a password in there?"

Mike again, "If there isn't, we'll be starting all over again." He touched her shoulder. "Let me back on my computer. Please."

Once again, they traded places and watched as Inessa pulled the 1Password app up on Josette's laptop. Then they each began writing out passwords and passphrases using the song's lyrics.

A few minutes later, they were ready to pass some of the possibilities to their Russian hacker.

"Paraphrase," Cary said. "When all my hopes are a heartbeat away. No spaces."

Inessa typed the words. "Nothing."

"Try it with spaces."

She tried it. "Still nothing."

"With hyphens."

More keyboard strikes.

"Nothing."

"Here's the next combination," Cary said, and read it off.

Still nothing.

With each of them contributing, rejections piled up. Ideas became crossed out words on multiple lists.

Finally, totally frustrated, Inessa had said she needed a bathroom break. Cary and Mike needed lunch. Going downstairs for a sandwich, neither could get Josette's password off their mind.

After they had ordered, Cary said, "It must be simple enough to remember, yet practically impossible for others to guess. I still think the entertainer/song idea is a good possibility." She stopped for a sip of tea and quickly downed a third of the glass the waiter had brought. Mike, his jaw dropped, watched in pretended wonder. When she finished, he made a show of moving his own glass away from her. Cary slapped at his hand with an exaggerated blow. "I wouldn't drink yours."

"I'm sure you wouldn't," Mike said as he scooted his glass even further away. They both laughed.

Getting back to business, Mike said, "Let's have Inessa try a couple more things before we abandon your song idea." He jotted a couple of notes on a napkin as they talked. "Maybe we'll try tacking on the numbers from one of Josette's addresses or some other familiar numbers—her parents address or maybe Landie's."

Cary was making notes too. She remembered the address at both of Josette's apartments.

"What other numbers might be possibilities?" she asked aloud.

Anything," he said with a sigh. "Possibilities are limitless."

The waiter arrived with their food, leaving them both to dig in. Only a few minutes passed before they were back at the computer upstairs.

"I'm going to try the address numbers," Inessa said as much to herself as to Cary and Mike. She was punching keys as she talked.

"Nothing."

Mike rose from the computer and walked to the window again.

Cary could tell he was exhausted.

"Let me try some other things," Inessa suggested. "I'm going to use a different phrase."

Mike heard typing and then her say, "Not it." She muttered something Russian again under her breath. He glanced at the screen thinking he probably wouldn't want to know.

He heard her punch more keys. Then, after a long pause, "That's it!"

Cary looked up, catching his eye. Then Inessa answered their unspoken question. "Pure luck," she said. "A different phrase and the old woman's house number. I reversed and split the number with half at the beginning and the other half at the end of the new lyric phrase."

Cary smiled at Mike, her hands out and open.

"Absolute luck," they heard Inessa say.

The 1Password app was open.

Cary breathed a sigh as she stood up. "We're in."

"Yeah."

"Do I deserve a reward?" Cary asked, a sparkle in her eye.

"Sure," Mike told her seriously. "I'll buy the sandwiches."

She swung at him, but not very hard.

He stepped inside, her arms flailing outside his own, and pulled Cary to him.

"Thank you. You're something, you know that?" He grinned. "Beautiful *and* smart."

She relaxed in his arms. "Thank you. Now, can I have my reward?"

"Sure." He kissed her. "I'll try to think of something special when we find the journal." He kissed her again.

Then they heard Inessa say, "Don't I deserve a reward too?"

~~~

It was late Friday afternoon, and the woman had come to the cemetery to visit her husband's grave. Now it was time for her to head back to the capital. The Arlington Metro Station was several minutes away, but she always enjoyed the walk.

The years had been difficult since Robby became one of thousands buried beneath the simple headstones and crosses at Arlington. This was the first time she hadn't cried as she thought of all that had been lost on that Sunday morning in the mountains of Afghanistan. Their life together could never be
~~~

reclaimed; she knew that. But knowing didn't make living without him any easier.

The rain continued to fall as she dodged puddles on her way to the station. Following her usual path, the woman spotted the lone individual she had noticed earlier standing near the Kennedy graves. Now he was staring at a single cross among the thousands displayed there across the sloping hills. She wondered if this was the grave of his son. The man was dressed for the rain, even wearing an Aussie hat.

He looked deep in thought.

She hurried on, leaving him to his solitude.

A multitude of others were waiting for the train when the woman reached the platform. The rain combined with the late hour had a crowd waiting for their ride.

The man she'd noticed a few minutes earlier strolled into sight. Hearing the train nearing the station, her eyes were drawn back to the individual in the Aussie hat. Walking at a normal pace, he was just reaching the loading area when his pace quickened. She continued watching him.

Walking faster now, he was rather close to the edge of the platform. Obviously, the man wanted to be one of the first to board the train—he and about fifty others.

Behind him, the train was entering the station. Forty yards and still moving at a fast pace, it quickly closed the distance.

The man glanced over his shoulder. He was joining the crowd now, still very close to the edge of the platform. When he glanced in her direction, their eyes locked for a moment. A few feet and several fellow travelers separated them, but his expression appeared sad.

Then suddenly, he stumbled toward the tracks and the oncoming train. Only later would she wonder if he could have been pushed.

She lost sight of him but heard a soft thud and screeching train wheels. Several individuals ran to the edge of the platform and looked over. Confusion abounded.

Adding to the uncertainty were screams all along the passenger deck. Among the loudest, she realized, were her own.

Gathering her wits while clutching her arms to her chest, the woman noticed a familiar object.

Near the very edge of the platform, the man's Aussie hat lay all alone.

# Chapter Nineteen

Back in the hotel room, Cary and Mike were celebrating their victory. After days on end of frustrating trial and error, they had finally broken Josette's code.

Leaning back in his arms, she said it again. "We're in."

It didn't matter to either of them that the result had come by the hands of Inessa the hacker and pure luck. What mattered was that they were now prepared to search her personal records for the congresswoman's journal. Both believed it was on her computer.

Mike was looking over Cary's shoulder at the monitor. She was right. Josette's 1Password app was open. They had been struggling to open it since early in the week.

"Signing off," they heard Inessa say as she released the Screen Share.

Cary and Mike talked over one another with their 'thank you's.'

A click and she was also gone from Cary's phone.

With an elbow, Mike gently moved Cary aside. Then he slid into the chair and began rolling the ball on the wireless mouse, clicking it occasionally before moving on. Indeed, they were in. His train of thought leaped forward immediately.

"It's going to take a lot of searching," Mike said, his eyes never leaving the screen.

Cary had turned, hands on her hips, and was watching him. *He's in another world,* she thought. *One that doesn't include me.* She breathed a long sigh and made a commitment to herself. *That's going to change.*

The hands came off her hips, and she moved to Mike's side.

Leaning on his shoulder, she asked, "Do you see anything that might be a diary or a journal?"

"No, not yet," he said. He was scrolling through files on Josette's computer. The Mac's Finder was open, and Mike was browsing for anything that might lead him to the illusive journal or diary.

As Mike searched through files, one by one, he was also thinking about the woman beside him, considering it multitasking in an odd way.

He surreptitiously glanced her way. Cary was focused on the screen. His eyes lingered for only a moment, but she noticed.

"What?" she asked. "Is something wrong?"

"No...no, nothing."

Staring into her eyes, he wanted to say "I love you," but he didn't. The next move was his; Mike knew that. But he couldn't pull it off. He watched her for a moment. Cary had made her feeling clear. She wanted a relationship—a lasting one.

After a moment, Mike turned back to the keyboard, but his thoughts remained on the tall, green-eyed woman beside him. It was hard to shake that one.

He thought, too, of Jack Robbins, his boss at the Marshals Service. And he thought of Jack's family. That was what Mike wanted.

Cary's voice pulled him back. "Anything new?"

He glanced her way. "Josette had a lot of files. The stuff we want could be in any of them."

"But now we have her passwords," Cary said as he turned back to the monitor.

"True, but that's just a beginning." Still staring at the monitor and pounding keys, he said, "Josette was smart. She would still have hidden the details, maybe in several files."

Watching, Cary could see that he'd opened the Mac's Finder app again and was searching through the applications. He was counting.

He glanced her way. "She must have a hundred different programs on here, and they each have their own files." Fatigue was evident in Mike's voice.

Cary was watching the monitor as he tapped into Josette's Word program.

"Whew…" Mike's nose was only a few inches from the monitor. There were dozens of files: upcoming cruises, bucket lists, to-do lists, some jokes, and other junk that only Josette might understand. "Finding this unknown senator will be akin to locating the proverbial needle in a haystack."

Cary was exhausted too. She willed herself to walk away from the computer.

Mike turned, watching her as she stood staring out the window. "Why don't you rest for a few minutes?" He motioned toward the bed.

"I don't need to sleep," she told him as an involuntary yawn overtook her. Cary clicked her phone and glanced at the time: 4:07 in the afternoon. And then she eyed the bed. *Thirty minutes wouldn't hurt.* Without further comment except an "Okay, maybe." She eased down on the bed, curling up on her side. Moments later, she felt a blanket gently spread over her.

*Aww…* A long yawn.

*A short nap couldn't hurt*, she thought.

After pulling the blanket over her, Mike went back to the desk and Josette's computer. He continued opening and closing files. Meanwhile, he kept a written list of the ones he'd discarded. He wouldn't open those again. A second list of files would bear further scrutiny. Slowly but surely, he began making progress.

Two hours after Cary's departure to sleepyland, Mike willed himself to stand and shake out the kinks in his arms and legs. Glancing at the sleeping figure on the bed, he smiled. She was doing pretty good for 'not needing to sleep.' After stretching one final time, he settled back into the chair. Smiling, hethought, *Seat's still warm. I don't take long breaks.*

His mind buzzed with possibilities. They were close—a sense that something was imminent. Mike couldn't imagine what it would be, but he'd had this feeling before. The strange sensation seemed always to precede some action or discovery.

The next named file was "Landie Notes." Mike considered skipping that one altogether. Josette had covered her tracks well, hiding whatever notes she had regarding the senator she'd been working with. She certainly wouldn't have them readily available in her grandmother's file.

Intending to move on, Mike decided he'd catch Josette's personal notes with her grandmother later. Then something caused him to hesitate, his hands poised above the keyboard. Reconsidering, not wanting to miss anything, he clicked on "Landie Notes." A few minutes in, he proved himself right as it wasn't much but Josette's thoughts and other things she wanted to discuss with her grandmother. Nothing there piqued his interest.

He clicked on the next file and then a dozen following that one. Spending two hours on them and finding nothing, he couldn't help but feel the time was wasted. Nothing he saw referenced a journal or the nameless senator. The big mystery was still out there.

As Mike clicked on the next file, a thought occurred to him. He leaned back in the chair, staring absently at the typical hotel art print on the wall above the laptop. Then he moved the cursor back to "Landie Notes" and clicked it open again. Once more he leaned back, thinking as his eyes wandered through Josette's notes. He scanned page after page, and folder after folder. Nothing.

~~~

Senator Rayburt sat deep in thought at his desk. As he often did, the senator slowly turned to face the wall of photos and awards at his left. He had accumulated the history depicted there over a thirty-
~~~

year stay in Washington. Dating back to the late 1980s, several of the photos included presidents of both parties.

*I've tried,* he thought. *Through the years, I've put the good of the country first, to vote according to the constitution.* He counted as major accomplishments the several times he had bucked his own party when the overall goal required it. *Now, by bucking the constitution, I'm putting everything on the line—the country and my own thirty-years of history.* The senator recognized he had questioned General Wisecroft's concerns because, deep down, he was questioning his own.

Rayburt had spent many sleepless nights arguing with himself. At last, he had come to peace on the subject. *We can't allow Iran to go unpunished. This takeover must be done for the good of the country.* He agreed with Zack Holden and the committee on thatone.

Leaning back, Senator Rayburt considered the personal consequences. *If we're successful, I'll become leader of the free world, saving this country in the process.* Another thought then crossed his mind. *If we're not right, I could end up with my head on a platter like John the Baptist.*

As the senator contemplated his future, his secretary buzzed. "General Farmington is on the line, sir."

"Thank you." Senator Rayburt turned back to his desk and picked up the phone.

"Are you alone?" Farmington asked immediately.

"Yes," Rayburt said.

"George is dead. The Marine Commandant is dead."

Leaning forward, the senator spoke only two words—a question. "An accident?"

"It looks that way."

# Chapter Twenty

Senator Rayburt's office was quiet, just the senator and General Farmington in the room. Farmington had arrived early for the Saturday evening meeting, wanting to field any questions the senator might have for him before the others arrived.

"I've been to George's office," Farmington told the senator. "I found and took possession of his set of codes. There was one other potential problem, but I've handled that too."

A slight shiver ran up the senator's spine.

"What problem?" Senator Rayburt was on his feet now.

"George called his secretary a few minutes before the accident," Farmington said. "He was obviously still at Arlington."

"And?"

"George gave instructions to type a letter of resignation, to be effective immediately."

"George was going to resign?"

"Yes."

The senator settled back into his chair. "You took possession of the letter?"

"I did," the general said. "I told George's secretary we would consider it null and void since General Wisecroft had never make it official."

"Wisecroft's secretary was okay with that?"

"He was pleased."

"How bad does this hurt us?" the senator asked, bringing attention back to the purpose of the meeting.

The Bear took a deep breath, exhaling it slowly before saying, "It's a blow."

He rose from his chair and took a couple of steps. Turning, he stared across the room for several seconds before glancing back to the senator. He appeared ready to give thought-out details.

"Our plans require the Marines to take the White House and the president," Farmington said as a matter of fact. "Ironically, it's set up to be part of the parade."

Senator Rayburt remained quiet, listening.

"Overall, it couldn't be more perfect," General Farmington said, a slight grin on his lips as he cut an eye toward the senator. "The president requested his limo and security vehicles be imbedded with the Marines for the parade."

"President Carrington enjoys festivities," the senator mused. "He wanted this one and he got it. Unfortunately for him, this will be his last parade."

General Farmington smiled. "Yes, it is interesting. Not many world leaders request the means to their own undoing."

The general continued. "The Marine contingent will begin its part of the parade from Pennsylvania Avenue in front of the White House. POTUS and the first lady will be ours once they are outside the residence and reach the marines on the street."

"Where will they be held?" Senator Rayburt realized he had not previously asked that question. Then, he felt a touch of shame for the overall deception. Allen Carrigan would never have expected this of him.

The general answered, "Initially, they will reside in quarters set up for them at Camp Lejeune. They'll be taken there from the White House immediately and on the president's helicopter."

The senator listened carefully.

"That's only until the dust settles," Farmington told him. "When we think it's appropriate, the President and Mrs. Carrigan will be moved to Camp David by night and by helicopter. We have a force assigned to guard them there. Their location will remain secret until the takeover is fully in place."

Senator Rayburt noticed the general had not said 'when it's safe, they will be moved.'

General Farmington stated finally, "We haven't planned past that. The situation itself will dictate much of our actions at that time."

"Does your force at Camp David know who they will be guarding?"

"Initially, only that it will be an important world leader," the Bear said. "Like everyone else, they will know when the announcement is made."

"What have you done to deter any possible action from Russia or China?" the senator asked.

General Farmington told him, "Ten days ago, I ordered Admiral Patron to immediately deploy two additional carrier groups and three nuclear subs to the North Sea off Russia. Another carrier group and two nuclear subs are already off China in the South China Sea. "We're making ourselves known." He added, "Admiral Patron will be here this evening if you need other information."

The senator's questions for General Farmington had been answered—at least for the  present. And  just in time.

There was a knock at the door. Army General Charles Avery and three other senior officers were shown into the senator's office.

"Good evening, Charlie." Rayburt said, shaking the general's hand. He then turned and greeted two generals and an admiral who had arrived with General Avery. The admiral, Eric Patron, Chief of Naval Operations, shook hands with the senator and took a chair.

The first topic of interest was, of course, the untimely death of General Wisecroft. Admiral Patron had been friends with the general. They had been at the Naval Academy together. Wisecroft had been a year ahead of the Admiral.

Discussion centered on the tragedy of the accident. The senator and General Farmington made eye contact several times during the casual conversation.

When they were seated, General Farmington leaned forward taking charge. The Chairman of the Joint Chiefs reminded Senator Rayburt about the duties of the three new officers, adding, "Everyone here is of like mind concerning the need for a change of command on Pennsylvania Avenue."

Farmington summarized the overall details of the takeover. He emphasized again the specific need to isolate the president at zero hour. Everyone agreed on the necessity for that single action to go without a hitch. Taking the president had initially been assigned to General Wisecroft. His untimely death had left a potentially destabilizing weakness in their plans.

The Bear zeroed in on the problem, defining and tentatively solving it quickly.

"I will assume the operational duties previously assigned to General Wisecroft. For the parade's purpose, I will be taking command of the Marine contingent assigned to neutralize the president." He glanced around for objections or questions. There was only silence.

Farmington continued. "Starting from the White House, the president's limo is scheduled to take a place between two sets of Marine Abrams tanks."

"What about his security detail?" Senator Rayburt asked.

"One car will be allowed in front of the limo and one behind it. Two others will follow the second set of tanks." Farmington looked at the senator who only nodded. "As we start to roll, the security detail will be separated from the president's limo by the Marine tanks and the personnel on the ground."

The meeting wrapped up with assurances by General Farmington that the change in command of the country would be finalized in the first few minutes after the beginning of the parade.

In closing, General Farmington told them, "Arrangements are also scheduled for an announcement of the takeover to reach the public as soon as it is complete. Delay would serve no useful purpose."

~~~

Public details involving General Wisecroft's death were few. Witnesses at Arlington said it appeared he stumbled and fell from the Metro station's boarding deck—unfortunately, in front of a moving train.

The general had simply changed into casual attire on that rainy Friday afternoon. That was not unusual for Wisecroft; he often went out to Arlington. It was a quiet place to think, he'd said.

Donning a raincoat and hat, the general had picked up an umbrella, and taken a Metro out to Arlington Cemetery.

On his way back, there'd been the accident.

Several witnesses had noticed the lone individual walking among the graves. One woman saw him standing near the John F. Kennedy gravesite.She had also watched him stumble off the platform and into the path of the train.

An army colonel who had been visiting his own son's grave recognized the general as he lay near the tracks. If not for that, Wisecroft might have gone unidentified for several hours.

The general left no communications in his office or at his residence. His wallet was left in the general's office safe.

It was that simple, and it was that complicated.

~~~

While Senator Rayburt was meeting with the Pentagon's top brass, Rage Doyle was involved in a conference of his own. Several hours after Rage had left a message for him, Eldon Patterson, his CIA friend, finally returned his call.

"I'm in Washington," Rage told him. "Can you see me? Something important has come to my attention, and I need your input. It's urgent," he added.

"If you think the situation warrants," Patterson said, "I'll take time."

They met at a small neighborhood café and ducked into a booth in a quiet corner. After ordering, Rage brought Patterson up to date, basically repeating the same details regarding the death of Congresswoman Kato he had laid out for Sladen. Patterson had listened, asking a question here and there.

Rage said in closing, "She wasn't killed in a robbery."

The Deputy Executive Director at the CIA was quiet for a few moments as if deciding what his reaction should be. Patterson took the time to loosen his tie and unbutton the top of his shirt. His suit coat was already on the chair beside him. Finally, Patterson leaned forward and said, "I was already aware that Radisson was the shooter of the congresswoman." Rage's surprised expression caused him to add, "A friend at the FBI called as soon as there was an identification. Radisson's an assassin. His involvement makes no sense unless the congresswoman knew something very damaging." He leaned forward. "I had not heard that a senator might be involved."

Rage reminded him, "If the congresswoman knew details about this senator's plans, and if she turned down his offer, that could be enough for someone to order her assassination."

Changing the subject, Patterson asked if identification of the senator was close.

"My people are searching for the congresswoman's journal," Rage told him. "We think she may have names there."

"Keep me in the loop," Patterson said.

"I will," Rage told him.

The meeting was over, and they headed for the door.

"Call if I can help," Patterson said as they parted outside on the sidewalk.

Rage glanced over his shoulder as he walked away. The CIA's Deputy Director hadn't moved. He was staring after Rage. When Rage looked back, Patterson gave a slight wave, then turned and strode off in the opposite direction, his hands deep in his pockets.

# Chapter Twenty-One

He was deep in thought. The stakes were huge and would be long-lasting. His immediate decisionand that of others would affect the country for years to come.

Although it was Sunday evening, the man was in his office. Sitting at his desk in the near darkness, he glanced at the time: 10:17 p.m. He picked up the digitally encrypted phone and tapped in a number.

A sleepy voice answered. "Hello?"

"I need to see you."

The individual on the other end immediately became alert.

"When?"

"Now."

"I'll be there in an hour."

~~~

As he strolled toward the Lincoln Memorial, Eldon Patterson saw his contact waiting on the steps leading up to the monument. Light bathing the statue of the sixteenth president softly illuminated the steps where Patterson took a seat a few steps below the other individual. Ten feet separated them, close enough to converse without raising their voices. Other late
~~~

evening visitors to the monument strolled nearby without paying attention to the two strangers.

Patterson was leaning back, his elbows bracing him in a casual manner. Over his shoulder, he said, "We have a potential major problem."

Continuing, he passed on details. "One of our former agents is digging. He's spoken to people and seems to have friends and connections throughout the services." He glanced over. "Based on things he told me, he already knows enough to be a major danger to the operation." Patterson paused, then, "I'm sure you know him—Rage Doyle. He's an old friend."

"Is that a problem?"

"No."

Sitting straighter, the individual said, "Raegene Dorryen Doyle. Yes, I do know him." The answer was low and slow. "He has contacts throughout Washington."

"We can't have him probing. He's dangerous."

"How involved is he?"

"He's investigating the congresswoman's death." Leaning forward and glancing about, Patterson continued. "He has others working with him."

"What do they know?"

"They know she was killed in a staged robbery. They also know who pulled the trigger." He gave details about William Conrad Radisson being identified.

"How did they get all that?"

Patterson explained that there was a security camera in the store's cooler. Turning a little, he ended with, "It gave them enough to determine the shooting was meant to eliminate the congresswoman and wasn't connected to the robbery."

"How did they find out about the third camera?" The questions were very direct.

"One of Doyle's people found a video from the third camera," Patterson said

"Do we know Doyle's people?"

"Only one. A Chief Warrant Officer out of the army's CID. His name is Heber Kean O'Connor. Goes by Herbie."

No response came from above for nearly a minute. "Tell me how they found and identified Radisson."

It took a few minutes to detail the identification of Radisson's body after he turned up in the Louisiana swamp.

Finished, Patterson heard an expletive uttered in the near darkness.

"I haven't gotten to the most dangerous part." He heard the individual shifting on the steps above.

"Tell me."

In a low voice, Patterson said, "They know there's a U.S. senator involved."

Expletives again. "Do they have a name?"

"Not yet, but knowing Doyle, they will."

"That can't be allowed. They'll have to be stopped." Then another question. "Do we know where they're located?"

"Yes. The River Suites hotel in New Orleans."

"Time is of the essence. Can you reach them?"

"With your help, I can. Do you have someone we can send?"

"I do."

There was movement behind him, then scribbling. Pen on paper. Moments later, a small note dropped over his shoulder. In the half light, he saw a name and a phone number.

"Tell this person what you've told me about their location. Give him particulars on each of them." Then the voice added, "We might already be too late to stop them in New Orleans. If not, O'Conner will be a good place to start." More rustled paper noises before a short list of questions regarding arrival time and a physical description was passed down. "Have this information ready before you call the number."

The last thing Elena Springer-Preston said to Patterson was, "Slow them down."

~~~

It was mid-morning, and Mike had been at the computer for hours. Cary was still asleep. Mike shook his head. He smiled as she snored softly and turned on her side. The long dark hair he loved to touch was spread across her face. Mike didn't remember what time he'd placed the blanket over her.

Everything was starting to run together. The screen had been blurry for some time. Close to exasperation, Mike leaned back again; his head was hurting, and his neck had stiffened. Almost in a daze, he rubbed at his burning eyes and slowly rolled his head back and forth on his shoulders.

*Maybe the congresswoman hadn't kept a journal after all.*

As he considered that possibility, there was a stirring behind him. Glancing back, he saw that Cary had awakened and was looking at him, a confused expression on her face.
~~~

"Where am I?" she asked aloud.

*She must have had a bad dream.*

"You're in a hotel room with me," Mike told her. Flashing a grin, he added, "We made mad passionate love, and then you went to sleep."

She took a deep breath and grinned back, appearing to gain her senses. Sitting up, she heaved those long slender legs off the bed and onto the floor. Then she narrowed her eyes, capturing his attention as surely as if she had touched him with a hot branding iron. "We haven't been making mad passionate love," she told him with a twinkle in her eyes. "I *would* remember that."

"Oh well, I tried," Mike said as he turned back to the monitor. A moment later, with an arm draped across each of his shoulders and her face close to his, she scanned the screen, nuzzling his neck. And then she bit his ear—hard.

"OUCH!"

Leaning away, his eyes on Cary, Mike touched the injured earlobe. "That hurt."

"That's what you get for lying," Cary told him. With her eyes still on his, she added, "You shouldn't say things like that unless they're true."

He stared at her for a long moment, not quite sure of her meaning.

But Cary had moved on and was now staring at the monitor. "Have you found something?" "Nothing," he told her, "but I still believe the notes are here." He gestured toward the monitor, "I just haven't found them."

Turning and sitting on the edge of the bed, Cary said, "I think it's time for me to get back to Knoxville and my job. At this point, I'll only be in the way here. You and Rage understand what's going on. I don't." She reached over and touched his cheek with her fingers. "Time for me to bow out."

Neither of them looked forward to parting. Still, they both knew she couldn't help further at this point.

Cary went to her room to make reservations and pack. She left Mike staring at the monitor, searching for a journal that might not even exist.

# Chapter Twenty-Two

Mike's phone buzzed a few minutes after eleven on Monday. He glanced at the caller—Rage.

Mike wasn't surprised. "Morning," he said to the boss.

"Good morning," Rage returned. "You sound like you just got up."

"I haven't been to bed," Mike told him. "Still looking for Josette's journal

"Sounds like you need to take a break," Rage suggested. "Take a nap and then you can get back to the computer. A little rest will sharpen your senses."

Mike yawned and agreed to a break.

"What about Herbie?" he asked as he made notes on his pad. "Is he coming back to New Orleans?"

"He's flying back this morning. Should be there by noon," Rage said. "I have a couple more people to see and then I'll be headed back too. Probably later today. I've done all I can here without knowing the name of Josette's senator."

"I'm working on it."

"I know you are."

"See you later then."

~~~
~~~

As the leading nucleus of individuals were only days away from a military coup to overthrow the U.S. government, Covid-19 continued to roll through America like a tsunami. Variants kept researchers busy searching for new vaccines. The crisis wasn't over. Contagious variants were almost as dangerous as the original Covid-19 virus.

The pandemic had not been considered in their plans at the beginning. As the virus again filled hospitals from coast to coast, it became apparent that various aspects of the situation could be used to an advantage. Senator Rayburt received daily briefings regarding details and statistics concerning its spread.

Non-exposure to others contagious with the virus was still considered one of the best methods of fighting the virus. For a second time, the further possibility of removing most of the population from public places was considered at all levels of government—federal and state. The senator brought that information to his planning unit in a hastily called meeting. As a group, they knew another countrywide stay-at-home order would be to their advantage as the target date for the operation grew closer. They also expected it would be a hard sell to the president and other leaders. Still, it was worth a try.

Senator Rayburt suggested contacting the White House and offering to have the military enforce such an order. From there, by agreement of the group, it fell to the Chairman of the Joint Chiefs of Staff to make the initial contact. To get things rolling, the Bear agreed to ask for a meeting with the president's chief of staff. To his surprise, the general was invited to the White House that same afternoon.

In his car and on the way, General Farmington sat in back reviewing his goals for the conference. First, based on the seriousness of the most recent developments, he wanted to know if the president would be in favor of a second informal shut down of the economy—a temporary stay-at-home order. With such a mandate, there would be a need for some sort of skilled formal enforcement. *Logically, it would need to be more than localized police and sheriff's officers.* Though calling the National Guard to duty would be the next reasonable step, it would be left to individual state's governors initially to make that call. *Some would do it,* the general believed. *Some would not.*

In earlier use of such an order, the population and the economy had suffered. Paychecks reduced drastically or were cut altogether. Businesses closed.

General Farmington's second goal for the meeting—to gain the president's commitment to federalize the National Guard if the situation warranted such a move. He believed he could present the condition to the White House chief of staff in such a manner as to procure an agreement calling for a new stay-at-home order. Both goals were based on the need to curtail movement of the population for a period allowing President Carrington and his team to be ousted.

Immediately, a new president would be installed along with his own cabinet and staff and backed by the military. With the military firmly in step with the new head of state, Congress would have no choice but to accept new leadership in Washington. *The next hour or two,* Farmington thought, *will be critical for our cause and for the nation.*

As his car neared the White House, General Farmington realized his driver had slowed and then come to a halt in traffic. They were held there for several minutes before starting to move again. The problem came into view, and the general smiled. Preparations were in full swing for the president's parade. Maintenance workers on cherry-picker trucks were installing flags and other patriotic decorations along the parade route. Washington, D.C. was starting to look festive.

When he arrived at the White House, General Farmington was shown into the Situation Room's conference area. He expected the president's current chief of staff, Jonathan Karist, to join him there. Before the general could take a chair, he heard voices in the hallway. A moment later the door opened, and President Carrington himself strolled in followed by Karist and one other individual who looked around, then stepped outside and closed the door. *Security*.

On seeing the president, General Farmington snapped to attention. President Carrington, in turn, reached out to shake hands and warmly greeted the general, a long-time acquaintance.

"How are you, Paul?"

"Fine, Mr. President." Relaxing a bit, he said, "I didn't realize I would be seeing you. I expected to speak with Mr. Karist." He glanced at the chief of staff.

"Jonathan told me the reason you were coming over, and he thought I might want to hear what you have to say." The president gestured toward the chairs surrounding the conference table saying, "I haven't much time, so I'll ask you to get right to the details."

"Fine, Mr. President." Seated, the general leaned toward the table and began.

"I think it's safe to say this pandemic and its serious implications has caught us all by surprise."

The president nodded but remained silent.

General Farmington then said, "If it's still as bad as medical professionals say, and if the new variants continue to spread as easily, the country is in for another several hard months at best. Once again, it will be necessary to shut down almost everything we consider normal. To slow the spread of the virus, most nonessential businesses will again be required to close. Initial layoffs will peak out far north of twenty percent." He took a breath. "Hospitals will be flooded again." General Farmington added, "As a fact, they already are."

The general relaxed a bit but kept a stern expression. "People will need to wear masks and stay out of public places until the medical community can catch up with this situation." He looked at both the president and his chief of staff, giving them time to consider his comments.

"How long would you think a complete shutdown could last?" the president asked.

"Your information is better than mine, sir," the general said, "but I would estimate at least sixty days."

The president listened but then had his own take on the subject. "Dr. Allerton thinks a shutdown may well extend past sixty days, maybe half a year. It will hurt the party's off-year election and my chances of re-election, but I would call for a long shutdown if it was necessary for the good of the country."

General Farmington nodded.

Continuing, President Carrington said, "I want to start with a voluntary situation in the beginning. If that doesn't produce the results we need, then we can make the shutdown mandatory."

Suddenly, the Bear didn't like where this was going. "But—"

"Hear me out." The president had his own plan. "We'll know if the voluntary works within two weeks. All steps could be in place at that point if a required shutdown is necessary."

General Farmington had expected some sort of response, but this wasn't exactly what he had hoped.

The general's thoughts were racing ahead. *We won't have the actual shutdown by Memorial Day, but the steps will be in place. The senator can pull the trigger at any point once he's in control.*

The Bear almost smiled. His basic goals were being met, and General Farmington had allowed the president to make his case for him. Without using those exact words, the president had nevertheless laid the grounds for a shutdown of the U.S. economy. It wouldn't happen before the takeover, but the new leader of the country could call for a shutdown at his discretion.

*Thank you, Mr. President.* General Farmington only nodded. *On to the next step.*

The general said, "There will be a number of governors unwilling to order a shutdown under any circumstances." The Bear hesitated for a moment, then asked the president, "Would you federalize the guard in those states?"

President Carrington turned to his chief of staff, asking, "Does my authority to federalize the guard cover this?"

"Yes…probably, Mr. President," Karist said, "but there will certainly be those in congress who will try to stop you."

"I wouldn't expect otherwise," the president said as he turned back to General Farmington.

"Yes, if the Covid-19 situation warrants, I'll federalize the guard to keep our people at home for a reasonable period."

*Thank you again.* The Bear mentally checked off goal number two. This was useful information for Senator Rayburt.

Farmington quickly communicated to President Carrington that the military could aid in enforcingsuch an order should the situation arise. He remindedthe president of the recent nationwide military maneuvers.

"We can announce and put regular troops on the ground again." Forward in his chair, the general expressed his thoughts. "The national guard can be visible early and regular military, under the guise of maneuvers, will be available as backup."

President Carrigan nodded, then turned his thoughts to the plans that were already in motion. "It will take several days of planning before we caninitiate such a move. Also, I intend to have the parade here in the capital on Memorial Day," the president said.

"Even *during* the pandemic?" General Farmington cautiously indicated surprise. "The holiday is only days away."

"The public needs something to look forward to," the president said. "I can have Dr. Allerton and his people begin the necessary steps for the shut down without immediately alerting the public."

"But what if the situation worsens before Memorial Day?"

"The parade can be cancelled up until the time it rolls, can't it?" The president was asking.

General Farmington smiled inwardly. *The president wants his parade.* "Yes sir, it can be cancelled at any time."

~~~

Herbie O'Conner had spent the weekend clearing his desk and making phone calls, several of them having connections to New Orleans. He wanted to concentrate on the congresswoman's circumstances when he returned to work with Rage and Webster. Calls over the weekend had indicated that Josette Kato was one of several young individuals in congress who were expected to be the new hope in Washington.

According to Herbie's sources, Congresswoman Kato had worked with several different senators both before and after her initial election to congress. Legislation passing through each of the houses of congress often required that representatives of the two houses work together for a compromise. Congresswoman Kato, working with representatives of both houses of congress, had been instrumental in the passing of several key pieces of legislation during her time in Washington.

Herbie had given his findings to Rage in a telephone conversation as he waited for his flight to board. Knowing which senator might have had reason
~~~

to have Josette eliminated had become even more difficult without her notes or a diary. Rage had thanked him and said he would see Herbie in New Orleans.

The taxi ride out to Dulles on Monday morning had been scary. Bad weather and heavy traffic made for a less than appealing ride. Hoping the flight to New Orleans would be better, Herbie settled into a window seat and buckled his seat belt.

The entire flight from Dulles and through Atlanta had been bumpy. Rain seemed to be falling all along the eastern seaboard and across the south. Dark clouds were everywhere, and Herbie could see bright flashes out the window. Some of the lightening appeared close by.

He breathed a sigh of relief when he felt the plane touch down on a New Orleans runway. Climbing over two other people, Herbie was one of the first to gather his bag and exit the plane once they stopped at the gate. Just as he reached the taxi stand, there came a downpour. The result was the need for a total wipe down. The friendly cab driver provided paper towels.

Arriving at the River Suites hotel, Herbie paid for the ride and started into the lobby. The covered entrance area was deserted and dry, but rain was falling in sheets only a few feet away.

Near the door, a man carrying an open umbrella was coming outside. He was dressed in a suit and wearing a rain hat and coat. The individual appeared surprised when he glanced up. Then he called Herbie's name in a questioning way, as though he wasn't sure.

"Herbie? Herbie O'Conner?"

Not recognizing him, Herbie responded with a curious, "Yes?"

"I thought so," the man said as he smiled and started to lower the umbrella.

Herbie stopped, expecting to say hello to someone he didn't really remember.

Under cover of lowering the umbrella, the man pulled a silenced Walther pistol from beneath his coat. All in the same motion, he fired two rounds into Herbie's left chest from point-blank range.

Death came before Herbie's body slumped to the sidewalk.

The downpour had covered the sound.

The shooter finished closing his umbrella and glanced down at Herbie's body as a van pulled under the portico and stopped. The man, his hat pulled low, unhurriedly walked over and climbed into the van's passenger seat. Then the vehicle drove off into the rainstorm.

~~~

Cary was finishing the packing when she heard the first siren downstairs. Then there were others.

Walking over and parting the curtains, Carywas surprised to see an ambulance and several policecars near the front entrance to the hotel. Rain was coming down in waves, the wind blowing it across theparking lot. A chill ran across Cary's shoulders.

Mike answered immediately when she dialed his room.

"Yeah, I heard them," he said. "I'll go down and see what's happening."

Cary went back to her packing.

~~~

The elevator was off the lobby. When the door opened for Webster, there were several people standing about talking in hushed tones. Some were obvious guests of the hotel. Others were hotel employees and still others wore dark uniforms—New Orleans police.

Recognizing one of the women behind the counter, Webster asked what had happened.

"Someone was shot out under the portico." She glanced that way. "It was during that last rainstorm. One of our guests found him."

Thanking her, Webster walked toward the entrance. He had taken a half-dozen steps before a policeman stopped him, saying, "Use one of the other doors."

Flipping open and showing his U.S. Marshals badge, Webster was allowed to pass. Seeing a covered body outside, a dark thought flashed through his mind. Webster suddenly had a sick feeling.

While working undercover for the U.S. Marshals, he'd seen death in many forms and all too often. It didn't get easier. Once again, the covered body there on the sidewalk was probably someone familiar.

Walking through the doors, he asked but somehow already suspected whose body lay covered on the pavement a few feet away.

Showing his ID to the officer outside, Webster was told the news he dreaded.

"Heber Kean O'Connor," the officer said matter-of-factly. He was reading from a small notebook. "Shot twice." Glancing at Webster, hequestioned, "Friend of yours?"

"Met him recently at breakfast in the hotel," Webster said. He wanted to talk to Rage before making any statements. "Security cameras get anything?"

The officer appeared surprised at the question but answered anyway. "The shooter was probably familiar with security. He managed to keep his face hidden."

The officer eyed Webster. "You know anything I should know?"

"Nothing," Webster lied, thinking he could straighten it out later.

An ambulance and several police cars were parked near the portico. Several EMTs and law officers were looking on.

Stepping a few feet away, Webster stood still for a moment before returning inside. Glancing again at the body, he was haunted as he remembered the lossof a young friend a few years earlier in Columbia.

While working undercover for the Marshals, Webster had managed to infiltrate the inner circle of the Merchant. The narcotics kingpin was one of the major suppliers to the drug pipeline in the southern United States.

Juan, the Merchant's young son, had taken to Webster and Webster to the boy. The father had been wary at first; Webster was an unknown, *and* an American. But Juan had quickly become friends with the tall young man. Webster spent significant time with the boy, and Juan quickly began speaking the new language. It was an ideal situation for Webster. He was on the inside in one of the largest cartels south of the American border.

There were other advantages to the friendship. The Merchant was preparing his son to follow him as leader of the drug cartel and wanted Juan to be fluent in English. How better to do that than have Juan spend much of his free time with Webster.

The arrangement had worked for Webster too, until the time came to bring down the drug kingpin and close his thriving enterprise. A raid on the Merchant's Columbian headquarters was scheduled. The problem arose when the Federal police fired their first shots five minutes early—five minutes before Webster would have had the boy safely outside the compound.

One of the Merchant's guards had grabbed Juan and attempted to flee, forcing the boy to accompany him. Both the guard and Juan were killed by the Federal Police as they ran along a roofline inside the compound. The Merchant had blamed Webster for Juan's death. Webster had blamed himself.

When the raid was over, Webster had been asked to identify the boy's body. Like the body outside under the hotel's portico, Juan had been covered, still and cold, the last time Webster saw him. The memory continued to cause nightmares for Webster.

Back upstairs, he knocked at Cary's room.

"It's Herbie," he said when she opened the door.

Cary immediately uttered, "Oh, no!" and turned away. She had figured it out too.

"He was shot twice at close range," Mike told her. "It was during one of those downpours. No one heard the shots."

"Poor Herbie," Cary said. "I liked him."

He stared at the sadness in her eyes for a moment, then shrugged and nodded, saying, "I liked him too."

Back in his own room, Mike dialed Rage's number. Waiting, he fell onto the bed and leaned against the pillows.

Rage answered on the third ring. He sounded tired.

"I have bad news," Mike told him.

"What?"

"Herbie. He was shot and killed here at our hotel."

Nothing for a few moments. Then, "When?"

"Twenty minutes ago."

"Any witnesses?"

"No," Mike told him. "No one saw the shooting, but the hotel's security cameras did get it on film. Unfortunately, the gunman had taken precautions. He was wearing a raincoat and had a hat pulled low over his face. No one even heard the shots. It happened during one of these short New Orleans thunderstorms."

"Did the gunman leave in a car, or was there a pickup?"

"Cameras caught a van picking him up, but there was nothing to identify it. The shooting was obviously well planned."

Mike heard Rage mumble something. He chose not to ask him to repeat it. Then he heard Rage say, "I'll contact his family." By the tone of his voice, Mike knew the matter was closed.

"Is Cary still there?"

"She is. She was packing to fly back to Knoxville when we heard sirens."

"Okay," Rage said. "Get her on a plane and then call me. You'll need to get out of that hotel too."

Mike heard the phone click. Rage had moved on.

Glancing around the room, Mike realized he could be out in ten, maybe fifteen minutes. He also knew Cary was almost finished with her packing when he left her room.

There was a knock—*Cary?*

She was standing there when Mike opened the door, her bags beside her.

"My flight is in two hours," she told him. "Give me time to pack," Mike said. "Then we'll call a cab."

"What about Herbie?" Cary asked, rolling her bags inside the door. "Someone needs to reach out to his family."

"Rage is taking care of that. They were friends."

~~~

Twenty minutes later they had checked out and were climbing into a taxi. At the airport, Mike, using his U.S. Marshals badge again, walked with her to the counter and then to her gate where they took seats in a quiet corner.

Waiting and sitting close, each looked into the other's eyes. "I wish I could stay," she said while reaching out to touch his face with her fingertips. "Will we always be saying goodbye?" There was a thin film of tears in Cary's big green eyes.

"I hope not," he said.
~~~

Mike could only manage a sad smile. He didn't like saying goodbye either.

They reached out, locking fingers.

Mike expressed the answer to her question again in a soft voice barely above a whisper. "I really hope not."

# Chapter Twenty-Three

For the second time in only a few weeks, military maneuvers were being held across the country. With only days left until the end of May, commanders of participating military units were honing their abilities at moving men and equipment quickly and with skill to wherever they might be needed.

General Farmington had been at Marine Corps Base Quantico for the last week. Only a short distance out of Washington, this was the location the general had chosen to organize the tank unit that he would command on Memorial Day. All conditions were positive for the president's parade. Farmington had spoken with the White House chief of staff several times and with the president himself on two occasions.

The general had been keeping up with developments concerning the pandemic too. The coronavirus, Covid-19, with its variants had not yet run its course, but with vaccines, medical professionals were cautiously optimistic. For the parade, social distancing and masks would be encouraged. Parade-goers on the streets were expected to be sparse, but the president's Memorial Day parade was scheduled to roll.

~~~

Before he left the airport, Mike dialed Rage's cell phone, getting an immediate answer.

"Are you out of the hotel?" Rage asked. "And is Cary gone?"

"Yes, to both questions."

"Good. We've obviously been compromised," Rage said. "Herbie was killed to slow or halt our search. We need to disappear."

"If you're right, where did the leak come from?"

"Most likely here in Washington," Rage said, adding, "The people I've spoken with are highly placed. I've known most of them for years, but none of them can be ruled out."

Thinking ahead, Mike said, "A possible connection here might have been through Josette's shooter." He hesitated. "That's unlikely though, since Radisson's been eliminated too, and it appears he was a loner. But if we knew who sent him here?"

"Good luck on that one," Rage said.

"Yeah…"

"I'll call again when I'm ready to leave Washington," Rage said. "We're going to need rooms, maybe even a suite. That would give us space to work."

"I'll handle it," Mike told him.

When his phone rang ten minutes later, Mike was surprised. It was Rage again.

"Forget looking for space in New Orleans. I've decided I want you to come to Washington. I'll call back with instructions in a few minutes."
~~~

"Ah, okay."

~~~

Elena Springer-Preston glanced at her personal phone when it rang. The incoming call had reached her at CIA Headquarters in Langley, Virginia. The Deputy Director for Operations seldom received calls on her private device. Those having access to the number could be counted on the fingers of one hand.

She punched the button. "Springer-Preston."

"They've moved out of the River Suites," the man said.

"I'm not surprised. Doyle would have known someone was getting close."

"I have people searching in New Orleans."

"I doubt you will find them there."

"We're looking hard," the man said. "Two individuals can't be allowed to stop the takeover."

"We went over this when we met. I understood it would be handled." She hesitated, her tone growing dark. "Is that not the situation?"

She listened again before stating, "Then I suggest we do whatever is necessary. I trust I'm perfectly clear this time."

~~~

The boss had said wait.

Webster made himself inconspicuous at a sandwich shop in the busiest area of the terminal. An untouched grilled cheese and glass of water had been pushed aside on the table. From his vantage point, Webster could see the shop's front door opening to the concourse. Though he could keep a watchful eye, his choice of tables would make it difficult for anyone to spot him without making themselves obvious. A second exit, this one to a side hallway, was only a few feet away. He settled in to wait for Rage's call.

It came sooner than Webster expected.

Without formalities, Rage immediately issued instructions.

"Book a flight out of New Orleans with connections to Denver. From Denver, go to Chicago and then come to Washington." He stopped for a moment giving Webster a chance to catch up. "Buy individual tickets for each leg of the trip. If anyone is tracing you, they will be looking in Denver and then Chicago before realizing you've landed in the capital."

# Chapter Twenty-Four

Cary had an idea as her flight leveled out at cruising altitude on its way to Knoxville. *I need to help,* she thought. *Rage and Mike are in this alone now that Herbie's been killed.* She stuffed the flight magazine she'd been absently browsing back into its pocket.

*I should be able to use my connections,* Cary reasoned. *But what can I do with marketing and advertising?* She even thought of calling friends in the news media.

*Nah. Too much, too soon,* she decided.

Another idea interrupted her thinking.

"Jimmy Dale!" She excitedly said his name aloud.

The elderly man sitting beside her almost spilled his coffee on the book he was reading. Glancing toward Cary, his eyes wide, the man asked, "Are you okay?"

"Sorry," she told him. "I had a light-bulb moment."

"I can only imagine." A mischievous grin curled the man's lips before he turned back to his book.

Looking out the window, Cary continued thoughts of this newest idea.

*Jimmy Dale, I wonder what you're doing now.* They had dated, and there had been a period when Cary thought they might have a future together. She had even accompanied him home one weekend. After that, they drifted apart, and she had lost touch.

During her last semester, Cary heard the FBI had approached Jimmy Dale about joining them. She didn't know if he had gone with the Bureau or not.

Looking out the window, she couldn't shake the idea. *If he is with the FBI, he might have contacts that would be helpful.*

A second and more immediate thought crossed her mind. *Should I be doing this without passing the idea past Mike and Rage? Probably not, but if I'm going to help, I gotta be willing to step out on my own. I'll call him.*

Up came her handbag from the floor. Checking her phone, Cary realized she must have deleted his contact information somewhere along the way. The alternative was to call Jimmy Dale's parents. She was relatively sure she still had their number in an old address book at the apartment.

Remembering his name, she smiled. *Jimmy Dale.* The double moniker being a sure sign of a boy from the south. Jimmy Dale was from Birmingham, Alabama.

~~~

The call was the first thing Cary did after slipping out of her shoes at the apartment.

"Grantham residence."

She immediately recognized the rich southern drawl of Jimmy Dale's father, smooth as molasses and butter on cornbread. She'd heard that description somewhere.
~~~

Explaining who she was, Cary was cut short by Mr. Grantham. "I know who you are, honey," he said. "We still chastise Jimmy Dale for let'n you escape." He chuckled and then added, "He's still available if you're interested."

Laughing with him for a moment, Cary was hastily back to her mission. "Where is he?" she asked. "I need to pick his brain on something."

Jimmy Dale's father was quick to answer, and his response took care of her immediate questions.

"That boy's in Washington now. Got himself a rip-roaring job with the Federal Bureau of Investigation. Seems to be doing well."

Without being quizzed, Mr. Grantham provided a street address, home and mobile phone numbers, and a personal email. She wondered if Mr. Grantham might have not been kidding when he'd asked if she might still be interested in his son. It was nice knowing Jimmy Dale's father remembered her.

Cary hoped she wasn't wasting her time. She hoped, too, that she wasn't out of line by pursuing another angle for Mike and Rage to consider.

After checking in at work, it was late afternoon before Cary could make a call to Jimmy Dale. She dropped back on the sofa, legs drawn up and under, and flipped a long, dark lock of hair over her shoulder. Her call to Jimmy Dale's mobile number was answered on the second ring.

"Cary Anne Warren?" he asked immediately, obviously seeing her name on his phone. "University of Tennessee? *The* Cary Anne Warren?" he asked in a light manner, his voice smiling. Cary remembered Jimmy Dale's smile.

"The one and only," she said. "How are you, Jimmy Dale?"

"I'm fine." There was a pause. "Better now."

He listened as she told him how she'd tracked him down. "It wasn't difficult. I told your father my name, and he was very accommodating."

"I bet," he said chuckling. "Mom and Dad mention you almost every time I'm home. Meeting you in that short visit, my parents decided you were the girl I should marry." He added in a serious tone, "Their views haven't changed with time."

"I'm *sorry*?" Cary wasn't sure what would constitute a proper reply.

"Not a problem," Jimmy Dale told her. "Islashed my wrists and moved on. Work is my mistressthese days."

She remembered heated moments together. Cary believed neither had been ready for a lasting relationship at the time. Several years had proven her right. He sounded okay too.

Cary decided it was time to move the conversation forward. "Jimmy Dale, I have something I want to pass by you."

"Okay," he said, "but if you don't mind, everyone calls me J.D. these days. Even Mom and Dad are reluctantly falling in line. I hope you're okay with that."

"Sure."

"Now, how can I help you?"

"You're with the FBI, right?"

"Yes, several years now." J.D.'s voice and words had turned very businesslike. "What's on your mind?"

"Can we speak confidentially? Off the record?" For good measure, she added, "Old friends?"

Hesitantly, he answered her. "Yes. I'll let you know if I change my mind. This sounds potentially like FBI conversation."

"I'll let you decide. Here goes."

Barely conscious of an indistinct click on the connection, Cary didn't give it a second thought. Their conversation was now being recorded.

"Are you aware of the congresswoman whowas shot in New Orleans recently?" she asked. "She was the granddaughter of a very good friend of mine."

J.D. was silent, so she continued.

"I know some people, friends, who are looking into the possibility that Congresswoman Kato was targeted and not the victim of a convenience store robbery gone wrong."

Still, he didn't say anything. Cary was a little surprised.

Then she asked half-heartedly, "Would this be something that might interest the FBI?"

His answer was slow in coming and didn't raise her hopes of helping Mike and Rage.

"My initial response is that this sounds far above my pay grade. My personal reaction is that I would think it's a local matter, something the New Orleans police would handle."

She wasn't willing to let it go that easily. "Would it be reasonable for you to refer me to someone higher up?" Then she told him, "One of my friends is in Washington now. I'm sure he would be open to a meeting."

There was a moment of quiet. Then, "I have an idea."

"What?" Cary was desperate. She wanted to help Mike and Rage, but couldn't help thinking, *I'm in over my head.*

"Let me make a couple of off-the-record inquires in the morning," J.D. said. I'll see if I can help."

Cary was unimpressed with his offer, but she had no other alternatives at the moment.

"Just hold tight," he told her. "I'll call if I'm able to find an interest here."

Cary thanked him but couldn't help feeling J.D. hadn't shown any real concern in Josette's shooting.

They spoke of life at the University for a few minutes longer, then voiced their goodbyes with J.D. saying he'd be in touch. He didn't leave her with high hopes.

~~~

Mike, following Rage's instructions for flights, arrived in the Capital late in the evening. He hailed a taxi and asked to be taken to a good hotel. Mike didn't know where he would be staying; he'd left it up to the cabbie. If anyone was looking for him, he'd made it a little more difficult.

"There's a nice Holiday Inn Express about three miles away," the driver told him adding, "It's out of the landing paths."

"Sounds good," Mike said as he relaxed back into the seat.

Thirty minutes later, he had checked in at the desk and carried his overnight bag and computer satchel to his room. Dropping his gear on the extra bed, Mike tapped a number into his phone and waited.
~~~

Rage answered. "Yeah?"

"I'm here!"

"I know," Rage told him. "I had someone watching for you at Dulles. He'll be keeping an eye on your door during the night. Get a good night's sleep, and we'll talk in the morning." The phone clicked.

One more call to make …

Next, Mike tapped her number into the phone and leaned back on the bed.

"Where are you?" Cary asked immediately. She sounded sleepy.

"Washington," he told her.

"The capital?"

"The capital," he affirmed.

"Why are you there? I left you in New Orleans this morning."

"Boss told me to come here. I do what the boss tells me."

"Oh," she said hesitantly. Then, she began a confession. "Ah…there's something I should probably tell you, and I hope I haven't overstepped my limits."

His senses charged to full alert, Mike swung his feet off the bed, propping elbows on his knees.

"Okay?"

After another moment of uncertainty, she let it go. "I called the FBI."

"Ah…the Federal Bureau of Investigation?" *I couldn't have heard her right.*

"Yeah," Cary said, a slightly indignant tone in her voice. "That FBI."

"Why?"

"College," she said. "I knew someone at the University of Tennessee who went to work for the FBI."

"This person is a special agent for the bureau?" Mike was digging.

"I have no idea what he's called," Cary told him. "I just know where he works."

"What did you tell him?"

"I asked if he had heard about the congresswoman who was shot in New Orleans." She detailed the remainder of conversation with J.D., concluding with the apparent lack of concern on her friend's part. "He said he'd get back to me if there was interest from his office. He appeared to think it was a local police matter."

Mike didn't want to alarm her but couldn't help being uneasy. "Keep your door locked."

"I will."

~~~

Cary placed her phone on the side table, fluffed the pillow, turned out the light, and slipped into an uneasy sleep.

It felt as though she had just dropped off when the apartment's doorbell chimed, rousing her. It rang two or three times before stirring her to complete consciousness.

She rose to her elbows and glanced at the clock. "What the...? Who's at the door this time of the night?"

The doorbell chimed again.

Cary climbed out of bed, not really alert, and headed for the door, one arm into her robe and then the other.
~~~

Looking through the peephole, she could tell there was more than one person outside her door.

"Who is it?" She wasn't about to voluntarily open her door to strangers in the middle of the night.

Outside, one of the individuals garbled a few words and held an object up to the peephole. Cary didn't comprehend any of it.

"I can't hear you." She said it loud and clear.

A deep voice outside said, "We're from the FBI." That was loud and clear too, and he repositioned a badge for her to see.

"Oh...Just a moment." Cary checked herself. *Yep, modesty's covered.*

She clicked open the two locks and cracked the door a few inches without removing the chain. She wanted a better look at her uninvited visitors.

Each of them was holding a badge for Cary's scrutiny, she stood firm, still not removing the chain. Two men and a woman stood watching her.

Pushing his badge toward her, the spokesman said, "I'm Special Agent Allen Stanford of the FBI." He introduced the others: Special Agents Don Jumpter and Marla Nepton.

Stanford asked, "Are you Cary Anne Warren, and are you employed at Trebeck Corporation?"

"Yes, I'm Cary Warren. What is this about?" she asked.

"We need to ask you some questions." The woman had spoken this time.

Cary shifted her attention. After a brief hesitation, she said, "Go ahead." Still not vacating the doorway, Cary waited.

"It will be necessary for you to come to our office," Special Agent Nepton said. "There are some things we need you to examine."

Cary couldn't imagine. *But they are FBI agents.* She thought of her earlier conversation with J.D. and wondered if that exchange had spurred a visit from the three agents standing outside her door. She made a quick decision. *I do want to help.*

"I'll have to get dressed," Cary said. She removed the chain and stepped aside, motioning them into her living room.

Moving toward the bedroom, Cary realized the female agent intended to accompany her.

"I can get dressed without help."

"Sorry," Nepton said, "but there will be someone with you at all times until you are returned to your apartment."

*Unbelievable!*

"Can I make a phone call?" she asked.

"We would rather you wait until we're finished with the questions," Nepton said. "Carry it with you but leave it in your handbag."

Cary did as she was asked and zipped the bag closed.

"Well, come on. Let's get this thing done," she said and walked to the bedroom where she hurriedly dressed. Special Agent Nepton followed along.

Ten minutes after the agents had arrived, the four of them walked out of Cary's apartment. In the parking lot, they climbed into a dark SUV. Cary was surprised when they headed toward Maryville and not toward downtown Knoxville.

She was even more stunned when they slowed and turned off at the entrance to McGhee Tyson Airport. Driving in, out, and behind various buildings, they ultimately reached an area where several aircraft were parked. The SUV stopped a few feet from a small jet. The aircraft's door was open, and the offside engine was whining. The special agents climbed out of the SUV and waited for Cary.

Sliding forward, one foot out the door and looking at Special Agent Nepton, Cary said, "I thought we were going to your office."

"We are," Nepton told her. "Our office is in D.C."

~~~

They landed in the dead of night. Cary and her escorts were met and driven several miles to the FBI Washington Field Office in central Washington. Arriving there, Cary was shown to a small windowless conference room on the second floor. Left alone, she heard muffled conversation and realized there were people just outside the door. A few minutes later, a young man brought her a cup of coffee and said someone would be with her shortly. He left immediately, pulling the door closed behind him. Conversation outside the door continued.

Using the phone in her purse was tempting. The only thing stopping her was the knowledge that the agents could return at any moment.

Another twenty minutes had Cary pacing up and down. Finally, she heard someone at the door. Two new agents entered along with Special Agent Nepton and followed by… *J.D. Grantham?*
~~~

Her surprise must have been obvious, but he chose not to acknowledge her, not even a hello.

Jimmy Dale continued his silence as they assembled around the conference table. Grantham gestured for Cary to be seated at one side of the table. He pulled out an end chair for himself. The others settled themselves across from Cary.

Once they were settled, Grantham finally turned to her and smiled. "Sorry to wake you at home, Cary, but circumstances dictate the situation. The decision to bring you here was made after our short conversation last evening."

She nodded, remaining silent.

"One last thing," he told her. "This question-and-answer session will be recorded."

Again, she nodded.

Addressing the other side of the table, Special Agent Grantham said, "As I told all of you earlier, Miss Warren and I were acquainted when we both were students at the University of Tennessee. I should add, since leaving UT, we have not spoken nor corresponded otherwise until she called me a few hours ago."

He continued. "In our phone conversation, Ms. Warren inquired if I was aware of the recent shooting of Congresswoman Kato in New Orleans. Further, she advised me that she had friends who are looking into the possibility that the congresswoman was targeted and not a random victim."

The agents listened to Grantham and then returned their attention to Cary.

Grantham moved the focus back to Cary. "I'm going to ask you some questions." He gave Cary all the normal warnings, including that she should tell the truth and only the truth and then asked if she understood.

She did and said so.

J.D. started easy. "Why did you become interested in Congresswoman Kato's death?"

"A relative of the congresswoman is a friend of mine," Cary said.

She was already sorry she'd called Jimmy Dale. *Rage and Mike aren't going to like this.*

Cary glanced at the agents seated across the table, and then focused on Special Agent Grantham.

*I'm really in over my head.*

She faced Grantham and said, "I would like legal representation, and I want to make a couple of calls before I answer any more questions." Cary leaned back in her chair.

Grantham was quiet for several seconds. Then he jotted something on his notepad, looked up at Cary, and pushed the pad over for her to see.

When she looked down, the words—a name— seemed to jump off the notepad. *Rage Doyle.* With widened eyes, Cary slowly placed a hand at her throat. It took an effort to not cover her mouth.

J.D. was staring at her when she glanced up.

"Is this one of the calls you want to make?" Grantham asked.

Watching her, everyone at the table could see the obvious.

"Yes."

~~~

The previous evening, Rage had spent an hour with his friend, Bob Cummings, the FBI's current
~~~

Associate Deputy Director. He had smiled when Cummings arrived. *A prizefighter in a suit*, Rage thought. His friend was neatly dressed in a dark suit, white shirt, and dark tie. The suit appeared ready to explode. Rage wondered what Cumming's biceps might measure. It had to be a big number.

During their conversation, Cummings affirmed what Rage already knew: local FBI operatives in New Orleans had helped identify the congresswoman's shooter. In a trade-off to gain more information than he gave, Rage threw out the basics of a theory about a potential governmental takeover. He spoke without giving details.

"I have reason to believe a coup is being planned by individuals within the government and the military," Rage told his friend.

Cummings appeared surprised and was immediately interested in details and names. He didn't mention that the bureau was also pursuing questions regarding Congresswoman Kato's death. Nor did he mention the recent phone conversation with one of his people. Everything, all theories, were open at this point. Special Agent J.D. Grantham had reached him as he exited his car to meet Rage. The conversation was brief.

Cummings was quite interested in whateverMs. Warren might add to their information regarding the death of Congresswoman Kato. "Bring her in," he had told Grantham, "and find out what she knows."He had hesitated for a moment. "I would be especially interested in her sources. And one more thing, find out if she knows Rage Doyle."

With that, Cummings had stepped out of the car and went to meet his old friend.

# Chapter Twenty-Five

Cary wished she'd never thought of calling Jimmy Dale Grantham. Life had been simpler before she'd dialed his number. She thought of all the days when she had gotten dressed and gone to her regular job at Trebeck Corporation. This day was not like that.

The notepad with Rage's name lay on the table in front of her. Grantham looked at her and said, "Go ahead. Call him." Gesturing at the other agents, Grantham told her, "We can get out of here and give you privacy." He stared at Cary for a moment before she glanced down at the time on her phone: 3:50 a.m. *Not a particularly good time to call someone like Rage...and what would she say?*

Looking up, Cary made her decision. "Go ahead and ask your questions." Arms folded across her chest, Cary glanced at the agents across the table, then back at Grantham. *I can take whatever you throw at me.*

An urge struck her to stand. Cary rose as she waited for Grantham's questions. Positioning herself behind the chair, she stood facing him with her arms behind her, a hand gripping the other elbow.

J.D. immediately zeroed in. "How do you know Rage Doyle?"

*Easy one*, she thought. "A friend introduced us."

"Would you care to be more specific?" Grantham asked.

"I don't really know much more than that." Her arms remained behind her, fingers now crossed out of sight of J.D. and the others. Inwardly smiling, she thought of all the times as a child when she had done this while swearing something was the truth when it wasn't.

"Okay," Grantham said, "tell us what you know about Congresswoman Kato." He stood up and began to pace back and forth behind the agents seated on the opposite side of the table. All the while, he kept his eyes on Cary.

"Josette, ah… Congresswoman Kato is…" She paused, "was…" Cary closed her eyes for a moment as she changed Josette's life to the past tense. "She was the granddaughter of a friend of mine."

Grantham stopped, stared at her for a moment, then asked, "Did you know the congresswoman personally?"

Cary stared back. "No. On a couple of occasions, we met briefly at the grandmother's house in New Orleans. I didn't know her personally. I mostly knew the congresswoman through conversations with her grandmother."

Grantham changed his line of questioning. "Have you met Rage Doyle on more than a couple of occasions?"

"Yes."

"And how did you first meet him?"

"As I said, I met him through a friend."

"Care to give us the name of this friend?"

"No, I don't." She held his stare with a defiant one of her own.

Grantham stopped pacing and stood behind his chair. He gazed directly at Cary for a moment. "Why can't you give us your friend's name?"

Cary had reached another decision. She answered Grantham, a sincere tone in her voice. "Because I won't involve others when this is obviously a fishing expedition." Cary glanced across the table. The other agents were watching Grantham.

J.D. stared at her for a moment, clearly evaluating what she had said and what she had not said. Experience led him to believe there are others involved in this.

"Are you sure this is all you are willing to tell us?" he asked.

She stood straighter. "I'm sure."

Grantham had been doing this long enough to know when he had reached a dead end.

He watched Cary for several seconds, enough to make the average individual squirm.

Cary Anne Warren didn't flinch. She stood facing Grantham, her arms remaining behind her now, one gripping the other at the fist. Her forehead was wrinkled, her eyes slanted.

Grantham knew he had gotten all he was going to get from her.

"Take Ms. Warren home," he told Special Agent Nepton.

He leaned over and turned the recorder off. To Cary, he said, "It was nice to see you. Sorry it had to be under these circumstances."

"Me too," she said. "Say hello to your mom and dad for me." Cary gathered her handbag, waiting for Special Agent Nepton to take the lead.

"Come," Nepton told her, leading Cary through the building and out to another dark SUV. They drove to the airport and boarded the same jet, returning to Knoxville. Another dark SUV delivered Cary to her apartment complex.

"Have a nice day," Special Agent Nepton said in parting.

As her bad dream drove away, Cary glanced over her shoulder to the east. The sun was just coming up over the Smokies.

*What will I tell Mike and Rage?* It had been a night that would be difficult to detail.

~~~

Though in ways she dreaded it, Cary couldn't wait to talk to Mike about the last several hours. Inside the apartment, she tossed her bag and jacket onto a chair and punched his number into her phone.

"Cary?" He was still sleeping.

*Tough! This can't wait.* "Guess where I've been in the last several hours?" she teased.

"Uh…"

"I'll tell you. I've been with the FBI in their Washington office." She said it matter-of-factly, as though this was an everyday occurrence for her.

She could hear strange sounds as Mike shook himself, then rolled his head back and forth, not fully awake. She had watched him do that.

"Washington?" Mike queried as the sounds ceased. "The Federal Bureau of Investigation?"

"Yes, and yes," she said, adding, *"That* FBI."
~~~

Still not convinced that he had heard correctly, Mike asked again. "You've been to Washington since we talked a few hours ago?"

"Let's take this slower," Cary told him, a condescending tone in her voice. "Like starting at the beginning."

She walked Mike through the entire occurrence, reminding him of her phone call to J.D., and then proceeding to the ringing doorbell after she had gone to sleep. He listened, asking only a few questions.

As she explained, Cary began to formulate a new plan for herself. She didn't mention her thoughts to Mike, wanting instead to decide about her future without anyone else's input.

When she finished her summary of the night's events, Mike cautioned Cary again to be careful. He said he would pass the things she had told him on to Rage.

Before they hung up, Cary asked about Mike's efforts to identify the senator.

A tone of defeat was in his voice. "I'm starting to doubt if I'm ever going to find her journal. I've looked everywhere I know," he said. "But I'll keep trying."

A call to her office at Trebeck Corporation gave Cary until noon to rest, have breakfast, and make another call.

She took a shower, letting thoughts settle and preparing for that next call. Deciding she was ready to make the leap, Cary slipped into her robe, leaned back on the bed, and dialed a number.

Rage Doyle sounded congenial when he answered. "Hello, Cary."

She wondered if that would last when he knew why she was calling.

"Mike phoned me," Rage told her. "Sounds like you had an interesting night."

"I did," she said, then she made a request. "I want to come to work with you and Mike. I think I can be an asset."

She waited for him to tell her no, to forget it.

"Have you talked with Mike about this?"

"No," Cary said. "I didn't realize I needed to."

"You do," Rage said. "He has an equal say on additions to the group."

"Oh."

"Get back to me after you've spoken to Mike." He paused. "Okay?"

"Okay."

The phone clicked off. She would have to get used to him hanging up like that.

After going to the kitchen for coffee, Cary called Mike again. She expected him to be irritated at another interruption, but he wasn't.

"When can you start?" he asked.

"What?"

"Rage called. We both have some reservations, but overall, we think you could be useful."

*Useful? Like they were adding a new tool, a computer, or whatever.*

Cary took a deep breath.

"So, when can you start?"

"I'll let you know after I go over to Trebeck. I'm going to request for a leave of absence."

"Good idea. If this doesn't work, you'd have a fallback position."

"Yeah, a fallback position. I'll call you tonight."

She did a Rage phone hang up, hoping Mike noticed.

~~~

He was running late for a new meeting with Sladen. The NSA chief of staff had asked to see Rage this time.

Walking along the sidewalk after an initial greeting, Sladen led the conversation.

"Any luck on the senator?"

"No."

"Can my people help?" Sladen asked.

"I don't think so." Rage glanced over. "We think we're close," he lied. According to Mike, they were no closer to an answer than when they were in New Orleans.

An idea occurred to Rage. "Terrible accident involving the Marine Commandant, wasn't it?"

"Yes, I knew Wisecroft. A good man." He glanced at Rage. "He'll be missed."

Rage detected no sign of deeper knowledge or involvement. He would guess Sladen didn't know more than he had said.

"Are your people still working out of Louisiana?" Sladen asked, changing the subject.

A second lie. "They are."

With the elimination of Herbie O'Connor fresh on his mind, Rage knew there was no advantage to be had in saying Mike Webster was here in the capital, or that Cary had left New Orleans. Until Rage could separate friends from enemies, he would be extra careful about the information he revealed.
~~~

It was obvious that Sladen was searching for fresh intelligence rather than bringing anything new to the table himself. *That's his job. My goal is to head off a coup.*

~~~

Mike needed a break.

Without mentioning his intent to Rage, he called for a taxi that morning and gave the driver an address in Georgetown. A short time later, his ride pulled to the curb in front of the massive old brownstone mansion that had become his work home after high school and ultimately, Mike's pathway to a future.

Climbing out of the taxi, he stood for several seconds admiring the three-story building and its grounds. Memories were strong here. A special few of the individuals inside had become mentors and his proxy family when Mike had no idea how to move forward with his life. They had encouraged him, pointed him to the future, and even made sure he had funds for an education he would have never thought possible. Smiling, Mike recalled having met Rage for the first time inside the halls of Frankin–Peterson Law Group.

Inside, Mike was a little surprised to see the lovely lady behind the reception desk. She recognized him, her smile lighting up the room. Diane navigated the big desk and had her arms around his neck with surprising speed.

"Mike! It's really you, isn't it?" After a big hug, she stepped back. "A few pounds added. It looks good on you. What are you doing here?"
~~~

"I've come to see my family," he told her. Mike noticed the ring on her third finger, and she caught him looking.

She touched it and looked up, saying, "I gave up waiting for you."

They had been an item for a time, even considering a future together, but Mike had believed his path was a solitary one. They had parted as good friends.

"Who do you want to see first? Mrs. Collins, I bet."

He nodded. "I wouldn't dare do otherwise."

Diane keyed the intercom and said, "Mrs. Collins, there is someone important here to see you."

The little woman, dressed smartly and walking fast, came bustling down the hallway, breaking into a run when she saw Mike. She hugged him too and received the same answer as Diane when she asked what he was doing there. Mike glanced at Diane; she was smiling. His family was happy to see him.

Mrs. Collins took him to her office where she asked how he was doing these days. They talked briefly before Mike asked for a few minutes of Mr. Frankin's time.

"He's been in a meeting," Mrs. Collins told Mike. "I'll see if he's finished."

He was, and Mike was ushered into the founding partner's office.

Greetings aside, Mr. Frankin asked what he could do for Mike.

Without qualms, Mike told his former boss why he had come and stated that Frankin's friend, Rage Doyle, had been heading up the search for Josette's killer. A coup and the unknown senator were discussed, and Mike was questioned regarding possible co-conspirators.

"We'll have a much better idea once we identify the senator," Mike said. "When we know where this is going, we will need access to well-placed individuals in the government who have the power to advise the president and stop a takeover. Is there a possibility you can open some doors?"

Jacob Frankin stood and walked around the desk, taking the side chair next to Mike. He reached over, a hand settling on the younger man's shoulder.

"Mike, if this is as serious as it sounds, I will do whatever I can." He glanced across his desk and out the window to the courtyard before looking back at Mike. "A coup would greatly change this country as we know it." Frankin took a breath. "Responsible individuals with the ability to keep that from happening must do what they can." He touched Mike's arm this time. "You can count me on your side."

Then Frankin asked, "Where is your headquarters?"

"A hotel room," Mike said.

He told Frankin about New Orleans and the information that had been collected regarding the shooting of Congresswoman Kato. He detailed her connection to the senator too.

Mike also told Frankin about the murder of Herbie O'Conner, and the fact that a holiday had been mentioned as a target date for action.

Frankin's reaction was subdued. "Hmm. Today's Thursday. Memorial Day is coming up on Monday. Is that a possibility?"

"We think it is," Mike said. "Especially considering the fact that the president has insisted on a military parade." He leaned forward in his chair. "What better time to take a leader down than when he's surrounded by the military?"

"You are assuming top generals and admirals are involved?" Frankin said.

"Yes. It couldn't be done without them," Mike reasoned. "They've lost the Marine Commandant. We're assuming he was involved."

"Yes, I saw that on the news."

Frankin was quiet for a moment. Then he suggested an initial way he could help.

"Do you think Rage would accept working space here in our complex? We have significant onsite security, 24/7." Then he was up and walking again. "We also have surveillance cameras on the streets in a one-block radius around the office."

It was an offer Mike hadn't considered or expected. He suspected Rage would be very interested in the suggestion. "Can I let you know later today?"

"Yes, and there's the guest cottage in back off the courtyard," Frankin added. "Three small bedrooms and plenty of additional workspace. Our security covers the cottage too. Unlike the situation in New Orleans, you and your people would be safe here."

A car and driver were assigned to Mike when he was ready to leave. Mr. Frankin said the transportation along with the cottage was theirs until the investigation was over.

Mike waited to call Rage until he was back in his hotel room.

"We have some help," he said when Rage answered.

"I need some good news. Tell me about it."

"We have a place to work, and it comes with security."

# Chapter Twenty-Six

Mike's phone rang immediately after he hung up with Rage. It was Cary.

"I've taken a three-month furlough," she told him. "What can I do to help?"

"Where are you now?" Mike asked.

"My apartment," Cary told him. "Where do you need me to be?"

Mike thought for a moment. "Here. Finding Josette's journal is imperative. Without the senator's name, we're running in circles. We've got to find her notes."

"I'll repack my bag and catch the next flight to D.C. When I know an arrival time and destination airport, I'll call."

"We have transportation." Mike told her about their new workplace and the car and driver. "I'll have him pick you up."

Mike checked the time on his phone. *Twenty after one. Thursday! Maybe eighty hours until this country is changed forever.*

In almost a whisper he said, "Hurry."

~~~

Another call to Rage and then Mike repacked his own bag. Finished, he opened the satchel, placing both Josette's and his computer inside. Mike glanced around the room. He was ready to move.

Rage met him at the brownstone in Georgetown. Mr. Frankin introduced them to his head of security, and they were shown to the guest cottage that would be their headquarters.

In the interim, Cary called. She was on her way and would arrive in the early evening.

Over a cup of coffee in the guest cottage's living room, Rage and Mike discussed strategy.

"Nothing works and no one is going to treat us seriously until we have names and connections," Rage said.

"It all hinges on naming the senator," Mike said. "Once we know him, we can begin identifying others involved at the top. We will be concerned with civilian or military individuals who have been meeting regularly with this senator."

"Keep working," Rage said. "In the meantime, I'll be looking for a break with people I know."

"Will you be moving here to the cottage?" Mike asked.

"No." Rage said. "I'll keep my room at the hotel. It's probably better for us to be separated for now. Besides, I still have people to see in the capital."

Rage left Mike crouched over Josette's computer.

~~~

A little after seven that evening, Mike's phone buzzed. If it wasn't Rage or Cary, he didn't plan to answer. He glanced at the display; it was Cary.

"I'm at Dulles airport," she said, "and I'm not seeing you."

She didn't sound happy.

"Look for a tall guy in a suit," he told her. "He's in the baggage area and carrying a call sign for Sara Jackson."

"Who's Sara Jackson?" she asked, "One of your past flings?"

He could hear her chuckle. Cary liked to tease him. Then she was serious again.

"I'm walking through the doors now. Wait, I see him. Hang on while I make connection." The phone was quiet for several seconds except for the muted sound of voices. "Okay, I'm with your driver. He says we should be at your location in 30 to 40 minutes."

"See you then."

Mike trusted the situation. The driver, Ernesto, Italian to the core and totally dedicated to Jacob Frankin, would keep Cary safe and deliver her to the cottage in due time.

Mike returned to the computer; hours were flashing by.

~~~

There was a knock at the cottage's door just after eight o'clock. Ernesto was there holding Cary's bags. She was there too, smiling big around the driver's shoulder.

"Hi stranger," she said, reaching to give him a peck on the cheek. Ernesto left the bags and hurried off to check in with the security detail. Behind the closed
~~~

door, Cary gave Mike a real kiss. They cared for each other. Being separated was difficult.

"Any new luck on the journal?" Cary asked as she made coffee with K-Cups.

"No," Mike said. "I feel like I'm missing something. That I'm close…"

Cary handed him a cup and took a chair, asking for a rundown as she made notes on a pad Rage had left behind.

Mike had a list of files he had examined without turning up anything resembling a journal.

They traded ideas, each trying to push the other into a breakthrough.

Taking turns at the computer, the hours slipped away. The weekend was almost at hand, and they appeared no closer to finding Josette's journal than when they began.

After a while, Cary took her notes and went into the living room where she continued to jot down ideas.

A third of the way down his latest list of ideas and now on his third cup of coffee, Mike left the computer, joining Cary. Midnight had slipped by, and they were a couple of hours into early Friday morning.

She was sprawled across the sofa, and Mike had a large chair and ottoman to himself. Both were quiet, thinking their own thoughts.

Suddenly Cary raised herself to her elbows, an idea obvious by the expression of hope and concentration on her face.

"What about? No. That would be too simple."

"What?" Mike said. "Nothing's too simple at this point."

She hesitated again. "A friend of mine back at UT told me how she saved secrets she wanted to hide. She kept a diary of sorts hidden on her computer by typing it at the end of some innocuous file or other set of information. She said it worked better if the main file was long and boring. Also, she left a large number of blank pages between her boring notes and the diary." She looked at Mike, uncertainty in her expression. "I can't imagine Josette doing that, not with something this important." She slowly shook her head. "That wouldn't be the answer, would it?"

Mike sat up in his chair. He remembered the strange sensations he'd had when looking at Josette's file concerning her grandmother. It was a big file, and he hadn't searched it all the way to the end. Too boring, too personal.

Glancing at Cary, he stood up and returned to Josette's computer.

He had gone through portions of the file several times. Everything he'd seen involved Landie in one way or another. Skipping through it again Mike was still relatively sure he hadn't missed anything. Yet, as before, something continued to bug him.

Leaning back in the chair, Mike wondered, *could something that easy have merit?* Without reasoning why—just a hunch—he guided the cursor back to the beginning of Landie's file. He moved it down through the pages, reading a line here and there. It was all about Josette's grandmother or herself in one way or another.

Reaching the end of the notes relating to Landie, he noticed a blank page following that one. He pulled the curser down finding another blank page and another.

He glanced up, catching Cary's eye. "What?" she asked.

His attention was down on the keyboard again. *More empty space.*

Page after blank page flashed by on the monitor.

Until finally, there it was: Notes.

At the beginning of a new page, thirteen pages from the last one referring to Landie. Mike counted the blank pages again wondering if Josette had left that number intentionally.

At least it was arranged like notes, but the type if that's what it was, could not have been larger than a 3-point font. *Unreadable.*

"Make it bigger." Cary was shaking his shoulder.

Mike brought the font to 12-point. When he finished, they looked at the page and then at each other. Neither had any idea what language Josette's notes were written in.

"It's certainly not English," Mike said without turning.

"No kidding." She thumped his arm without taking her eyes from the monitor. "Run it through a translation program," Cary added.

"How?"

"Let me do it." She pushed him with her hip.

A few minutes later, Mike, looking in surprise, had watched her pull up a language translation program on Josette's laptop. Page by page, Cary had copied and translated the information they had found.

"It's Kurd," she told him. "About ten percent of Iranians speak the language."

Mike was astonished. "How'd you know that?"

"Part of the job at Trebeck these days," she said simply.

Both zeroed in on the notes with Mike back at the computer.

First came details for meetings that had been held. Set up in a table with columns, there was a date, then a list of the individuals present. Positioning the cursor over the dates and scanning downward, Mike saw that Josette's notes began a few months earlier on the 16th of November. Those first entries were minimal. Individuals present usually included Josette and "the senator" or just "the senator and me." Initially, only the two of them. No name for him.

"I think you hit it," Mike said. "This is what we've been looking for."

He leaned in toward the computer again, Cary at his shoulder. *The senator? Surely, she'll name him.* After a few entries, Mike became less confident.

Glancing at the final two columns, he punched Cary with a finger. "This one gives the location of each meeting, and the last column is the main discussion topic."

Cary was already ahead of him. "The initial November meeting was in the senator's office. It was just the two of them at that point."

Taking a moment to read, Mike was into the details. "The discussion involved a new piece of legislation targeting Iran's oil sales to the Russians. The senator obviously wanted to curtail those transactions. Glancing at Cary, Mike said, "Josette was expected to pursue an effort toward the same goal in the House of Representatives."

Cary was nose to nose with the monitor. "Her next note indicated objection." Cary pointed to the remark's column. Josette had left a personal note. "In my opinion, we need to remain on workable terms with the Iranians." Then Josette had added a second note. "I think the president is right on this one."

"Hmm, potential conflict." Mike said it, reflecting both their thoughts.

Mike took a few moments to get focused. Then, glancing toward Cary, he said, "We've found it. This is it. This is Josette's journal!"

"It is, isn't it?" Cary glanced at Mike and then back at the screen. "Perfect!" She was reading again. "It really is." Cary was on to other entries "What does it all mean?"

Mike was back to the keyboard with Cary draped across his shoulders. Both were reading and pointing.

"But who's the senator?" Cary asked, her eyes never leaving the screen.

Mike moved the cursor as they continued reading. There were several meetings about legislation involving the Iranians. The senator was in favor of measures forcing the Middle Eastern country to cancel all business and contact with the Russians.

Other issues concerning Iran's neighbors were also discussed. Israel, the Palestinians, and their threatening military actions were discussed at length according to the journal. Josette, based on her written remarks, did not always agree with the senator, but she seldom appeared to have voiced her differences to him—only on a few occasions, according to her own notes.

Mike and Cary remained huddled close to the monitor, reading every comment, often pausing to discuss a point.

"She doesn't agree with the senator on some crucial issues," Cary said after reading a couple of pages of Josette's notes.

"He doesn't seem to notice most of the time," Mike said without looking up.

"Yeah. I agree."

Further into the journal, Josette's notes changed. Others began attending the meetings. Those names were there. General Farmington, the Chairman of the Joint Chiefs of Staff, was almost always in attendance. Others included Army Chief of Staff, General Avery, and the Commandant of the Marine Corps, General Wisecroft.

The meetings, overall, could be construed as planning for an action of some sort.

Admiral Patron, Chief of Naval Operations, often joined using secured conference calls.

"I wonder if General Wisecroft's death was a blow to their planning?" Mike wondered aloud.

He was moving on. Another interesting item had caught Mike's attention. He was pointing to the screen.

"General Riverdale, the Vice Chairman of the Joint Chiefs of Staff, hasn't been mentioned. One other member of the Joint Chiefs is also absent, Allen Smith, Chief of Space Operations."

Mike turned, commenting, "Why would they be left out?"

Cary held out her hands, palms up.

They both noticed that the location for the meetings was seldom the same. Military offices and other less conspicuous locations were used from time to time, even personal residences on occasion. When there were only two or three attendees, the senator's office was most often used. According to her notes, Josette had attended many of the meetings.

But there were also notes on several she had not attended. Her information indicated the senator often discussed topics with Josette that had been touched on at meetings she missed.

One of the last entries involving these meetings and attendees was a brief weekend gathering held in Gulf Shores, Alabama. The senator and several top generals were there, but the name of another person caused Mike and Cary to glance at each other. This individual was a woman—Elena Springer-Preston.

"Preston is the Deputy Director of CIA for Operations," Mike said slowly. "Rage will be interested in that."

"Maybe she's the individual mentioned in Josette's note at her apartment."

Mike looked at her, a blank expression on his face.

"You know," she said. "The one I found in the cleaner bottle!"

"Oh, that one," he said, finally remembering.

Cary wasn't satisfied with him only remembering. "Josette thought the senator was taking advice from someone other than the Joint Chiefs. Maybe it was Springer-Preston."

"It didn't sound that way to me, but I'll mention that to Rage."

As the dates came closer to the present, Josette appeared to harbor more objections to the intentions of the senator and military officers.

"They're planning a military coup." Josette had typed those words in a remark's column only a few weeks earlier.

That was the first time she had expressed a solid accusation regarding a military takeover. Before this, her remarks had only included hints.

Mike and Cary each glanced at the other. She was now in a chair pulled close to his side. Leaningback, their eyes returned to Josette's statement.

"Wow," Mike said finally, "a takeover."

"A U.S. senator..." Cary added, "... and we don't even know which one."

Mike looked at her, hesitating—*thinking*—then saying, "And with most of the Joint Chiefs cooperating."

Cary nodded.

Mike glanced at the date of Josette's final notes. "These entries were in the last days before she was killed."

As Mike pulled the cursor down, the screen filled with the next page of notes. As if the monitor was a magnet, Mike and Cary were both drawn forward again, scanning the full page.

"He wants me to join them," Cary said, reading.

Mike chimed in, reading down the page. "Senator Rayburt really thinks I might consider being a part of this—"

The sentence was halfway down the page.

"He stopped me today as I was leaving and asked me to come with him. The senator said things would be different in this country with him in the Oval Office. He said we could do it with the help of the right people."

Cary breathed deeply; this came as a total surprise. Senator Wayne Washington Rayburt had been in Washington for years, a political star and a very popular one.

On a lighter note, every woman she knew—herself included—thought Senator Wayne Rayburt was one of the most handsome men in the capitol.

Several entries about the secretive plans for the Memorial Day takeover followed the discovery of the senator's identity.

Mike and Cary paused several times to glance at each other. It was difficult to believe the information written in Josette's notes. The plans they were reading about were already in place. The coup was scheduled for the coming Monday, three days from now. Senator Rayburt planned to be sitting in the Oval Office approximately seventy-two hours from now.

The details were explicit, giving times, instructions, and names of the individuals involved at the top. Most of the Joint Chiefs were there including the Chairman, General Paul Farmington. The Marine Commandant was there too, but Mike and Cary knew about his untimely death. General Wisecroft would not be leading the marines in the parade or using Abrams tanks to detain the presidential limousine with the president and first lady inside.

Pages of notes followed. They were often difficult to follow because the narrative involved Josette's thoughts and opinions of the individuals, the plans, and the objective of the takeover.

The congresswoman said as much toward the end of her notes.

Josette's last entry sent a shiver through Cary. The congresswoman wrote, "Given our differences, I think he immediately regretted asking me to join them." Then she went on. "I told him my initial reaction was to continue in congress, but that I would consider his offer and give him an answer when I return to Washington on Monday. The senator knows I'm scheduled to fly home tomorrow."

Cary glanced at the date of the note, then pointed it out to Mike. "Josette made this entry early on the day before she was killed that evening in New Orleans." They sat staring, eyes locked on the other, each with their own thoughts.

"Interesting coincidence," he said softly.

"Yeah," she added, "a deadly one."

# Chapter Twenty-Seven

"Rage has been waiting for this."

Cary nodded as Mike reached for his phone. It was early on Friday morning.

Rage was in his Washington hotel room, just before leaving for breakfast when his cell phone rang.

"Hello."

"It's Senator Wayne Rayburt."

"What?" Rage wasn't sure what Mike was telling him.

"We located Josette's journal. It was buried inside another file on her computer. She names Rayburt as the senator who wanted her to go to the White House with him. Josette had added a note that she thought he regretted asking her to join them. Rayburt's heading up the takeover."

Rage was quiet for a few moments. "You're sure she was naming Senator Rayburt."

"Very sure, and the takeover is scheduled for Memorial Day. That's Monday," Mike told him. "And there's something else you should know."

"What?"

"In addition to top generals from the Joint Chiefs of Staff, the Deputy Director of CIA for

Operations is one of the co-conspirators. Elena Springer-Preston."

Rage was silent for several seconds before saying, "I'm surprised. I recently met with Eldon Patterson from the CIA. The fact that their Deputy Director is involved may explain Herbie's shooting. Patterson has probably been working with Springer-Preston all along."

Rage was quiet for a moment. Then he said, "I might as well have signed Herbie's death warrant."

"Do you think the note Cary found at Josette's apartment was referring to someone other than the Deputy Director?"

Cary was listening over Mike's shoulder. She tugged at his sleeve. "Springer-Preston was already on board. Josette was almost certainly referring to a third party."

"Cary thinks it was someone else."

"I doubt it," Rage told him. "But let's keep an open mind."

Rage was ready to move forward. "Go through the journal searching out every item of information about the takeover. And do it fast."

Mike was making notes.

"Has Cary been able to help?" Rage asked. "She has. She's the one who brought in the Russian hacker. Together, they broke Josette's password code." He winked at her and added, "She also had the idea that made it possible for me to find the journal."

She smiled at Mike.

"Dig through the journal," Rage ordered again. "Find every detail relating to the takeover, no matter how small. We're going to have to convince some important people that a coup is imminent." Almost as though he was trying to convince himself, Rage paused for a moment. Then he said, "That isn't going to be easy. Obviously, they'll do anything to stop us."

Then just before the expected hang-up, "Be careful."

~~~

Mike emailed Cary a copy of the journal and Rage's instructions to search out every piece of information about the takeover.

"No matter how small," Rage had said.

Cary and Mike each combed independently for every reference involving the coup. Josette even had notes on the military maneuvers that had taken place over the last few months. They stopped several times to briefly discuss a point one of them questioned.

Finally, believing they had everything, Mike emailed a copy of their combined list to Rage. He followed up a few minutes later with a call.

Rage answered immediately. "Good work. I'm going to pass the generalities of this by the FBI and NSA, my goal being to reach the president. We only have Josette's notes as evidence. Let's hope someone believes us."

"Would you have any objections if I discuss this with someone we both know?"

"Who?"

"Jacob Frankin."

After a pause, Rage said, "Probably a good idea. He knows important people in this town. He also knows where a lot of bones are buried. Mr. Frankin can open doors you and I don't know exist."
~~~

"Cary and I will talk to him," Mike said. "I need to introduce Cary."

"Let me know how the meeting goes."

Then Rage was gone.

~~~

The young congresswoman's notes regarding the takeover attempt had been revealing. When Rage was given the names of those involved, he mentally noted each and then sat in deep thought for several minutes. Then he was ready to make things happen, or in this case, to stop others from making things happen.

Punching Sladen's number into his phone, Rage waited.

When Sladen answered, Rage told him, "We have a name."

"The senator?"

"Yes."

"Who?"

"Not on the phone," Rage said. "Let's meet, maybe go for a walk."

"Where?" Sladen hesitated. "I'm near the capital now."

Rage was on top of the idea quickly. "The Mall? Jefferson Memorial?"

"That's fine," Sladen said. "In an hour? Five o'clock."

"I'll be there."

Hanging up with Sladen, Rage, in his mind, was working on more than one solution. He didn't like the idea that their only evidence of a coup in progress was Josette's notes. Rage pulled up Google Earth Pro on his computer and searched for the closest significant city to Gulf Shores, Alabama. The coastal Alabama beach
~~~

town was among the last meeting locations for Senator Rayburt and his top people.

It took only a couple of minutes: Pensacola, Florida, was closest, only 34 miles from the popular tourist destination. A name immediately came to mind. Gerry Sanders, a friend and former policeman had recently moved to Pensacola.

Rage checked; he still had a mobile number. Ten minutes later, arrangements had been made for Sanders to take a drive and check on a couple of things. To aid him, Rage pulled photographs of Senator Rayburt, General Farmington, and the other Gulf Shores attendees, and then he emailed them to his friend. If a covert meeting of the senator and his people could be verified, this would strengthen the theory of a coup in the planning. The particulars laid out in Josette's journal would have independent backup.

~~~

It had taken more time than expected to peruse through Josette's notes. They examined the notes wanting to be sure nothing material had been missed, nor any meaning overlooked. Morning had quickly become late Friday afternoon. Satisfied they had gleaned every point of information from Josette's journal and notes, Mike called Diane at the front desk in the old brownstone mansion and was told that Mr. Frankin could meet with them at six—an hour from now.

Arriving a few minutes early, they were met by Mrs. Collins. Mike introduced Cary to the lady who had taken him under her wing when he was but a boyand had been instrumental in making him the man hehad become. He had also explained that Mrs. Collins
~~~

was office manager for the entire firm and private assistant to the senior partner.

Waiting in the reception area, Mike watched Edith Ann Collins as the two women became acquainted. A warm feeling flowed over him. This elderly woman was so much more than just a friend.

Mrs. Collins fussed over Cary while teasing them both about being alone in the cottage. "You should have a chaperone," she said, a slight grin on her face.

At six, a buzzer sounded on the front desk, and Mrs. Collins walked them to Mr. Frankin's office door. "You are on your own," she said, smiling at Mike. "Make your case."

~~~

Shaking Cary's hand, Mr. Frankin appeared quite taken with her. He asked about her family and was given the short version of her life to date. Expressing sympathy for the loss of her parents, he quickly moved on to the reasons for this meeting.

Gesturing for them to sit, Frankin turned to Mike and asked if he had made progress since their recent conversation.

"Yes sir," Mike told him. "A coup is definitely being planned. We've identified a senator and several top generals and admirals. And a top CIA operative." He paused, then said, "On a positive note, we have also identified a couple of top military personnel who appear to have been left out of the planning."

Looking up from his notepad, Frankin pushed back his glasses and asked, "Are you confident of your source? After all, you are basing everything on this journal and the fact that the congresswoman was killed
~~~

in what you think may have been an assassination. There is always the possibility it really was a common convenience store robbery."

"We're confident it was a directed killing," Mike said with a glance toward Cary.

She was nodding. "Rage Doyle is sure too. And Herbie O'Conner was convinced."

"I don't want to know names," Jacob Frankin said. "If I can arrange something, you can present your case then. Allow me to consider the possibilities. I'll reach out to some contacts and get back to you in a few hours."

Mike nodded. He had presented his best argument.

"Will you and Cary be staying overnight at the cottage?" Mr. Frankin asked. "And what about Rage?"

Mike glanced at her, noting a slight nod.

"Yes, sir. We'll be staying," he said. "Rage will remain off site. He has meetings."

Mr. Frankin nodded, assuring them, "I'll be in touch, and I'll have the security people watch the cottage closely while you're there. Try to get a good night's rest. You could find yourselves very busy over the next couple of days and nights."

~~~

Back at the cottage, the two realized they had not eaten since early morning. Searching through the fridge, Cary found a pizza. They got it on a stone and into the oven, then made coffee while they waited.

An hour later, a single slice of pizza was all that was left. They were each on a final cup of coffee. Cary was on the sofa again, and Mike in the chair facing her. She reached out, brushing the back of his hand with
~~~

fingertips. Their eyes met—the look—for both, one of caring and passion.

That moment lasted…

Mike was the first to speak. "We'll get more done if we don't touch."

Reluctantly, Cary withdrew her hand. "Unfortunately, you're right."

"We're at a standstill," Mike told her. "Until we hear from Rage or Mr. Frankin."

"We should try and get a few hours of sleep," Cary said, yawning. "I'll take the guest bedroom. We won't sleep if we're together."

"Well?"

"Well, we need the sleep," she stated, smiling. "Mr. Frankin is right. Once this thing breaks, we will probably be awake until it's over."

Standing and leaning over, Cary reached for Mike. She cupped his neck in her hand and touched his lips with a tender kiss. Cary could hear his reaction—a deep, ragged intake of breath—and could feel her own.

Turning, she dropped into his lap. A deep look into each other's eyes and then they kissed again, passionately this time.

After a few seconds, a hand on each of his shoulders, Cary leaned back, breaking the hold they had on each other.

In a breathless whisper she said, "We can't do this now."

She felt him relax. *He understands.*

"Help me up," she said.

Mike shook his head. Then, with a slightly wicked grin, he smiled and pushed Cary to her feet.

They both understood what they had to do in the coming hours, and they both understood what they couldn't do.

# Chapter Twenty-Eight

Rage had reached the Jefferson Memorial a couple of minutes before five. The Mall was virtually deserted, a few lone individuals here and there.

He could see Sladen approaching from the opposite direction. A wave and then a bumping of elbows.

Rage verbalized it, "You can't be too careful."

"You can't," Sladen agreed. Turning, he fell into step.

Without intention, they walked east along the path around the Tidal Basin.

As they strolled, Rage began to feed bits of information to his friend.

"We've made some discoveries," Rage told him. "The congresswoman's journal."

Sladen glanced over. "You've found her notes?"

"Yes."

Sladen gestured for him to continue.

"She names the senator," Rage told him. "And others."

"Who is he?"

Rage told him.

"Wayne Rayburt?" Sladen stopped, turning toward his friend. "Senator Wayne Rayburt?" Sladen appeared genuinely surprised.

Rage was watching him closely.

"Yes," Rage said, continuing. "And the congresswoman names several military leaders who are connected to the coup."

"I would expect top military people to be involved," Sladen said, shaking off the shock. "Were there any surprises?"

"There are others," Rage said, "but yes, the congresswoman did name one who came as a shock."

Sladen stopped and was standing still, waiting.

"There was a meeting down at Gulf Shores, Alabama," Rage told him. "One of the attendees was the Deputy Director of CIA for Operations."

There was real surprise in Sladen's voice again. "Elena? Elena Springer-Preston?" The Chief of Staff at the National Security Agency was clearly taken aback. "I know Elena. We correspond often. I can't believe she'd be involved in a coup attempt."

"I have someone on his way to Gulf Shores as we speak," Rage said. "He should confirm a meeting took place there recently."

Rage had begun walking again.

"In addition to the senator, several generals were at the meeting along with Deputy Director Preston."

He stopped again, turning to Sladen.

"Overall, it looks like the Chairman of the Joint Chiefs and most of his top people are on board with the coup. That covers the army, navy, air force, and marines since General Farmington has basically taken command there since Wisecroft's accident."

"What about the other members of the Joint Chiefs?" Sladen was trying for a full picture.

"There are only two. Neither is mentioned in the information we have," Rage told him.

Sladen, a finger scratching at his chin, said, "That could mean either of two things. One, they're not involved, or two, other duties kept them out of the meetings."

"I don't think they're involved," Rage said. "Congresswoman Kato's notes were very in-depth. She would have mentioned them."

"You are probably right," Sladen pointed out, "and if you are, then they could be instrumental in stopping the takeover. Assuming they aren't involved, these individuals might be temporarily replacements for some of those involved."

"How would you suggest using them?" Rage wanted to hear Sladen's ideas before giving his.

Arms outstretched and palms up, Sladen said, "This is out of my field of knowledge." Looking at Rage, he added, "Your experience with the CIA makes you the natural."

"I have some ideas," Rage said noncommittally though he was already developing the basics of a plan. "Can you get us in with the president once we have a strategy?"

"I can get us close. We'll have to convince others around POTUS to get the president's attention and an appointment." Sladen stopped and turned back toward the Jefferson Memorial. "Where are you keeping your people?" he asked as they strolled back.

"Hotel rooms," Rage lied. He was the only one in a hotel at this point, but he wasn't willing to tell anyone about the guest cottage in Georgetown. He remembered Herbie.

"One last thing," Rage said. "The congresswoman left a strange comment in one of her notes."

"What sort of comment?" Sladen asked.

"Her note read that she thought perhaps the senator was being guided by individuals other than the Joint Chiefs. And she commented, 'online video conference meetings.'"

"He could have been talking with another source. A private video conferencing program could be their method." Sladen hesitated. "But who?"

"Yeah," Rage said. "Who? I agree and we're looking at the possibilities."

The two men parted at the memorial, each going their own way back to transportation parked on darkening streets.

~~~

As he walked, Rage became aware of distant footsteps. An individual appeared to be following him a hundred yards back. Still a block from his vehicle, Rage turned a corner, quickly picked a secluded spot, and waited.

The man never knew Rage was waiting.

After checking for identification and finding none, Rage left the individual unconscious but alive and resting comfortably behind a cluster of neatly trimmed bushes near the sidewalk.
~~~

Except for a sore neck, the man was undamaged from the encounter. He would tell his supervisor that the target obviously realized he was being followed.

~~~

On Rage's suggestion, Gerry Sanders went directly to the airport at Gulf Shores. Later, Sanders would travel to the Cuban Towers where the meeting in question had been held.

Already into the evening, the day staff at Jack Edwards National Airport had gone home several hours earlier. The night agent checked scheduling for the days of the meeting. "Ellie Brogan would havebeen on the front desk that particular Saturday and Sunday."

A call to the woman's home informed them Brogan was out to dinner with friends but could be reached on her cell phone. Two calls to Brogan's mobile went unanswered. On the third call Brogan answered, listened, and agreed to come directly to the airport.

Sanders explained the situation and asked if she objected to having their conversation recorded. She didn't.

"We're attempting to verify that twoindividuals flew into your facility on Saturday of that weekend and out on Sunday." He slid five photos in front of Brogan—four men and one woman.

She immediately leaned forward; her eyes locked on the senator's photograph. She put that one aside and shuffled through the other photos. After giving the other four photos a good look, she picked one and dropped it beside the senator's.
~~~

Picking up Senator Rayburt's photo, Brogan turned to Sanders asking, "What does this one look like? Physically, I mean. A description?"

Sanders was prepared; Rage had sent that information, too. "He's 6'5" and 225 pounds."

Brogan looked at the Rayburt photo again. "He was the tall one," she said. "I thought I had seen him before." She glanced at Sanders. "Who is he?"

"A politician," Sanders told her.

"He looked familiar. I probably saw him on the news."

"Yeah, probably."

She picked up the second photo. "This is the man who was traveling with the tall one."

It was General Farmington—The Bear.

Sanders took a verbal statement from the woman and had her sign a note affirming her identification of the two men.

~~~

At the Cuban Towers, Sanders found the going more difficult. To start, there was no front desk.

He reverted to knocking on doors. Starting next to the condo utilized for the clandestine meeting,Sanders knocked on a half dozen doors before getting any result at all. No one answered at three; the other three were vacationers who had only recently rented the units.

The seventh door provided possibilities.

John and Minnie Vorstead had been coming to Gulf Shores annually for a decade and had rented the same condo each year. They were from Minnesota and enjoyed escaping the chilly weather back home. Minnie said they also enjoyed long walks on the beach.
~~~

The couple had stayed longer than normal this year. Despite precautions, both had come down with a mild case of the covid. Clear now, they would be headed back to Minneapolis next week.

"I need to ask some questions about one of your recent neighbors," Sanders told them.

He was immediately invited into the Vorstead's living room which looked out on the beach in the distance. Once seated, he asked if he could record their conversation. Sanders told them his questions involved a local inquiry.

The Vorstead's were very willing to help. "You betcha," Minnie said. Her husband nodded enthusiastically.

As they had walked by the front bedroom, Sanders glanced that way and noticed the curtains were open. Two teenagers engaged in animated conversation were walking by.

Sanders asked about the room. It had two windows looking out on the walkway. A recliner and a small table with books indicated a place to relax and keep up with whatever might be going on outside.

"Is that your reading room?"

Minnie answered. "Reading and," she pointed to her husband, "sleeping for John. He takes his naps in there." John chuckled as he nodded his agreement.

"My wife keeps up with our neighbors from there too." It was Minnie's turn to nod.

Sanders started his questions. "Were you here in mid-February?" he asked. "Particularly on the weekends?"

"Oh, sure," Minnie told him. "We leave the weekends to the tourists. About the only time we get out is to go for groceries. Oh, and sometimes to walk the beaches early in the morning to pick up shells."

He was concerned about his next question because of the time interval. Next, Sanders asked if they had been at the condo on the Saturday and Sunday in question, back early in the new year, and had they noticed anyone coming in or out of condo number 1418 next door? Minnie Vorstead thought about it for only a moment and was then quick to answer. "Yep, and yep." There was no doubt or hesitation in her voice.

Minnie's husband was agreeing with the constant nodding of his head. "Yep," he said finally when he could get a word in. Minnie was a talker.

She did the explaining. "There were five of them, don't cha know. Four fellas and a gal. I keep the curtains open in our reading room, so I see people coming and going."

This was good information, and it had been volunteered.

"Two of the men stayed at the condo. One of them was really tall," she said, adding, "if that's important. The other two and the gal came a little later. The two men first, then the woman. She was alone. Looked like she'd been playing tennis. Had on the outfit, don't cha know." Minnie took a breath. "Later on, the gal left by herself, and the four men went out to eat."

Sanders realized he must have had a questioning expression.

"I heard them talking 'bout restaurants and seafood when they passed the window," she said, pointing back toward the front room. "The gal was in her tennis outfit, but I already told you that. The four fellas were dressed for golf. Shorts and pullovers. The first two fellas had golf clubs when they arrived, but the only time the clubs came out of the condo was when they were leaving on Sunday."

Sanders asked if Minnie and John would sign a short statement saying they had agreed to the interview and having their answers recorded. "You betcha" again from each of them.

Finally, he pulled the photos from their envelope. Without knowing their names, the Vorsteads identified the photos: Senator Rayburt, General Farmington, General Avery, General Wisecroft, and Elena Springer-Preston.

Minnie Vorstead pointed to the photo of Senator Rayburt. "He's the tall one."

Sanders nodded.

As soon as he reached his car, the information and the recordings from both interviews were transmitted to Rage. Finished, Sanders glanced at the time: 9:50 p.m., an hour later in D.C.

~~~

He was going through his notes later that evening at the hotel when an email notification sounded on Rage's phone. Checking it, he smiled.

Gerry Sanders indicated he had been successful on his journey to Gulf Shores. He had sent several files. Glancing at the time, Rage pulled them off his computer and on to a flash drive when he reached the hotel. He could print them at the business center downstairs.

Thirty minutes later, the files were on paper. Rage called Sladen.
~~~

He wanted to follow up even though he had been followed after their last meeting. Rage needed to be sure of his friends going forward.

Sladen was surprised to hear from him so quickly. Rage told him about the files he had received from the gulf coast.

"Now we have third-party corroboration of that meeting," Rage said. "The coup is close, almost certainly scheduled for Memorial Day: in conjunction with the President's parade."

Slow to answer, Sladen replied, "You're right. The president will be riding in the midst of the military. Even his secret service contingent can't save him there."

Rage thought it was time to mention his earlier encounter. "I was followed when I left you earlier," he said to Sladen.

"Tonight?" Sladen sounded genuinely surprised and alarmed.

"Yes, this evening," Rage repeated.

"It wasn't my people." Sladen sounded sincere. Pausing for a moment, he added, "Perhaps they were watching me but decided you were the better target."

"Maybe."

Rage let it drop and moved on. "We have to get the president's attention."

"I'm already working on that," Sladen said. "You convinced me earlier."

"What's your plan?"

"Give me a few hours, then we'll talk. I may need you with me later."

"Okay," Rage said, "but hurry."

~~~
~~~

Back at his hotel, Rage called his CIA contact. There was music and muted conversation in the background when Eldon Patterson answered. "I'm at a private party," he explained. "Hold for a moment."

Seconds later, Patterson was back, immediately asking, "Have you identified the senator?"

The question didn't feel right. "We're close," Rage said without details. "Probably within hours." He was unwilling to give Patterson a name, especially with Elena Springer-Preston involved in the coup.

"Do you have any idea?" Patterson was anxious.

"No, but we're close," Rage repeated. Then he asked, "When we have a name, can you get the president's attention?" He didn't tell Patterson that he had also talked with Sladen at NSA.

"I can probably get a meeting with the Secretary of State," Patterson said. "We can try to convince him that a coup is in progress. After that, we'll see."

Rage didn't tell him that someone else was also working on getting them into the White House.

"Someone has to listen," Rage said. "If Monday is their target, we only have a few hours."

"I'll get back to you in the next two hours," Patterson said. "I'll be getting some people out of bed."

Rage could detect uneasiness in Patterson's voice as he answered.

"Let's hope one of them is the president," Rage said.

He glanced at the time before closing the phone. 11:31 p.m. Time was short, and a door had closed. Patterson was on the other side.

~~~
~~~

Secretary of State Jäger's jet had been in the air for nearly twelve hours. Most of the nearly 6,000-mile journey from Tel Aviv was behind them now. The top-secret flight would be landing in less than an hour.

The secretary's mission to quell the Middle Eastern turmoil had been less than successful. Even a side trip to Tehran had not been encouraging. Conflicting goals and angry voices on both sides appeared primed for war. As he stared out the plane's window at a sleeping Washington, the Secretary of State was convinced President Carrigan had no more than a week to avoid actual combat between the two opposing forces.

At that moment the secretary's personal phone buzzed in his pocket. Glancing at the screen, Jäger recognized the caller and smiled. He would take a call from this individual any time.

"Hello, Jacob," he said. "How are you?" Then, "It's late. Shouldn't you be sleeping?"

"Some nights are too busy for sleeping," Jacob Frankin said. "This is one of them."

"I assume then, that this is not a pleasure call."

"It isn't," Frankin replied. "I've been trying to reach you. I need the ear of the president, and time is of the essence."

"I've been unavailable," Jäger said. "Can you give me a general idea of the reason you need to reach the president?"

"Discussing the subject over an unsecured line is not a good idea," Frankin said immediately.

Secretary Jäger was quick to detect his caller's urgency. "Give me five minutes. I'll get back to you."

"Thanks."

Five minutes stretched into seven before Frankin's phone rang.

"Jacob Frankin here."

"It's me," Jäger said. "We're on a secure line now. What do you have?"

The secretary had arranged for the call to be recorded, a fact he did not mention to his friend.

Speaking up, Jacob Frankin was not a man who wasted words. "Are you aware of an immediate plot to overthrow the president?"

Of all the subjects Secretary of State Jäger might have expected, this was not one of them.

"Is this a joke?" The Secretary of State knew it was not. Jacob Frankin did not deal in jokes. "I'veheard nothing. What do you know?"

"A trusted citizen has come to me with details involving a senator and several members of the Joint Chiefs of Staff," Frankin told him. "I believe this individual has reasonable evidence to warrant advising the president to the danger."

"Do you know details, names of the individuals involved?"

"I did not ask," Frankin said. "I believe it better if the president hears the evidence and names first-hand from those who have made the investigation."

"Let me think," the Secretary of State said.

Frankin listened, hearing voices in the background advising others to prepare for landing— the sound of a seatbelt clicking closed. *He's on an airplane.*

Then Secretary of State Jäger was back. "Can you have your source available in an hour?"

"Yes," Frankin told him. He wasn't as certain as he sounded. And he needed to add one small piece of information. "Actually, there are three individuals the president would want to question," Frankin said.

"Three?" Jäger had been caught off guard. He was thinking. "Still doable. Have them ready to go to the White House at 5:00 a.m."

Clarifying the situation, the secretary said, "I'm in the air now and will be going directly to the White House. I'll have your people picked up and brought there."

Frankin gave him details and a location.

~~~

An hour later two men and a woman stood waiting at curbside in front of the Brownstone Mansion in Georgetown. A pair of dark SUVs drove down the street and pulled to the sidewalk beside them. Four unsmiling men stepped out of the lead van, two on either side of the individuals on the sidewalk.

One of the men spoke. "Where did you go for your last vacation?"

Rage Doyle answered. "Big Island, Hawaii."

"What was the weather like when you were there?"

"Cold and snowy."

A door on the lead SUV reopened. The three individuals were patted down and had their weapons removed. Rage's briefcase was opened and examined. Finally, Rage, Mike, and Cary were allowed to enter the van.

"Your firearms will be returned when you leave the Oval Office," Rage and Mike were told.
~~~

No one spoke during the drive. It remindedCary of her ride to the cemetery when her mom and dad were killed.

Soon, they were passing through the gates to the White House. The SUVs pulled under the portico, and the doors were opened. Rage and his people were invited to step out and follow a tall woman into the building.

Inside, they were escorted to a waiting area and told to make themselves comfortable. Rage, especially, was uncomfortable waiting, pacing back and forth as hours passed.

Glancing at the time, Rage was growing more distraught by the hour. Midmorning had passed without them being summoned. They had no way of knowing the gravity of the conversation in the Oval Office.

Finally, Secretary of State Jäger came for them.

"Follow me," he said simply and led Rage, Mike, and Cary to the Oval Office.

President Carrigan was standing at a window behind his desk. Looking out, he appeared deep in thought.

Cary was reminded of photos she'd seen of JFK.

The Secretary of State stood with the others, waiting. The president's chief of staff remained near the door. Rage also recognized the chief of the White House Secret Service detail.

Finally, the president turned, and Secretary Jäger said, "Mr. President, these are the people I spoke to you about."

Facing them, President Carrigan said, "Secretary Jäger tells me you have information I should know."

The Secretary of State shuffled his feet. Tension was evident on the faces of everyone in the room.

Glancing at Mike and Cary before answering, Rage turned and said, "Mr. President, we believe a military coup is in place to forcibly remove you from office two days from now."

The president was quiet for a moment. Then, "Your evidence?"

Mike answered him. "Sir, Congresswoman Josette Kato was killed in New Orleans recently. Initially, her murder appeared connected to a convenience store robbery. We don't believe that. We think her shooting was an assassination."

"Why would someone need to eliminate a congresswoman?" he asked.

"Because, Mr. President," Cary answered the question. "Congresswoman Kato had worked directly with those who are planning the takeover. She had been involved on other projects with the senator who's behind the planning. She heard comments and saw other information concerning that planning. Though she was not involved, the congresswoman overheard enough to know that plans were in the making."

"And how do you know this?" the president asked, skepticism strong in his voice.

Rage answered this one. "The congresswoman kept a journal, a private diary of sorts. It's quite detailed."

The president appeared surprised. "Why haven't I heard this before," he asked, glancing at his chief of staff.

Rage answered. "The information was buried on the congresswoman's computer. We've only located the journal in the last few hours," Rage told him. "We've also verified details of a secret meeting mentioned in that journal."

"Then you think the takeover is real?" The president was concerned.

"Yes sir," Rage said, "we do."

"Okay," the president said. "Name some of the individuals involved."

Rage started at the top. "Senator Wayne Rayburt is leading the planning."

A moment of sincere shock claimed the president's face. His eyes were drawn, his lips a bit parted.

Rage continued. "Senator Rayburt expects to be the next president. He has the chairman and most of the Joint Chiefs of Staff on board with him."

President Carrington stared at Rage for a moment, genuine disbelief in his eyes. Standing until now, the president turned to his chair and dropped into it. After a moment, he gestured for the others to sit. Secretary Jäger and Rage took side chairs leaving the others to the large sofas. The chief of the White House Secret Service detail remained near the main door.

"I've known Wayne Rayburt for thirty years," the president said. "He wouldn't do this." The following quiet was deafening. "Would he?" The president was thinking aloud. Then he was up again.

Standing abruptly and walking to a window, he stood there quietly looking out, lost in the moment. He was within himself—alone in his thoughts.

Then Cary did something without consideration, surprising everyone in the room, even herself. She rose from the sofa and walked to the president's side. Touching his arm, she whispered, "You're not alone, Mr. President. Good people across the country are with you."

Looking at her, the president sighed, then said softly, "You're right. I'm not. The voters of this country trusted me to make decisions for them, not Senator Rayburt nor the military." He smiled at Cary before turning to face the others.

His eyes back on Rage, Webster, and Cary, he said, "Thank you for your input and advice. Now I must decide if I can trust your findings and how to go forward."

To Rage he said, "I will need a copy of your investigation and the congresswoman's journal."

"Yes, of course, Mr. President."

Cary opened Rage's briefcase and passed a copy of their work and Josette's journal to the president.

President Carrigan took the papers and stared at Rage for a moment. "Aren't you the individual Lyndon Johnson called The Author."

"Yes sir."

"I thought so," the president said. "You arrange things."

Rage nodded.

"Your talents may be called upon in the next few hours."

"Yes sir," Rage said again, nodding.

To them all, President Carrington said, "We'll talk again."

The president's chief of staff ushered Rage, Mike, and Cary out of the Oval Office and back to one of the dark SUVs. They were driven to the brownstone where they had been picked up earlier.

Saturday's late morning sky was cloudy when they stepped out onto the street. Cary was more into the moment than either of the men and could see that thunderstorms appeared on the schedule for the day. She'd never liked dealing with the rain.

Cary listened to Rage and Mike's conversation while at the same time noticing the scarcity of people on the sidewalk going about their weekend routine. As she prepared to don her mask, Cary noticed a mother and a toddler daughter who were passing. She smiled; the pair were wearing identical Minnie Mouse covid masks. Noticing the attention, the mother's face smiled under her mask, the corners of her eyes wrinkling. She explained, "It's the only way she'll wear hers."

"If it works, use it," Cary told her. Flipping the long hair back, she slipped her mask's ear bands on and turned back to her friends. They were discussing details of a plan already in motion.

~~~

When the others had gone, the president poured coffee for himself and Secretary Jäger. They seated themselves across from each other on the sofas.

"What do you think, John?" the president asked. He had leaned forward, his coffee in his hands.

Without hesitating, the Secretary of State said, "I think their argument is more than a reasonable possibility. If the congresswoman's journal is real, and
~~~

I believe it is," Jäger glanced at the president, "then you have only a matter of hours to stop the senator."

Jäger, still holding his coffee, stood up. Pacing while giving his thoughts, he continued. "From the start Senator Rayburt has adamantly opposed our Middle Eastern policy. And I've heard rumblings and offhand comments that several military leaders from all branches were lining up with the senator's theories about Russia and its backing of Syria."

Jäger added, "And the military has recently been active with maneuvers both here and abroad. General Farmington can bring the entire military on board." He set his cup down. Looking his old friend in the eye, he said, "The activity could certainly be preparations for a military takeover backing Rayburt."

"You're right." President Carrigan said after a few moments of thought. The president set his own cup aside. "Assuming the congresswoman's journal and notes are accurate, then a coup could easily be in play."

"Yes," the secretary said, "I agree."

Standing and returning to his desk, the president picked up the phone and summoned his chief of staff.

"Find Senator Rayburt," the president told Karist. "Tell him I need to see him right away. Mention the Middle East."

Hanging up, the president glanced at Secretary Jäger. "I think we'll know where he stands when I present the results of your trip." Carrigan said. "The tip-off will be when I demand his backing."

Nodding, Jäger looked at his watch. "I need to brief my own people," he said. "I'll ask Karist to let me know when the senator is expected."

As the door closed behind the secretary, the president sat down at his desk. Leaning back, fingers touching his chin, President Carrigan thought of Truman. *Boy, was he ever right. The buck certainly does stop here.*

~~~

Saturday was ebbing away. It was late afternoon, and the senator had just arrived at the White House.

The president and Senator Rayburt were seated across from each other in the Oval Office. Secretary of State Jäger stood nearby.

"How are preparations for the parade?" the senator asked matter-of-factly.

"They're going fine," the president told him. "Covid will limit the crowds here in Washington, but television coverage will show the nation we're ready to enforce peace anywhere across the globe."

Senator Rayburt smiled. "Yes, we need to know our military can handle anything." He added, "Anywhere."

Another sip of his coffee and the president changed the subject.

"Wayne, the situation in the Middle East has gotten even worse since we last talked." The president watched his old friend. "Secretary Jäger has just returned from a top-secret mission to the area."

Senator Rayburt appeared only mildly surprised.
~~~

The secretary spoke directly to Rayburt. "Senator, war is only days away unless we intervene." He glanced at the president, then back to Senator Rayburt. "In my opinion, backing and passing the president's bill is the only way to keep the peace. Everyone in that area and interested parties elsewhere need to see that we are serious in our efforts to halt the conflict."

The president made his pitch. "Wayne, we need your vote on Tuesday. If you come on board, several others, both in the senate and the house will follow. We need this bill, Wayne."

Senator Rayburt was standing now. "I don't think I can do that." He turned and walked behind one of the sofas. Without facing the president directly, he said, "Unless..."

President Carrigan's eyes darted to the senator. "Unless what?"

The senator appeared to be considering a possibility. "I have envoys in the Middle East, too. They expect to wrap things up and report back to me early in the week. Tuesday or wednesday." Rayburt turned and addressed both the president and secretary. "I need their information before deciding." He took a moment to look at each of them. "With new intelligence, perhaps I *can* back you. I will tell you then." He added, "I can delay a vote on the floor until then."

President Carrington had his answer. Rayburt was stalling, waiting for the coup on Monday to put him behind the president's desk.

"Thank you, Wayne," the president said, adding, "Keep me informed."

With the senator gone, Carrigan turned to Secretary Jäger. "I'm going to stop this takeover. Do whatever you need to stop war in the Middle East." He added in a grim voice, "I suspect my task will be more difficult than yours."

# Chapter Twenty-Nine

Rage had just checked the time when his phone buzzed. He was on the sofa at the cottage. It was 9:15 p.m. *It's Saturday night*, he thought. *The parade is 36 hours away.* Rage had a different, more grim thought. *It could be the last parade in the country as we know it.*

Recognizing the caller, Rage answered. "Hello?"

"Mr. Doyle?"

"Yes."

"This is Jonathan Karist, the president's chief of staff. President Carrington would like you and your people to return to the White House as soon as possible." He added, "I will send a car for you."

A basic plan was forming, but it needed work. The three of them had been laboring since returning from the White House. With Rage leading, they had agreed on the necessary points of a plan. Each of them would be responsible for certain actions. Details were still in the development stages.

Time was short, and now the president was calling.

~~~
~~~

Mike and Cary were left outside in a waiting area while the boss was in the Oval Office. Early hours of Sunday morning were quickly passing by.

Rage spent thirty minutes alone with the president and his chief of staff.

With Karist nearby, President Carrington sat across from Rage and told him, "I've read your CIA file, and I'm going to ask you and your people to do something for which I think you're uniquely qualified. Your special skills are needed in the next thirty hours."

"I understand," Rage told him.

Turning to Karist, the president said, "Bring his people in."

When Mike and Cary were seated, the president addressed the three of them.

"If it had not been for you people finding the evidence, we may not have known about the coup until it happened. Senator Rayburt and his military leaders might have accomplished their goals without opposition."

Rage nodded.

"Now," he said, "I'm going to ask you to stop the senator." The President stared at Rage. "Can you do that?"

"Yes, sir. We can."

The president glanced at his chief of staff. "Mr. Karist has capable people in this area, but the three of you have first-hand knowledge of the details." Carrigan studied Rage for a moment and then Mike and Cary before saying, "And you have Mr. Doyle as a leader."

The President of the United States stood up. "Let's do it."

In a voice more confident than his thoughts, Rage asked, "Will we get the full cooperation of your office? Also, we'll need support and assistance from your people?"

"Yes," the president said. "You will get whatever you need." He glanced at his chief of staff, who was nodding.

"Okay," Rage said. "First, we don't know everyone involved in the coup. Given that factor, we will need to break the lines of communication up and down the military chain of command. We can do that by isolating certain individuals."

The president nodded.

Mike picked up the narrative. "Second, since we don't know all the conspirators, we'll be forced to concentrate on those named in the congresswoman's journal. If we can isolate them and their initial efforts, we stop the takeover."

Again, the president nodded.

"Time is in short supply," Rage said the obvious to the president. "We'll need to concentrate on General Farmington, the Chiefs of Staff, and the few others we know. The goal will be to short circuit any execution orders going to field commanders."

The president listened, waiting.

Thinking of the plan that had been formulated in recent hours, Rage said, "We'll need access to your personal secret service contingent, certain members of the domestic staff here in the White House..." He paused, thinking, "...minute-to-minute access to you and those around you. And others as the situation accelerates."

He continued, looking at the president's chief of staff. "We will need a detail room away from the natural flow of White House traffic. We'll need communications, a large conference table, white boards, at least a half-dozen desks, and more as the situation accelerates."

Glancing at Cary, Rage told Karist, "Ms. Warren will give you a detailed list."

The president's chief of staff was making a list as Rage moved from item to item.

"There are offices and a conference room near the Oval Office," the president said. "Our people can reroute foot traffic. Jonathan will be your liaison." He gestured toward Karist. The chief of staff nodded.

The president repeated what he had said earlier. "You'll get whatever you need."

Finally, turning and looking Rage in the eye, President Carrigan said, "Mr. Doyle, we only have time to bet on one horse in this race." Hesitating for a moment, he pointed to Rage, a hand on his shoulder. "You're that one horse."

~~~

Time was flying by.

Several individuals were summoned to the Oval Office by the president's chief of staff. Some were already in the White House; others were rousted from their beds. Karist had been taking notes as Rage laid out his plans.

Glancing at those entering the room, Rage recognized Secretary of State Jäger and his chief of staff along with Jack Lanney, the Director of the Secret Service.
~~~

The president asked everyone to be seated and opened the meeting by introducing Rage.

"Some of you know Mr. Doyle," the president said. "He has served our country honorably for many years. Ordinarily, we would handle the situation I am going to describe internally, but time is of the essence and Mr. Doyle and his people are experts."

Gesturing toward Rage, the president made his announcement, "Mr. Doyle has agreed to head an effort to quell a military takeover of our government."

There was surprise, even doubt on several faces.

Then, with the shock factor gone, individuals glanced at each other and around the room. Now everyone knew why they were there.

Eyes quickly focused on Rage.

The president continued. "Mr. Doyle is to have a free hand. Whatever he and his team needs will be made available." He gestured toward his chief of staff. "Karist will coordinate." Then the president emphasized, "I say again, whatever Mr. Doyle needs, he gets. Time is scarce. This takeover appears focused on the Memorial Day parade. That means we have less than thirty hours." There was no argument.

Rage rose from the sofa. "We'll be in touch," he said as he headed for the door.

~~~

The SUV that had brought them to the White house now took them to a dark street in Georgetown. It left the three of them on the sidewalk after Rage had given instructions for a pickup.

Security personnel routinely checked their IDs and walked them to the guest cottage.
~~~

Webster opened the door and led them inside. He checked the time— Sunday morning, 4:23 a.m.

Cary headed for her bedroom to freshen up. "A few minutes," she said as she disappeared.

Rage walked directly to the kitchen. Coffee time.

"Have you had any sleep?" Mike asked the boss.

"No time," Rage told him. He motioned toward the closed door. "Is Cary okay?"

"She is." Mike yawned and checked his watch again. "We had about three hours earlier," he told Rage.

As Mike poured their coffee, Cary's door opened. "Good morning, gentlemen. I feel better now." She swept in and took Mike's cup for herself.

He gave her a dirty look.

She smiled as she took a sip. Then, glancing at him, she said, "Could use a little more sugar."

Rage gave them both a dirty look. "We have our work cut out for us," The Author said. Time for business.

Both Mike and Cary leaned forward.

"We've been asked to direct efforts to stop the coup," Rage repeated the obvious.

Mike and Cary exchanged glances. They were there and understood the significance of the situation.

Then he gave instructions. "Gather everything you'll need. We won't be coming back here until this is over."

~~~

The sun was peeking over the horizon when they returned to the White House. The president's
~~~

chief of staff met them and led them to their offices. The space was large and had been outfitted with the requirements list Cary had jotted down for Karist. There were desks with computers, monitors, television screens, and telephones everywhere, as well as a room with a conference table and a dozen chairs.

Walking through, Rage and Mike nodded to each other, satisfied.

"Let's get to work."

The president's chief of staff left them with assurance that he was only a short distance away and at their beck and call. "For the duration," he added.

Rage turned back to Mike and Cary.

"Grab a pad and let's get started," he told them.

At the conference table, Rage repeated the agenda. "As I said on the way over, we have two basic tasks," he said, "both of equal importance."

Rage continued. "The first is to protect the president."

Both Mike and Cary nodded.

"To do that," Rage said, "we have to keep him out of reach of the takeover."

'I'm working on that," Cary said.

He nodded, acknowledging her, concentrating, explaining his overall plan in depth, re-emphasizing certain points to each of them. Cary had an important part in the overall plan.

When Rage was finished, Cary smiled and relaxed back into her chair. "It's basic, but it could work." Then she made a couple of significant suggestions for her area of responsibility. Finished, she leaned back again. "What do you think?"

"I think you have a mind for this kind of work," Rage said.

"Yes." Mike was on board too, agreeing after listening.

Rage asked her, "Do you need others?"

"The fewer who know what we're doing, the better off we are," she said. "I can do it. All I need is the supplies."

"Give Karist a list and tell him what you're planning. He may argue but you're in charge in this area. The president should know, too." Standing, Rage added, "Then do your thing early on Monday. If you can make this work, the senator's going to be in for a big surprise."

Sitting down again and leaning in, Rage said, "Our second chore is to isolate Senator Rayburt and his military leaders. We need them under our control without them realizing it." He continued. "It has to be done in a way that keeps them from communicating down the chain of command." Rage stood and began pacing, thinking. "The Joint Chiefs can't suspect what's happening." He glanced at Mike. "Same for Senator Rayburt."

For the next two hours, the team discussed and planned their unorthodox details.

~~~

Sunday morning, 11:45 a.m. Midday was almost upon them.

Action was accelerating around the White House. Four Abrams tanks, escorts for the presidential limousine, were already on the street outside the gates. All along Pennsylvania Avenue and the parade route, workers using Cherry Pickers and other equipment
~~~

were busy putting last touches on street decorationsfor the parade.

The president was in the Oval Office and had been there since early Saturday. Secretary of State Jäger joined him before dawn on Sunday. The old friends were comfortable together, often saying nothing, and at other times softly discussing the world's problems. They had watched reports coming out of the Middle East. Updates for the president were steadily coming.

Clashes along the border between the Palestinians and Israeli troops were becoming routine. Rocks and Molotov cocktails thrown at Israeli tanks and troop carriers were the norm.

Outright war was only an incident away.

The president was near the end of a long political rope. Something had to be done. Envoys were working both sides of the conflict, but results—few in number—were slow in coming.

~~~

At mid-afternoon on Sunday, a call went out to Senator Rayburt, five other senators, and several representatives from the house. Each of the Joint Chiefs were summoned, including General Farmington who would arrive following the parade. Several other high-ranking military officers were also asked to be present for the newly called Monday morning meeting. The NSA, FBI, and CIA were all represented. Rage Doyle prepared most of the list and mentally checked off Bernie Sladen, Bob Cummings, Eldon Patterson, and Elena Springer-Preston. Others, not normally called to the White House, were asked too.

According to the memo, a Middle Eastern planning session with the president was on tap
~~~

immediately following the parade. Attendees had been asked to come early, before the parade, to avoid parade traffic. They would view the Memorial Day parade from the Cabinet Room at the White House. The extremely important strategy meeting would be held immediately after the parade. Time was short, and the president wanted input from the military and those who were knowledgeable regarding the conflict.

Senator Rayburt smiled when he read the president's notice. A thought crossed his mind. *He's playing right into our hands.*

In the senator's way of thinking, President Carrington was literally inviting those who would unseat him in for coffee. The downside was having individuals present who were not involved in the takeover. *But we can deal with that.*

The senator would sleep that night with the knowledge that Monday would bring an entirely new situation for him—one he had dreamed of for thirty years.

*That,* the senator thought, *requires a salute.* Rayburt went to the small wet bar in his office and poured himself a double shot of Old Pepper Straight Rye Whiskey on the rocks.

"Ahh..."

# Chapter Thirty

Early Monday morning was exceptionally busy at 1600 Pennsylvania Avenue.

Several important events were scheduled: the Memorial Day parade, set to roll at 10:00 a.m.; a state dinner for the Czech Republic's Prime Minister in the evening; and the presidents hastily called Middle Eastern crisis conference had traffic constantly flowing in and out of the White House grounds. Preparations were at a frantic pace.

When the attractive blond who routinely brought fresh produce to the kitchen fell in line with florists and other deliveries, she was recognized and waved in without opening the doors on her small van. She smiled and blew the guard a kiss as she breezed past the checkpoint. At the secluded kitchen ramp, she backed slowly to the dock. The smile was gone.

A Secret Service agent appeared from inside and hurried out to the truck. After a quick but thorough 360-degree inspection of the area, he opened the rear door of the van. In quick succession, sixteen individuals dressed in business attire with several carrying briefcases, unfolded from the cramped space, and slipped out of the van. Moments later, the twelve men and four women had disappeared into a side entrance to the kitchen.

The Secret Service agent led the group through deserted halls and back doors to the offices utilized by Rage Doyle and his team.

On their arrival, Mike Webster quickly walked to one of the newcomers, shaking hands and smiling. "Welcome aboard, Jack."

Mike called Rage over and introduced him to Jack Rollins of the U.S. Marshals Service. They talked softly for a few moments before Rollins led his team to the nearby conference room. Mike returned to his conversation with Rage.

"Are the marshals set to go?" Rage asked. "Do they need anything?"

"Ready and up to date on the schedule," Mike told him.

"Where is Cary?" Rage glanced about the busy office, appearing to search for her.

Mike caught his attention. "She's dealing with the presidential detail. There were some specific questions before the parade."

<div align="center">~~~</div>

The president's request to selected senators had produced results. Individually, they began arriving shortly after nine in the morning, Senator Rayburt being one of the first. Members of the Joint Chiefs of Staff had also arrived early.

The senator asked the president's chief of staff if he could have a few words with President Carrington before he and first lady joined the parade. Shown into the Oval Office, Rayburt got right to the point. "Any positive changes in the Middle East?"

"No," the president told him. "In fact, my envoys tell me the situation appears to be gettingworse."

"Sorry to hear that," Rayburt said, adding, "but my contacts agree."

Senator Rayburt thought of the latest short conversation he'd had with Zack Holden. The committee had continued to be positive regarding the takeover, but something Holden repeated from earlier conversations had continued to be troubling. It had most recently been on the senator's mind since the early video conference with Holden that morning.

Rayburt's thoughts had to do with the board's contacts in Russia and China. Initially, the senator had been told that closely aligned individuals in those countries listened to their leaders and passed information on to the board. Early on, Holden and the other board members had said the board answered to no one—no stockholders or anyone else, to use Holden's words. The senator remembered explicitly. The idea had thoroughly impressed him.

Over the ensuing years and especially most recently, Senator Rayburt had begun to wonder. In recent meetings, Holden had twice passed on specific instructions to Rayburt regarding the takeover. The instructions had come directly from Russian contacts of the board and had been thinly veiled as advice.

Based on conversations with Holden and other members of the committee, there appeared to be six of these close links in Russia and another three in China. Wondering if these contacts were oligarchs, the senator researched top business leaders from the two countries. What he found bothered him. In both governments, several of these immensely wealthy family leaders were reputed to be close to the country's leaders. It didn't take a great leap in thinking to see how the oligarchs could in fact be a major factor in the leadership of these countries.

The senator mentally shook himself. He needed to concentrate on the present. Still the  conversation with Holden remained on his mind.

"The parade and takeover are only hours away now," Holden had said. "Are you sure everything is arranged?" What he said next—the repeated warning—was the thing that Rayburt found troubling, the thing that kept bouncing around in his mind.

"There's no room for error." Zack Holden hadsaid those approximate words several times since the board advised him to consider a takeover of the U.S. government. Rayburt had been left wondering what repercussions there would be if the coup should fail.

As the president talked on, Senator Rayburt listened while at the same time thinking his own thoughts.

*Everything is in place.* The senator was sure of it. Even if the parade was canceled at the last minute, the original plan for taking the president would become effective. The Middle Eastern conflict had provided the means. A presidential trip to the Pentagon regarding the struggle would have afforded the military an ideal opportunity to seize and relocate the president to Camp David. From that act, Senator Rayburt could literally have walked into the Oval Office.

President Carrigan had finished his comments regarding Israel and the Palestinians. "We'll discuss the details in depth after the parade," the president said as he slipped into his coat.

"Yes," Rayburt said, "we'll do that." He smiled and touched the president on the shoulder as Carrigan headed out the door to join the first lady for the parade.

The senator returned to the Cabinet Room, joining other attendees gathered there. Standing at the end of the conference table, General Avery and Admiral Patron appeared to be in a tense conversation. The admiral was emphasizing points by punching the air with an index finger. Standing a head shorter than Avery, he was making his points upward.

Senator Rayburt scanned the room. Several of his military people were already present. Others who were not involved in the takeover had arrived too. General Riverdale was there. The Vice Chairman of the Joint Chiefs was standing alone near a door. He appeared deep in thought as he watched one of the screens showing preparations for the parade. Though they had been ultra-cautious, Rayburt wondered if the general might have gotten wind of the takeover.

As Senator Rayburt studied the general, Riverdale glanced up, catching, and holding Rayburt's eye for a long moment. His expression was serious with brooding eyes.

*He knows...* the senator thought. *Riverdale knows, but it's too late. In a couple of hours this will be a different country.*

Riverdale had been a thorn in the senator's side since President Carrigan nominated him to the Joint Chiefs. The general's views in several areas opposed those of Senator Rayburt and the Joint Chiefs who backed him.

The senator's longevity and influence had served to check Riverdale's several attempts at forcing him to vote in ways that would have weakened Rayburt's steady move to power over the years. Within hours, Riverdale would be free to purchase some fishing equipment for use in his retirement. His days of command would be at an end.

Rayburt smiled. Power was intoxicating.

Glancing back, Senator Briston had joined General Riverdale. The senator was a steadfast conservative from the south. He would certainly be against a military takeover. Briston could buy fishing equipment too.

*Only a few hours now.* Senator Rayburt breathed a sigh of relief.

~~~

The president's limo was parked and idling under the White House portico. A door was open and waiting for the president and first lady.

Outside on Pennsylvania Avenue, four massive Marine Abrams tanks moved into a line. Sufficient space for the president's limo and security detail was left between the two middle tanks. The procession was about to begin.

Parade watchers were on both sides of the street outside the gates. The crowd noise could be heard all the way to the White House though presence on the street was less than packed. Sounds of the Navy Band warming up with "Hail to the Chief" could be heard too. The parade appeared only moments away.

Several military bands were playing patriotic tunes. Marching units from the Army, Navy, Marines, and National Guard were interspersed among the
~~~

bands and would be showing their abilities at precision marching and weapons handling.

High school bands and marching groups from several states added to the festivities. There was even a bagpipe marching group from Scotland.

Out on Pennsylvania Avenue, General Farmington's jeep pulled to the curb near the tanks, allowing him and his new aid, Marine Colonel Ainsworth, to step down to the street. Surveying the situation, the general motioned for the opening between the middle tanks to be reduced and watched as the space closed to twenty yards. Then, followed by the colonel, the general walked over to mingle with the three platoons of ground troops who were standing at parade rest adjacent to the tanks. The Marines, dressed and shined for the procession, quickly broke ranks, and gathered around the Bear.

Ever alert, General Farmington continued to glance toward the activity off the White House portico. The area was overrun with Secret Service. Continuing to look that way, he caught a fleeting glimpse of President Carrigan and his dark-haired wife as they hurried out and ducked into the presidential limousine. Secret Service cars immediately took up their positions. The five vehicles slowly began the drive out to take their place among the tanks.

Cheers went up from the crowd as the presidential limousine and its escort exited the White House gates. Everyone wanted to wave at the president and first lady.

General Farmington ended his casual break with the troops and returned to his jeep. He needed to stay close to the tanks in advance of the street takeover.

The stage was set.

With practiced ease as they reached the street, two of the security cars peeled off and fell in line behind the fourth tank. The remaining two—one in front of the presidential limo and another behind—pulled into the space left for them between tanks two and three. Smoke filled the air as giant Honeywell turbine tank engines revved, readying to power the combat vehicles away from the curb.

The tanks were huge, over 30 feet long, 12 feet wide, and 8 feet tall. The tracks alone were nearly as tall as the presidential limo. Parade goers along the street couldn't keep themselves from pointing and exclaiming about the size of the tanks.

The Bear surveyed the area one last time.

The president's parade was ready to move.

Standing in the jeep where he could be seen from the tanks, General Farmington raised his arm, rotating it in a rolling motion. He smiled; the takeover was beginning.

Moving slowly and carefully, the tanks, along with the four secret service vehicles and the president's limousine, moved into the street as a precision unit. Change didn't come until the tanks had reached the middle of Pennsylvania Avenue. There, a strange transformation took place. It happened with a sudden threatening swiftness.

Dwarfing the presidential limousine, tanks two and three abruptly angled and moved to the side of the secret service cars immediately in front and to the rear of the presidential limo. With engines roaring, the two tanks veered toward both security vehicles, forcing them to move away from the limo or be crushed.

Simultaneously, tanks one and four moved to join the others in a tight formation surrounding the presidential limousine.

Secret Service agents on the ground appeared to be caught off guard; this was not an exercise for which they had prepared. Acting confused, the agents could be seen dodging and attempting to reach the president. Two agents were struck and knocked to the street by the rapidly moving tanks. Parade goers rushed forward in some jeopardy, dragging the downed agents away from danger and to the sidewalk.

Screams could be heard from onlookers. Several nearby marching bands ceased playing as their members scattered. Sirens sounded, but there was no way to avoid or overcome the seizure by the tanks.

Pandemonium was suddenly the order of the day.

Secret Service agents piled from their accompanying cars only to be confronted by a trio of forty-three-man platoons of Marine ground troops and their commanders. The marines had moved into protective positions of their own. Moments before, these soldiers had been a part of the president'sparade. Now they were standing or kneeling between Secret Service agents and any access to the president's car. Weapons were ready for action; the lock and load command had been given. Behind the Marines, the president's limo was now hidden inside a fortress ofarmor.

General Farmington climbed atop the lead tank, standing with legs spread and balancing, his hand was on the .45 Colt automatic at his side. The general switched on his mike and began speaking. It was loud.

"Attention, Secret Service." He paused. "Mostof you know I'm Army General Paul Farmington, Chairman of the Joint Chiefs of Staff." It took several seconds for the general to gain their full attention.

He glanced toward the White House. *They probably hear me.*

Parade goers were snapping photos and shooting videos with their phones and cameras—an opportunity of a lifetime. A four-star general, tanks, Secret Service, and close to a hundred and fifty armed marines. Some of the onlookers had even edged to within a few feet of the tanks and other military activity in the street.

Colonel Ainsworth and a squad of the marines forced them back to the sidewalks.

A few picked up on the general's words intended only for the Secret Service.

The general was into the main points of his speech. "Men and women of the Secret Service, at this moment there is an ongoing change of power in the White House and the U.S. government." He allowed a few seconds for this dramatic statement to penetrate their thinking. Their allegiance, the general knew and understood, was to the current president.

In those moments of waiting, a vision of what must be happening in the White House flashed through the general's mind. He glanced back at the limo and wondered how soon-to-be ex-President Carrington was going to react to the change in power.

In the crowd watching and listening along the street, confused expressions prompted questions. "What did he say?" "A change of power?"

Though weapons were drawn and ready, the president's Secret Service detail now appeared to be warily directing their attention to the general. As he spoke, the situation quickly became evident. Though these men and women would lay down their lives for the president, useless sacrifice made no sense as long as they could stay close to their president.

Then—within the plan—General Farmington eased the pressure of the situation. Climbing down to the street, he gestured toward nearby Secret Service agents, even taking a step in their direction.

"Here are your instructions," he said. "Listen closely."

The general gave them a moment.

"We are going to return to the White House. You will be allowed to move with the limousine and its tank escorts, but you will be guarded by the marines. The president and first lady will remain inside the limo until we're back at the entrance. Once there, I will escort President Carrigan and the first lady inside."

Continuing, the general laid down the rules. "The president's car will travel inside the perimeter of tanks until we reach the gates. The tanks will remain on the street. Marine ground troops will surround and escort the president's limo until we are under the White House portico. You will be guarded and remain outside the perimeter of the marine security."

The general paused for a moment. Then, "Any effort to reach the limousine and the president and first lady will be dealt with in the harshest manner."

Once again, he swept an arm toward the Secret Service agents. "Are we clear on how this operation is going to happen?"

There were disturbed expressions but no contradictory words.

*This is almost too easy,* the general thought.

"One last instruction. This one isn't easy, but it is necessary." General Farmington knew his next order would be difficult for the agents to accept.

"In order to save lives, I am requiring all of you to clear your weapons by removing magazines and clearing chambers. A marine will stand with each of you as you empty your weapon. Your ammo and magazine will be handed over to the marine." He added, "Hopefully, this will be a deterrent in case someone decides to be a hero."

Secret service agents glanced back and forth among each other and at General Farmington. This situation hadn't been covered in their training. They were unsure how to proceed, and they were facing three platoons of armed and ready marines. There was no reasonable way to approach the presidential limousine.

The general continued. "You will holster your weapons after all ammo is removed and handed over to the marines."

There was a quick conversation between the general and his colonel. After a few moments, General Farmington nodded and looked back toward the Secret Service agents, saying, "My aid, Colonel Ainsworth, will walk among you verifying that my orders have been followed."

The colonel quickly passed among the agents and marines overseeing the clearing of their weapons. Satisfied, he signaled the general.

General Farmington finished by saying, "Thank you for your cooperation, people. Let's finish this without blood being shed. Now we move back to the White House."

With that, the general gave the rolling motion with his arm. Idling tank engines roared to life. With careful consideration for the president's limo, the procession slowly turned back toward the gates and the long circular drive.

Secret Service agents moving outside the marine guard accompanied the presidential limo. A squad of marines jogged ahead of the limo. Reaching the portico, they had orders to move everyone back and clear the area. The Secret Service contingent stood a few feet distant and had been joined by White House agents.

General Farmington—The Bear—looked forward to escorting the deposed president into the White House.

A few minutes later, the procession was back under the portico.

"I'll take it from here." Farmington said as he moved toward the presidential limo.

# Chapter Thirty-One

The Cabinet Room was crowded. Civilians and military alike had watched as the parade began and then halted as marine tanks took command of the presidential limousine.

Several of those present moved a step or two toward the big screens. Something signific was happening outside, and they didn't want to miss the action.

Many had come expecting to watch the president's parade and then attend the meeting concerning the Middle East.

This was much more. The situation had obviously changed. Instead of watching a parade, they were now viewing the action taking place out on Pennsylvania Avenue. A few knew a military takeover was in its initial stages because they were involved. Others didn't know or only suspected. The eyes of almost everyone were glued to the screens.

Viewers—involved or not—suspected President Carrigan's administration was in its final minutes.

~~~

General Farmington and the marines were in control. As planned, the presidential limousine was being escorted along the circular drive and back to the White House.

Conversations among those inside the Cabinet Room were becoming animated. More questions were being asked than answered.

Glancing across the room, CIA Director Drake caught the eye of Senator Rayburt. A slight nod by the senator was the only indication the two men even knew each other. They would be working much closer in the coming weeks. Drake would replace the elderly John Jäger as Secretary of State. Drake planned a much stronger stance on the problems facing the U.S. in the coming days.

Having watched the almost invisible exchange between the senator and the Director of the CIA, Mike Webster smiled inwardly. He had been sure the CIA was involved.

~~~

Slowly, the president's limousine, guarded by United States marines, returned to the White House portico. The president's secret service detail was there too but appeared to be separate and guarded by the marines.

The time had come for a change in administrations.

Senator Wayne Rayburt glanced around the Cabinet Room and then stepped to the podium that had been set up near the conference table. Portraits of George Washington and Harry Truman stared down on the Senator from the wall of the end of the room.

Taking the microphone and adjusting it, Senator Rayburt called for everyone's attention. The buzz settled slowly as eyes shifted to the senator.

"Ladies and gentlemen, military leaders, and others." He paused for a moment. Then, "A military takeover is under way to replace President Carrigan and his cabinet." He continued but could now see by widened eyes and surprised expressions that many of those in the room were immediately in a state of disbelief at what they were hearing.

"What you've seen on the monitors is the detention of the president by U.S. Marines. POTUS isnow under control of the military. At this moment, the president and first lady are being returned here to the White House where they will be held under house arrest for the next several hours."

He paused to allow his important audience to consider the situation.

Senator Rayburt's leaders kept their eyes on the senator. Those outside the senator's circle glanced about and wondered who among them might be actively involved in a takeover.

As he scanned the room, Senator Rayburt noticed the Vice-Chairman of the Joint Chiefs of Staff watching him, alert to his every word. A chill ran across the senator's shoulders.

General Riverdale remained cool; he was listening but without expression...and seemingly without fear.

*Did he know?* Senator Rayburt could only guess. *What could he have known? And does it matter?*

Unexpectedly, the senator heard the door behind him open. He glanced over his shoulder. The president's chief of staff stepped out and stared directly at Senator Rayburt.

Then Karist took a couple of steps into the room and announced in a loud voice, "Ladies and Gentlemen, the President of the United States."

To everyone's surprise, President Carrigan strolled into the room. Many who were waiting glanced at the monitors. They had been led to believe that President Carrigan and the first lady were in the presidential limousine. There were gasps of surprise and glances back and forth among several of those in the room.

Senator Rayburt took a moment to glance at one of the monitors. The president's limo had halted under the portico. The senator watched, a stricken feeling in his stomach, as marine's broke ranks and formed a protective line from the vehicle to the White House entrance.

Turning back to the room, Rayburt could feel the walls tumbling.

President Carrigan had been followed out of his secretary's office by several men and women dressed in business suits. These individuals quickly and prudently positioned themselves near the president and at strategic locations around the room. The three doors in the Cabinet Room were given special attention. Without it being said, everyone recognized the Cabinet Room was now under lockdown.

Senator Rayburt and Elena Springer-Preston stared at each other, sudden dread in their eyes. General Avery and other military leaders involved in the plot were watching too, obviously dismayed, squinched eyes and wrinkled foreheads betraying their thoughts.

Carrigan stepped over and held his hand out for the microphone. Senator Rayburt locked eyes with the president for a moment before the senator turned, keeping his body between the president and the mic. President Carrigan stood his ground, his hand out again, waiting.

Though it felt longer to those watching, the standoff lasted only a moment or two.

Jack Robbins of the U.S. Marshals Service—one of the individuals who had entered the room with the president—walked over and extended his hand to Senator Rayburt.

"The microphone, please," Robbins said. "If you don't hand it to me peacefully, we will physically take it from you." Robbins was backed by two others in his group, a man and a woman. The three individuals said nothing more, but their intent was evident. They were there to back the president. Senator Rayburt stared at them for only a moment before taking a half step away from the podium and handing the mic to the president.

Looking into the senator's eyes, President Carrigan said, "I would never have expected this of you, Wayne. It's beneath you and your oath and everything you've ever stood for." The president paused. "You and your people appear to have forgotten that the ballot box is the way we make changes in this country." Then the president took Senator Rayburt's arm and moved him to the side.

The microphone was live and near enough for everyone in the room to have heard the president's rebuke of Senator Rayburt.

Subdued, but with blazing anger in his eyes, Rayburt turned and headed for the nearest door. Without being obtrusive, two U.S. Marshals shifted slightly to block him.

With nowhere to go, Rayburt turned back to the room, standing alone, arms folded across his chest, to face the president. The senator could feel the hot stares of several involved in the coup. Like Senator Rayburt himself, there was nothing for them to do but wait.

Finally, the president turned to the room and its dazed occupants.

Thumping the mic, President Carrigan looked out over his audience. "Ladies and gentlemen, no one will be allowed to leave this room until we are assured those involved in this coup attempt have been neutralized." After a pause, the president continued. "If you have attempted to use your mobile phone or any other electronic device, you have found them inoperative. Measures have been taken to block or scramble all outside communications to or from this room." Several individuals glanced at their mobile phones.

The president continued. "First, I will take a few moments to explain the situation as it stands." The president glanced at a far corner of the room. Rage, Mike, and Cary were there, still and quiet.

Gesturing in their direction, the president said, "Just hours ago, due to the efforts of a few concerned individuals, we became aware of the plans of Senator Rayburt and the leaders, military and civilian, who were allied with him."

The president took a few moments to pick out several in the room with his eyes: the CIA people, several members of the Joint Chiefs of Staff, and others.

Staring at the senator then, the president continued. "At this moment, the justice department is preparing applicable charges against Senator Rayburt." Shifting his attention about the room again to the military leaders siding with the senator, the president said, "General Farmington and other conspiring members of the Joint Chiefs will face proper military court martial charges."

Pausing, the president singled out Drake, Patterson, and Elena Springer-Preston. "Additionally," he said, "several officers and other operatives at the CIA will be facing charges along with the senator."

Elena Springer-Preston found an empty chair and slumped into it, her dream of becoming the Vice President of the United States gone. She brushed the back of a hand across her face.

~~~

Outside under the portico, General Farmington walked to the president's limousine when it stopped. He expected to be the one to escort the president into the White House and out of the presidency.

When the general opened the limo door, he was shocked. POTUS and the first lady climbed out—except it wasn't them. General Farmington ducked his head to look inside. There was no one else in the limousine, only the two individuals who greatly resembled the President and Mrs. Carrigan.

At that moment, the general's aid, Colonel Ainsworth, left his post with the marines and hastened
~~~

to the general's side. Secret Service Director Jack Lanney appeared and stood shoulder to shoulder with the colonel. A dozen secret service agents quickly joined them forming a wall of bodies around the three men.

General Farmington felt sweat pop out on his forehead. Something was very wrong. He glanced around. The marines were standing at rest, and it appeared he was being watched by everyone under the portico. Immediately, the general realized no one there was going to intervene on his behalf—not his colonel, not the marines, certainly not the Secret Service, no one.

Everyone was avoiding his eyes—everyone but his aid and Jack Lanney of the Secret Service.

"Come with me, Sir." Colonel Ainsworth touched his arm.

Stepping back, his eyes glaring, the Bear said, "Get your hands off me, Colonel."

Ainsworth slowly dropped his hands but continued standing defiantly close, only inches away. The colonel's eyes were drawn tight and bored into the generals.

"You were my hero," the colonel said.

When Ainsworth made no effort to move, Jack Lanney pushed his way between them.

The Secret Service Director softly informed Farmington, "It's over, General. President Carrigan is in charge inside the White House." Leaning into the general's line of vision, Lanney added, "The president has asked us to escort you to his office."

General Farmington stared at the Secret Service Director. The director stared back.

During the stalemate, a large marine Chinook helicopter noisily touched down on the lawn a hundred yards away. More marine troops charged out the aircraft and placed themselves between the increasing crowd and the activity under the portico.

General Farmington looked that way. He could see the coup was falling apart.

Lanney watched the fire slowly subside in the general's eyes. He gave the situation a few moments. Then, "Let's go inside, General."

Without further argument, the Chairman of the Joint Chiefs of Staff turned, his head lowered, and took the first steps of the rest of his life.

~~~

Inside, General Farmington was escorted directly to the Oval Office. When they entered, several individuals were standing silently around the room. Some were on the senator's team; others were not. General Avery was near one of the doors to the hallway.

Senator Rayburt stood behind one of the chairs near the sofas. The president lingered at a corner of his desk. Others were scattered about the room.

Escorted in to face the president, the Bear stood waiting, tension mounting.

President Carrigan had been reading from several sheets of notes he was holding. "Sit down, General," the president said, motioning to one of the chairs in front of his desk. Carrigan returned to the notes.

General Farmington made his way to the chair.
~~~

No one spoke to the general or even looked his way. The Bear had never felt so alone in a room full of people.

Several minutes after the general was seated, the president dropped the notes on his desk and said, "Put your activation documents on the desk, General."

Farmington wanted to glance at General Avery, who held the remainder of the codes. He wondered if Charlie had been asked for his pouch.

The president anticipated the unspoken question.

"General Avery has already surrendered his codes, Paul. Yours are worthless without them."

The Chairman of the Joint Chiefs was still reluctant to give up the data. General Farmington had planned that he and General Avery would initiate the takeover without further communications with Senator Rayburt. It would only take an email from each of them to a top-secret website at the Pentagon. The codes would be connected electronically, and orders would flow down the chain of command to all the proper locations

That wasn't going to happen now; this was evident.

Reluctantly, but without further delay, General Farmington slipped a hand inside his coat. He came out with the leather folder containing his section of the code. The general starred at it for a moment before placing it on the desk. His eyes followed the pouch as the president handed it to his chief of staff. Karist was already holding an identical pouch.

There was nothing else to say. The coup was over.

Senator Rayburt was watching from across the room as Farmington looked up. The general saw a slight, sad nod.

The president addressed General Farmington directly again. "As I've told other individuals that are involved in this takeover attempt, you will spend tonight under guard in your home. Until charges are levied tomorrow, you will remain there."

President Carrigan continued as he eased into his chair. "Admiral Riverdale and other general officers will assume joint chief's duties until new nominees can be confirmed."

General Farmington nodded.

The president was obviously finished with him. Two of the marshals escorted the general from the room.

~~~

After dismissing General Farmington, the president had the Oval Office cleared. Only Senator Rayburt, Elena Springer-Preston, Secretary of State Jäger, Jonathan Karist, and three secret service agents remained.

The Secretary of State settled in a chair away from the others and listened. Karist stood near a door to the hallway with a notepad and pen in hand.

Senator Rayburt remained standing as Deputy Director Springer-Preston was motioned to one of the now vacant chairs facing the President's desk. Preston seated herself without comment. The senator didn't.

"Am I under arrest?" he asked from the middle of the room.
~~~

"You're being treated no different than the others," the president said. "Before sending them away, I told them the same as I'm telling you."

The president, still standing by his desk, motioned the senator forward a second time. "Yes, Wayne, you are under arrest. What did you imagine?" the president glanced at each of them. "When you and Deputy Director Preston leave this office, you will each be returned to your home and detained there under house arrest until you are formerly charged. That will be tomorrow according to the DOJ."

The president gave each of them a hard look. "Would you expect less?"

Senator Rayburt walked to the chair the president had indicated earlier, dropping into it with an audible sigh. His confrontational manner was gone. Glancing up at the president, he shook his head in response to the question.

"Do either of you have comments?" the president asked.

Neither the senator nor Deputy Director Preston spoke.

President Carrigan settled into his chair, breathing a deep sigh.

"I've never imagined this situation," the president said. Focusing on Senator Rayburt, the president continued. "Wayne, do you really think a military coup is the best answer to the nation's international problems? You couldn't have decidedthat solely on your own."

Senator Rayburt looked at President Carrigan. As he did so, the senator thought about the last several meetings of the committee. In each of them, he had been warned that there was no room for error. In his mind, the situation couldn't get worse than this.

He responded to the president's comment. "No, it's not just me." A pause as Senator Rayburt collected his thoughts, wanting to redirect the conversation. "Mr. President, you certainly know your foreign policies are unpopular throughout the country. I'm not the only one who thinks so."

"I understand," the president said, "but we both know the constitution does not include rules for a military takeover. If you or anyone else disagrees with the policies of an elected group of leaders, you can vote them out of office."

"But Mr. President—"

"I'm sorry, Wayne." The president was shaking his head as he spoke. "I don't choose to continue this conversation. I'm not going to get into a policy debate with someone who has committed treason."

The president stood, telling the senator and everyone else, "I have a parade to attend."

A nod to his chief of staff was all that was required. When Karist opened the nearby door, three men and a woman entered the Oval Office. Two of the men walked directly over to Senator Rayburt; a man and the woman walked to Deputy Director Preston's chair.

Senator Rayburt and Elena Springer-Preston each stood without comment and left the Oval Office with their escorts.

# Chapter Thirty-Two

While they were waiting for the parade to begin, news anchors across the country had searched for something to report. An hour into the delay at the White House, the talking heads were thirty minutes into speculating that something significant had to be amiss.

News reporters had been allowed as far as the portico. There were cameras everywhere all the way along the circular drive to the gates and out onto Pennsylvania Avenue. The anchors had gotten a quick look as the president and first lady initially entered the president's limousine under the White House portico. Then they watched the limousine and security detail vehicles drive out and join the marine contingent with its four Abrams tanks.

The reporters and camera people had beenfooled then; they were more cautious this time.

The president and first lady would once again be with the marines and their tanks for the parade. Cameras caught every detail as they left the White House and joined the procession.

Once everyone had been in place that first time, the cause for speculation presented itself. There had been action involving the tanks and the president's security detail. The press had been kept at a distance, but they could see that something out of the ordinary was happening.

In what appeared to be a practiced operation, the four marine tanks had separated the presidential limo from its security detail. That done, General Paul Farmington, the easily recognized Chairman of the Joint Chiefs of Staff, appeared to take command of the situation. The general spoke a few words to the president's security detail at which time they appeared to examine and clear their weapons.

Shortly after, the president's limousine, his security detail, General Farmington, and the marines made their way through the gates and back to the White House. For the next hour and a half, everything was rumor and guessing.

Either the president or Mrs. Carrigan was ill— that came first. Next in speculation came a crisis somewhere around the globe. From there, all sorts of possibilities were floated among the news people.

A military coup was even mentioned by a relatively new female correspondent for one of the national TV news networks. She was laughed at, kidded, and ridiculed until the actual takeover attempt became common knowledge; then, suddenly, she wasa rising reporter.

~~~

After a long delay, the presidential limousine finally exited the White House grounds for the second time that day. It returned to Pennsylvania Avenue and its original position among the tanks. The president's security vehicles took their place too.
~~~

The Navy band began to play marching songs, and the parade was ready to begin.

Past presidential parades customarily moved at a brisk pace. That practice makes it difficult for parade-goers to catch a glimpse of the president and first lady. Speed also brings difficulty to those who would cause harm to the president.

In a break from norm, this parade moved very slowly, and the president was visible. Carrigan knew rumors would circulate regarding the attempted takeover. The president wanted parade goers and the nation to see him and know he was still in command.

The president could see parade watchers, most wearing masks, and they could see him and the first lady. Everyone could wave. The president and first lady were both wearing their masks.

~~~

In a different sort of outing, the ride to Senator Rayburt's home in Lanier Heights took only minutes. Though it was over quickly, on this day it seemed longer than usual. Despite all the times he had made the drive, the senator was quiet, looking out and absorbing the view. Rayburt knew the trip could be his last to the big house.

Arriving, the driver parked the dark van near the front door.

The circular driveway was impressively long, and the house was huge.

"You live alone?" one of the guards asked as they climbed out of the van. Kris had viewed the surroundings as they came up the driveway.
~~~

"Yes, I do," the senator told him, sadness in his words. Senator Rayburt glanced at his massive house and slowly shook his head.

"Do you have domestic staff that we should expect to encounter?" the head guard asked.

"I do," the senator replied. "Two women. They cook when I need it and keep the place clean." He added, "I also have a full-time gardener."

As the senator was explaining the help, the gardener came around the house pushing a wheelbarrow holding hand tools and a bag of potting soil. When he saw Senator Rayburt, the gardener left the wheelbarrow in the driveway and walked over.

"Afternoon, Mr. Senator," he said, reaching out to shake hands with Rayburt. A big smile was on his face.

"Good afternoon, Wilson." The senator shook the man's hand. The gardener waved a friendly greeting to the men with the senator.

"Howdy," he told them, then turned and sauntered back to his chore.

"Wilson runs things outside the house," the senator said as the man walked away.

Inside, the two women came to the foyer to meet the senator and his guests. After a quick introduction they returned to their duties.

"That's everyone," Rayburt said when the women were gone.

"You'll need to give everyone time off while we're with you," the senator was told. "We'll handle any necessary cooking."

"That's fine," the senator said. "I won't need them where I'll be going anyway."

The four U.S. Marshals had stayed close to the senator as they left the van and entered the house.

Inside, the marshals and Senator Rayburtpaused at the first floor living room area of thesenator's home.

Rayburt shook his head as the lead marshal explained the routine. It had come to this—*a prisoner in my own home.*

"You will be allowed to sleep alone," Robbins told him. "We'll have you on security cameras that we're installing. The one exception will be your bathroom unless it has more than one door."

Senator Rayburt shook his head. "It doesn't."

A fresh glimmer in his eyes went unnoticed by the marshals.

Robbins continued. "We'll go through your personal quarters very carefully. Bathroom, closets, bedroom, everything. Any potential weapon youcould use against us or yourself will be confiscated. Understood?"

The senator nodded.

Robbins continued. "We have a warrant and will be searching your entire house."

Rayburt nodded again.

"Before we begin, are there any firearms or other potential weapons in your quarters or anywhere in the house?"

Settling into a large recliner, Rayburt sighed deeply and remained quiet for a few moments, obviously thinking.

Finally, "There's a .45 ACP under one of the pillows on my bed, and a pump shotgun inside and above the door to my closet." He added, "They're both loaded."

"Okay?" Robbins waited.

"Other than those, it's normal stuff. Razor and scissors in the bathroom, and the normal in the kitchen." Hesitation again. "That's all, unless you count ties and belts as weapons." The senator released another deep sigh along with a sweeping hand indicating the entire house. "That's all."

"Okay," the lead marshal said. He motioned for Webster to stay with the senator and for the others to follow him. They started toward the stairs.

"You'll want to take the elevator," the senator told him. "My bedroom is on the third floor." He pointed toward a hallway. "The lift is down there."

Robbins stopped for a moment, thinking. Then, "Why don't you show us around? Then, we'll do our search."

Senator Rayburt nodded and took the lead.

To begin, he walked them through the first floor and garage.

There was the living room where they had been standing. French doors led into a formal dining room with a significant table large enough to seat a dozen. From there they filed into the kitchen. The women they had met earlier were sitting at the counter talking and enjoying a cup of coffee. They waved, then continued their conversation.

A mud room, accessible from the kitchen, led to the large garage.

It was huge—four bays. Only one housed a vehicle, a medium sized SUV. A glance brought an explanation from the senator. Rayburt looked at

Robbins and said, "I have a BMW sedan that I drive to work when I'm not being picked up by a limo. The BMW is parked at the Senate office building." He took a moment then to glance at each of the four marshals before sarcastically saying, "I don't normally get an escorted ride home."

After a short walk-through, they re-entered the house and took the lift to the second floor.

This floor reminded Robbins of an upscale hotel. Immediately outside the lift door was an open lobby area branching into two hallways. The senator said this floor was for guest bedrooms. He had five, each with its own bath. "Two," the senator told them, "are small suites."

A large recreation room was at the end of one of the halls. There was a theatre area with room for the dozen that had 'come for dinner downstairs,' and several shelves of books. A pool table was on one side of the room along with two game tables and a large round, polished-wood card table. A well-stocked bar was on another wall.

Robbins had already noticed a hundred places to hide a weapon on the first two floors. Shaking his head, he motioned back toward the lift.

The senator's third floor was, in most respects, a large, luxury apartment.

"I spend most of my home time here," he said.

There was even a kitchen—small but adequate. The bedroom and bath were off a significant living room. It was easily 20 x 30 feet. At one end, a broad recliner faced a big-screen TV. Two sofas and four stuffed chairs comprised a rather large conversational grouping centered around a wood-burning fireplace.

Off in another corner set a cabinet with a sink and small refrigerator that obviously served as the senator's private bar. An ice bucket and an unopened bottle of Old Pepper Rye Whiskey set on the counter near the basin.

Separated from the living room by French doors, another large room served as a study and library. A desk, shelves stacked with books, another fireplace, several chairs, and side tables could be seen from the living room.

Opening another door at a corner of the living room, the senator stepped aside saying, "This is my exercise room."

Jack could see how the senator could stay so fit. Though small, there was every piece of equipment necessary. Several could be used for multiple purposes, as was obvious by the signs of wear and tear.

Also off the living room was a small balcony overlooking a side yard. Large trees were visible across the lawn. An Adirondack chair, a lounger, and a side table furnished the space.

The senator pointed and then led the marshals into his private quarters. He stopped near the door and gestured for them to enter. Webster remained with the senator.

The bedroom and bath were both large. A king-sized bed and other dark furniture gave the appearance of this being a man's space.

Robbins immediately began the search for weapons by gathering the pistol from under the senator's pillow. He removed the magazine, emptying it, and cleared the weapon before handing the rounds and magazine to Kris.

"Get the shotgun," Robbins told L.J. On the elevator, he had motioned again for Webster to stay with the senator. Robbins noticed that his friend was watching the senator carefully.

"No other weapons?" Robbins asked the senator. "I don't like surprises, especially those involving firearms."

"No. These are all." Rayburt sounded sincere, but Webster would be watching him. Taking people at their word could be dangerous. He had learned that the hard way over the years.

L.J. returned from the closet with the shotgun. He emptied it and dropped the shells on the bed.

With the two acknowledged weapons in hand, the marshals began a thorough search of the house and four car garage. L.J. started with the senator's third floor suite. Kris took the second floor, and Jack began a search of the main floor, garage, and outside the house.

Webster suggested he and the senator wait in the recreation room on the second floor. Allowing Senator Rayburt to choose his own, Webster pushed a desk chair over in front of the door and sat. From there, he had command of the room and the only way to enter or leave.

"Mind if I read?" Senator Rayburt asked.

"Sure," Webster told him. "Choose a book and let me pull it off the shelf for you." He wanted to make sure there were no hidden weapons. Webster added, "Pick a spot to sit that's away from the bookcase until it's been searched."

"I can do that," Rayburt said and was soon settled in a corner of the room near a window. Webster noticed the senator had chosen a thick Ken Follett story. When Webster checked it, there was a bookmark well into the pages. Obviously, this wasn't the first time the senator had read from the novel.

~~~

L.J. was busy in the senator's third floor living room. He methodically opened and closed doors and drawers. Seat cushions were being moved about too.

Robbins could hear the action when he came upstairs to check progress. What he didn't hear was any exclamation of victory. Obviously, no new weapons or anything else of importance had been found.

The search went on for another three hours before Robbins decided there were no other weapons to be found. Kris had carefully worked his way through the second floor. He combed the recreation room while the senator watched from his corner. It was the last room to be explored.

The senator's house was equipped with a CCTV security system. There were cameras covering much of the interior. Outside, the system included coverage of the driveway, the gate, and most of the yard. There were two monitors—one on a small table near the senator's bed and another on the first floor at a small desk in the living room.

The marshals had brought new equipment with them for the senator's bedroom. Kris installed two new cameras, and using the systems software, connected them to the CCTV monitors. Another monitor was installed in the living room of the senator's private suite. The marshals wanted to keep a very close eye on their important detainee.
~~~

~~~

The search for additional weapons and installation of the new security equipment concluded a little after 9:00 p.m. Nothing new was found. The senator appeared to have been honest about the weapons.

Rayburt's cook prepared a light meal for them. It would be her last. The senator called her aside, gave her the bad news and asked her to inform the others. Their services would not be required over the next several days.

After dinner, the senator informed Robbins that he would like to have a shower and get some rest.

Robbins felt this was a reasonable request. His people could use some downtime too.

Duties for the night were laid out. Webster would settle in the third floor living room near the senator. That would also put him near one of the security monitors. He could get some rest there and still be able to enter the senator's bedroom and bath quickly if the need occurred. The lock on the senator's bedroom door and the one on his bath had been removed. Better safe than sorry.

Individual radios and security monitors and cameras were checked; everything was working.

Robbins would take first watch at the downstairs monitor and be alert for problems throughout the house and outside. Kris and L.J. would get the first rest. Duties would alternate every two hours. The marshals were prepared for the night and moved out to their assignments.
~~~

On the lift, the senator again expressed his desire for a shower. He glanced at Webster and said, "I could use about a half hour under very hot steam and water and twelve hours of sleep."

As the lift door opened, Webster nodded agreement, thinking he could use that too. Webster knew he wouldn't be getting either anytime soon—the shower or the rest.

~~~

Watching the senator move about his bedroom on the third-floor monitor, Webster saw nothing out of the ordinary. A man preparing for a bath. Emptying his pockets first, the senator slipped out of his tie and button down and then his trousers, tossing them on a nearby chair. He headed for the bathroom in his undershirt and shorts.

~~~

*The one solitary room in my own home where I can be alone,* thought Senator Rayburt as he pushed the bathroom door closed.

Once inside, the senator walked to the large steam shower. Opening the door, he stepped inside and a moment later was adjusting the volume to heavy steam. Satisfied but cautious, Rayburt waited a few seconds until the enclosure began to fill with hot mist. Then the senator stepped outside the shower and quietly closed the door. Standing just outside, he disrobed.

Out of his undershirt first and then his shorts, Rayburt left undergarments where they fell outside the shower. *If the marshal checks, he'll see the shorts and think I'm in the shower.*

Grabbing a towel, Rayburt draped and tucked it around his midsection and headed for the big walk-in closet. Inside, he quickly adjusted the position of shelves and hangers in a practiced rotation with pauses and watched the shoe section of the closet slide behind other shelves. The senator always smiled when he opened the cloak-and-dagger desk space. It was so quiet—the expensive hydraulics used by the contractor made the shoe rack's motion totally soundless.

Finally, at the built-in desk behind the closet wall, Senator Rayburt immediately brought his computer online. There wasn't much time. The marshal waiting outside in the living room would check on him if he was too long returning to the bedroom and camera view.

One set of keystrokes was all the senator needed, and then a quick reply from the other end. The simple set of communications had been set in place years ago. This was the first time they had been used.

The special gaming App was pulled up, the senator used the memorized keystrokes. Then he waited.

Less than two minutes later, the answer came.

"One hour."

That's all the message said. That was all he expected.

~~~

The senator had wanted to accumulate a billion dollars before he left Washington. He was short, butnine hundred million was a pretty good number considering the circumstances. *I'll be running, but the trip will be first class.*
~~~

Arrangements for a significant surgical change in his appearance had been made three years ago. No one knew about those preparations. Senator Rayburt and his plastic surgeons in Rome were the only individual's privy to that information. Tentative arrangements had been made during a senate research trip that included the Eternal City. A significant deposit was being held in one of the names on the senator's hidden accounts.

There was no wife or significant other to encumber his movement in the years to come. He hoped his ladies in Washington would understand.

Rayburt also hoped he wouldn't be bored with the journey he expected.

He glanced one more time at the passageway leading to the spiral staircase and outside.

*I could walk out now,* he thought, *but I'd be on my own. Maybe I could make it, but maybe not.*

Senator Rayburt decided to trust the plan.

Now—first things first.

The shower and then prepare to make his way to the end of the tunnel in an hour.

With a few more keystrokes Rayburt erased recent history from the computer and closed it down.

There was no cause for him to notice the individual standing in the near total darkness of the walled exit to the tunnel downstairs.

~~~

The senator returned to his closet and closed the hidden opening. He hurried to the shower, hanging the towel on a hook at the door. Stepping inside, he turned the steam shower on hot, wishing the 118°F steam could sting his body and wash away all the
~~~

things that had gone wrong since he asked Congresswoman Kato to join the coup.

*I knew better,* he thought. *I KNEW better.*

How many times had he said that to himself?

The steam shower was doing its thing; Rayburt's skin tingled as condensation rolled off his body in large burning rivulets. Dense steam quickly filled the enclosed space. Only moments passed before it was impossible to see the shower door only eight feet away.

The senator stood facing the wall, feet well back, his hands and arms bracing him as he leaned forward. After a few minutes, he turned and flipped down the teak bench. Seating himself, elbows to knees, he then leaned forward, took a deep breath, and relaxed as much as was possible.

Under normal circumstances, this was a favorite time of every day for him. Several minutes could pass without him moving.

He was relaxing. At least, something was going right.

# Chapter Thirty-Three

The towel-wrapped and silenced muzzle of the .22 caliber pistol was only an inch from his right temple when the trigger was pulled.

Death came instantly.

Senator Rayburt hadn't heard the shower door open or close.

The marshal resting in the suite's living room had not heard those muffled noises either. The steady swish of the steam shower covered all other sounds.

Taking no chances in case someone surprised him, the man carried a second silenced weapon in a shoulder holster. The shooter was very precise; he had done this before.

He stood aside, allowing the senator's body to slide forward off the bench and onto the floor under its own momentum. Natural was always best. Then, with gloved hands, he separately took each of the senator's hands and placed them around and on the flat surfaces of the weapon. He even took a moment to remove the magazine and place fingerprints there.

Then, taking Rayburt's right wrist, the shooter placed the pistol in his hand and closed the senator's fingers around its grip. Finally, he placed the towel-wrapped weapon on the wet floor near Rayburt's outstretched fingers. No prints other than the senators would be found on the weapon. The entire execution including planting fingerprints had taken less than two minutes.

The single spent cartridge lay nearby on the tile floor.

~~~

Relaxing in the living room of the senator's third-floor suite, the marshal glanced at his watch. Sitting near the security monitor screen, Webster had watched Senator Rayburt enter the bathroom intent on taking a shower. That was twenty-four minutes ago. He decided to check on things.

When a loud knock at the door brought no answer, Webster entered the bedroom. Normal sounds of a shower were coming from the bath. *Reasonably loud.* The senator probably had not heard him knocking.

*He's probably enjoying the hot shower,* Webster thought. He turned back toward the living room and then had second thoughts. *Better check.*

Webster knocked at the bathroom door. Still no answer.

The marshal entered the bathroom.

When a loud rap at the shower was met with silence too, Webster could feel a tingle at the back of his neck. He immediately pushed the door open.

At first glance, nothing seemed amiss.

The steam shower was on, and the enclosure was filled with a heavy mist. The upper wall of glass appeared as though it had been painted a soft shade of gray. The mist obscured everything. Nothing inside
~~~

the shower enclosure was visible. The only presencethe marshal noticed was the sound.

He called out. "Senator Rayburt?"

Still no answer. Webster could feel adrenalin pumping through his body.

Reaching out, he pushed the shower door out of the way. A heavy fog-like cloud billowed out, rising toward the ceiling, and permeating most of the bathroom.

As the mist thinned, Webster saw the body. Rayburt was face down, sprawled on the floor at the end of the shower enclosure, unmoving, and bleeding from a small head wound at the right temple. A thin trail of red made its way to a nearby drain.

A towel-wrapped and silenced pistol lay near the senator's fingertips.

A quick touch to the carotid artery verified what Webster was already thinking. The senator was dead.

Standing and turning off the shower, Webster pulled the radio from his pocket.

"Jack, you better get up here," he said with a steady voice and as much excitement as he ever exhibited. He added, "Better bring L.J. with you."

"On our way," the head marshal told him.

~~~

While he was waiting, Webster visually explored the bathroom and shower. Careful where he stepped, the marshal could see nothing out of the ordinary except the pistol near the senator's fingertips.

*Where did he get it?* Webster searched his mind for an answer. He knew L.J. had combed the senator's suite and found nothing.
~~~

Webster heard the elevator's doors open. Moments later Jack Robbins and L.J. entered the bathroom. Gesturing toward the shower, Webster pointed to the senator's body.

"That's how I found him—dead. I checked for a pulse."

"You heard nothing?" Robbins asked.

"Nothing but the steam shower," Webster said. "There were three doors between us." Hesitating, he said, "I only checked on him because he'd been in the shower for a long time."

Robbins stooped, examining the silenced pistol without touching it. He recognized the Dead Air Mask 22 HD silencer on the weapon. Robbins wasn't surprised the senator would have the best.

L.J. bent to examine the weapon too, mumbling something under his breath.

Robbins glanced his way. He was having the same dark thoughts.

Dreading the conversation, he would soon be having with Rage, Webster suggested they call Kris to the third floor and bring him up to speed before reaching out to anyone else. The senator certainly wouldn't be rushing them.

"Call Kris," Jack told L.J.

Then the head marshal turned to Webster. "Where did he get that pistol?"

Webster had no idea. "L.J. turned everything on this floor inside out," he said, adding, "I don't see how he could have missed it." He pointed toward the weapon.

"Walk through again," Robbins told him. "Maybe you can tell where he was hiding it."

~~~

Rage was getting some much-needed sleep back at his hotel when his phone buzzed. He picked it up and glanced at the display. Webster.

"I have bad news, boss."

"What?"

"Senator Rayburt got hold of a pistol and shot himself."

"Bad?"

"As bad as it can get," Webster said.

He heard mumbling. Webster didn't ask Rage to repeat whatever he'd said.

"Where?"

"In the bathroom at his house." Webster explained how he had found the senator and the circumstances concerning his suicide. The fact that no one heard the shot took some clarifying.

Finished, he waited for Rage.

"Have the local police been called?" the boss asked.

"No. We only found him a few minutes ago."

"No doubt about it being a suicide?" Rage asked.

"None," Webster said.

"How did he get hold of a weapon?"

Webster had been walking through the senator's suite since he got Rage on the phone. He leaned on the closet door. He hadn't found any hiding places.

"I'm searching again as we speak," Webster said. "Obviously, we missed something somewhere." His tone indicated the marshal was already taking the blame for the senator's suicide.
~~~

Webster was in a back corner of the senator's closet when they hung up.

~~~

The local police and the FBI were called. News people came from every direction. A U.S. senator was dead—one that was rumored to be involved in a military takeover attempt.

Everyone wanted a piece of the story.

It was four o'clock in the morning before a coroner's wagon took Senator Rayburt's body away. An autopsy would be performed later that day. The senator's body would then be returned to his home state for burial. The service would be private; only a couple of relatives and a few very close friends would attend.

~~~

The gun used in the senator's suicide went to the FBI's forensics lab at Quantico, Virginia. In an in-depth exam, the senator's fingerprints were the only ones on the weapon or its magazine. That was not a surprise, but one interesting factor did arise.

There were no fingerprints at all on the ammunition. Even the spent cartridge was clean. After discussion, the accepted explanation was that the senator must have worn gloves when he loaded the weapon. No further examination was scheduled.

No powder burns had been found on Senator Rayburt's hands during his autopsy. The easy explanation had been the towel he had obviously wrapped around the weapon to quiet the sound. Powder burns and residue was evident there.

~~~
~~~

Six weeks after the failed coup attempt, a small private dinner was held at the White House. Rage Doyle, Mike Webster, and Cary Warren were the special guests of President and Mrs. Carrigan. Also attending were Jacob Frankin and Secretary of State John Jäger. Jack Robbins represented the U.S. Marshals and their role in preventing the takeover.

The president thanked them for their efforts as a group. Then, Rage, Mike, and Cary received private words individually for exposing the coup. Lyndon Johnson's tag for Rage Doyle was cited several times throughout the evening. The Author was President Carrigan's new special friend.

~~~

In the days following the dinner at the White House, hanging details of the coup were carefully cleared away. Several additional individuals, civilian and military, were connected and arrested. Those already under indictment often found it to their benefit to add to the information already known and, in some cases, implicating others. Rage Doyle and his two aides gathered and organized details into a report for the DOJ and the president.

Further gratitude was shown in a letter of commendation to each of the three individuals, and a significant payout from the U.S. Treasury to their business organization, Strategic Private Investigations.

With the coup behind them, Rage opted to return to his cabin in the Tennessee mountains. Mike and Cary, after some discussion, decided they would like to spend a few days together in New Orleans.

At the suggestion of the president, Secretary Jäger made a jet available from his department to
~~~

deliver them to their destinations—Rage to Knoxville, Mike and Cary to New Orleans.

Rage was planning on getting some writing done in his personal journal.

Mike and Cary had set their sights on total relaxation and some quality time together.

~~~

Cary suggested taking a room at a small hotel in the French Quarter. They could walk to many of the places each wanted to visit. Café Du Monde and St. Louis Cathedral were already on the agenda. Cary said she could already taste the beignets and café au lait.

They spent five glorious days and nights, leaving the quarter only three times during their stay.

~~~

The first outing was a taxi ride to Landie's home in Metairie. She was expecting them; Cary had called.

Though it was midmorning, Landie had prepared for their visit.

Cary's elderly friend opened her door as Cary and Mike walked up the sidewalk. The heavy smell of chicory coffee and freshly baked sweet rolls lured them directly to Landie's kitchen. The rolls she had baked were delicious along with the coffee. Mike smiled and said he'd had enough but couldn't resist a third roll when Landie offered the last one to him.

"What have you been doing?" she asked when they returned to the living room.

"We spent some time in Washington," Cary said. She had already told Landie about the leave of absence to work with Rage and Mike.

Mike picked up the explanation, saying, "We passed on the information we had about Josette's diary." He glanced at Cary. "That's about all we can say. The people we met about the diary said everything was top secret."

"Were you there during that senator's attempt to take over the government?" Landie asked. She looked at Cary. "I thought I saw you in the crowd at the president's speech after the parade."

Cary laughed and tossed her hair. "Heavens, no." she said. "That was only for insiders."

"It sure looked like you." Landie appeared doubtful, but let it pass.

"I had planned to visit Josette's grave today," she told them. "Would you go with me? The cemetery is nearby."

A glance and a nod from Mike and then Cary said, "Of course, we'll go with you."

"Greg left a car in case you said yes. Mike, will you drive?"

He nodded. Mike had already learned you don't say no to Landie.

~~~

Josette's was a simple grave—a small headstone and a slab of granite. The congresswoman's name and the dates of her birth and death were accompanied by a single line. "She served her country."

Cary and Mike waited quietly as Landie placed a small bouquet at the base of the headstone. The elderly grandmother had picked the flowers from her backyard garden.

As Landie rose to her feet, she looked their way and softly murmured, "I miss her every day."

~~~

Mike and Cary's next excursion included a streetcar ride out to the end of the line and back. The ride carried them out St. Charles Avenue and through the Garden District to Carrolton Avenue and then to Airline Drive. Several times Cary pointed to old mansions, many, she said, dating back to the mid-1800s. She had googled facts about the area.

They both grinned, passing the street where they escaped their captors on a dark night when they were searching for clues in the death of Cary's birth mother.

Cary leaned into Mike and whispered, "That was the first time I really considered you as more than the man who took my job."

He took her hand. "Sorry." Then, "But I did give the job back to you."

He laughed when she poked his ribs.

Along the way, they each pointed to the convenience store where Josette had been assassinated. Nothing was said for several blocks, their thoughts recalling the turbulence of recent weeks. It was a somber moment.

~~~

The last outing was to deliver a dozen roses to Janice Talmer's grave. They chose a sunlit, late Saturday morning to visit the grave. Cary had found the roses in a small grocery store in the French Quarter when she went out for a solitary walk. Returning, she held the flowers up for Mike to see. "I want to take these to my birth mother's grave."

Mike immediately got to his feet. "Let's go."
~~~

Cary told the taxi driver which cemetery they wanted. Arriving, she leaned forward and asked, "Could you pick us up in an hour?"

"I'll be here," he said and drove away.

"Which way?" Mike asked. "I don't remember." All the paths looked the same to him.

"Follow me," Cary said, turning and startingout. Mike was momentarily left behind. He jogged a few steps, catching up.

Cary remembered that first time. A reporter friend had located her mother's grave and brought her here. Mike had accompanied her.

At Janice Talmer's grave, Cary was startled to find roses already spread across the top of the plain tomb.

*Surprised? Yes, but not too surprised either.* She had found roses spread across the grave this way the first time she had come here. *Johnny Periot...*

Cary's birth father was still sending flowers to Janice's grave.

She laid her roses next to those from her father in much the same arrangement as he had done for all those years. Finished, she stood silent for a while.

Mike walked away, giving her a time alone with a past that had never been. Cary caught up a few minutes later, gently taking his hand and saying, "Let's walk."

Mostly without speaking, they strolled slowly among the thousands of above-ground gravesites in the cemetery. Sometimes they would stop to read a date or an inscription, but mostly they just walked.

A few minutes before the cabbie was due to pick them up, Mike asked if she would like to revisit Janice once more before leaving. Cary nodded, and they turned that way.

Touching the roses again as if they could be better arranged, she spent another few moments at her young mother's grave.

Very soon, Cary looked up catching his eyes and saying, "Thank you."

She reached for his hand again, and they walked to the gate where the taxi was waiting.

~~~

Mike had their ride drop them at Ruby's Grill on the edge of the French Quarter. Each opted for a burger, fries, and a drink. The burgers were huge; neither could finish theirs.

Ruby's Grill was the first place they'd had dinner together. That fun night seemed ages ago though only a few years had passed.

They left the restaurant laughing again about the size of the burgers, but both agreed they were great. Hand in hand, they walked the several blocks back to the heart of the Quarter.

It was midafternoon when they reached Jackson Square. Cary suggested they find a shaded empty bench and rest for a few minutes. Mike thought that was a good idea.

They could see the front of St. Louis Cathedral from where they sat. As they watched, a long black limousine pulled near the entrance and stopped. Doors opened, and a bride stepped out. Several bridesmaids quickly followed. Obviously, a wedding was at hand. The bells in the church's tower chimed four o'clock as the wedding party made their way through the huge main cathedral doors.
~~~

Cary and Mike watched as obvious tourists continued to enter the cathedral through a different door. Several had pointed at the wedding party before going inside.

Mike had a thought. *The strangers are probably slipping in to watch the ceremony.*

Tapping Cary on the shoulder, Mike raised his eyebrows in a questioning expression.

She looked up. "Let's go." Cary was up and moving before he could verbalize the question.

On tiptoes, they slipped inside and found a spot where the action down front could be easily seen. The dozen onlookers at the back, including Cary and Mike, were quiet and still.

It was beautiful, both the church and the wedding.

Mike couldn't help glancing at the ceiling—vaulted and painted lavishly with scenes from the Bible. There was a white background for the art, but not really white; more like a surface that produced its own creamy white light.

Pews stretched along the marble floor on both sides and to the elegant front of the church. Both sides were filled with guests for the wedding, the bride's perhaps a little more than the groom's.

Glancing her way, Mike could see Cary was fascinated with the bride and the ongoing ceremony.

Others, tourists came and left, but Cary watched, indifferent to everyone else. Even Mike seemed outside her area of interest as she listened to the vows being said by the couple down front.

He was interested, too, but in a different way. Watching Cary, Mike thought of his own life to date and of Cary's. In a world full of people, they were both alone.

He glanced at her again. There was a thin glaze of tears in her eyes. Then he realized, there was a problem with his eyes too. Looking at her one more time, he made a decision.

Reaching out, he touched her chin, turning her face toward him.

Softly, he asked, "Would you …?"

She looked up, faint tears in her eyes, "Yes."

# Chapter Thirty-Four

Across the capital, autumn leaves were turning when Senator Jacquelin Atkinson returned to Washington. A few days of R and R in her home state had done wonders, both physically and emotionally. The race for a second term in the U.S. Senate had been arduous, but she had won. With the relaxing time at home, she was finally recovering.

A full term under her belt and a few months past the most recent election, Atkinson was finally ready to settle down to living and working in the capital. Hopefully, this would be her home for years to come. The senator had already contacted a realtor and was prepared to actively search for a condo of her own.

It was after nine in the evening when Jacquelin arrived at her apartment. Dinner and drinks with friends had taken most of the evening. The senator showered and slipped into her pajamas, a robe, and some comfortable slippers.

Pouring a glass of Riesling, she set it on the coffee table and reached for the jumble of pamphlets and other information the realtor had dropped by her senate office. He was pushing her now to decide. Having found several choices that met her criteria, he was ready to show them and get her signature on the dotted line.

Before diving into the pile, she took a sip of the wine. "Ahh…"

Over the next thirty minutes, Jacquelin picked three units she would like to see. All were 3/2s, and each of them was reasonably close to the Capital—thirty or forty minutes. She would set aside time and call the realtor early tomorrow. Senator Atkinson needed this behind her.

Yawning, she made two piles: the three condos she wanted to see and four she didn't. With that chore completed, she was ready to call it a night.

At the kitchen counter, she poured another half glass of the wine and carried it to the bedroom with her. Leaving it on the nightstand beside her book, Senator Atkinson prepared for bed. Teeth brushed and her robe on a nearby chair, she returned to the bed and her book. Downing the wine, Jacquelin decided to leave the book for a night when she was more rested.

Five minutes later, she was fast asleep.

~~~

The senator didn't find the envelope until shewas leaving the apartment the next morning. It  had been slipped under the door from the hallway outside. Only a corner was visible; most of the  packet  had lodged itself under the welcome mat.

Thinking it was solicitation of some sort, she started to toss it on the small table that normally held her keys. A second glance stirred her curiosity. The envelope looked too formal to be solicitation.

She opened it.
~~~

Upended, a dozen folded legal pages—a deed—and a key dropped out of the envelope and into her hand. Further scrutiny of the information indicated the deed gave Senator Jacquelin Atkinson ownership of a condo in an upscale community only a short distance from the Capital.

Checking the envelope again, Senator Atkinson found another item, a single page with a handwritten message.

It read:

*Dear Senator Atkinson,*

*I'm sure you are surprised at receiving this interesting envelope. I will be happy to explain.*
*Please arrange with your secretary to accept a telephone call from Chicago at 10:00 a.m. this morning. In the meantime, please do not discuss the contents of this envelope or the upcoming call with anyone.*
*I look forward to speaking with you.*

*Zack Holden*

# About the Author

Joe Shumock grew up in rural Alabama, attending the same school for the first twelve years of his education. Joe was a good student but not a great one. Sports held a higher priority. It is also suggested that none of his teachers would have expected Shumock to write a book, certainly not several. Getting Joe to write a 300-word paper or book report was a mission of hope.

He did enjoy reading, though.

Popular writers of the time caught Shumock's attention and prompted him to wonder if he could write a book (or books). Later in life, he seized an opportunity and wrote his first, *A Letter to Die For*.

Shumock's current story is titled *The Last Parade* and is played out mostly in and around Washington D.C. An attempted takeover of the U.S. government must be dealt with.

Here's hoping everyone enjoys reading this latest.

# Acknowledgments

The Last Parade began as an idea in early 2019. It was researched and written into a story, then edited, and a cover designed. Finally, it's going to print.

In the beginning, friends let me bounce ideas off them. That was a start. From there came the research.

The overall project became much larger than I initially anticipated. This story required I visit or research the Senate Office building, the White House, the Oval Office, and Arlington Cemetery among other locales. I'm probably more familiar now with some of these locations than the staff who works there.

As with each of my previous stories, many have encouraged me along the way, and many times I've heard, "When is it going to be ready?"

Well, to all who have waited, "It's here."

~~~

I want to take this opportunity to thank a few who have been actively involved in the final product.

Again, I'll begin with Wayne South Smith, my editor. He may not realize it, but time, association, and experience have brought me to think of him not only as an editor, but also as a friend. Without Wayne, I have no doubt this would be a different book. His recommendations and careful editing have added greatly to the final manuscript.

Next, I would like to thank Patsy Breland Shumock, better known as Pat, my wife. She encouraged me, listened to my revisions, took my temperature, discouraged me, and has otherwise been there when I needed her. Thanks, Pat.
~~~

It was difficult coming up with a cover for The Last Parade. Everyone involved had an idea. We threw them all into a hat, and Virginia Mathers used them to design a cover I believe portrays my story quite well. I'm very proud of the result.

As always, I apologize to those I've missed. "Thank you," to all, both named and unnamed. The Last Parade is a part of all of us.